Dancing on Coals

Ellen O'Connell

This book is a work of fiction. Names, characters and incidents are the product of the author's imagination. Any resemblance to actual events or persons is strictly coincidental. Some of the places mentioned do exist; however, descriptions may have been altered to better suit the story.

Copyright © 2011 by Ellen O'Connell
www.oconnellauthor.com

ISBN-13: 978-1466441187
ISBN-10: 1466441186

All rights reserved. No part of this book may be used or reproduced in any manner whatsoever without written permission, except in the case of brief quotations embodied in critical articles and reviews.

ALSO BY ELLEN O'CONNELL

Mystery
Rottweiler Rescue

Romance
Eyes of Silver, Eyes of Gold
Sing My Name
Rachel's Eyes, a short story

Dancing on Coals

1

Arizona Territory
Spring 1881

FOUR PASSENGERS IN a stagecoach instead of six improved the experience from hellish to miserable. No longer crushed between a drummer stinking of whiskey and a cowboy spitting streams of tobacco juice out the window, Katherine tried without success to find a comfortable position on her expanded share of seat. Overhead, the driver shouted to the horses, cracked his whip, and the stage lurched into motion, leaving the Tucson station behind in the dust.

Her two-day respite in the rough town hadn't been long enough. In days past Katherine had endured the press of meaty thighs, knobby knees and scrawny shanks in the full coach, hating every minute. Now she missed the support of other bodies wedging her in place as the coach rolled like a ship on wind-whipped seas.

This leg of her journey home promised to be even more exhausting than the last. How soon would the stage stop in another town with a hotel?

Catching herself planning another stop with the last hardly out of sight, Katherine almost laughed. One stop in New Mexico, she vowed, maybe two or three in Texas. She did want to get home this year, didn't she? The thought sobered her. Not wanting to dwell on it, she studied her new traveling companions instead.

Señor Estrada, a portly silver-haired man, sat across from her, eyes glued on the wide-brimmed hat in his lap. Since climbing into the coach, he hadn't raised his head. His worn black suit and hat were Mexican in style. Even if the few words of broken English he'd used to introduce himself weren't all he knew, the other passengers probably intimidated him.

Large, loud men with dark hair and bushy beards, the Hochners, father and son, undoubtedly intimidated a lot of people. Heavy work boots, canvas trousers and coarse wool shirts emphasized their aggressive manner, and their demanding behavior in the depot this morning hadn't recommended them as amiable fellow travelers.

Before either one of the pair could drag her into unwanted conversation, Katherine decided to find out if her guesses about Señor Estrada were correct.

"*¿Siempre es tan caluroso el Marzo, Señor Estrada?*"

He jerked his head up, his pleasure at meeting someone he could speak with in his own language evident. His reply was slow and careful, as if he feared her Spanish would prove too limited for conversation.

"Not always, but often, señorita. This is a warm climate. You speak Spanish well."

Katherine shook her head slightly. "I know my Spanish is different from what's spoken here, but at least I can understand and make myself understood."

"Most certainly. You speak with elegance. May I ask where you learned?"

"In Cuba, Spain and the Philippines. My family is in shipping, and as a girl I traveled around the world. I picked up a little of several languages and more of Spanish and French."

"You're far from the sea. What brings you here?"

The story Katherine had told so often slipped off her tongue easily. "One day I realized I'd been around the world several times but had never seen my native land west of Philadelphia or south of New Jersey. So here I am on a grand tour—from New York to California through the middle of the country by rail and now back home through the South."

Surprise flashed across Estrada's face. "Your family allowed you to undertake such a journey alone?"

"Everyone in my family is a traveler. No one has a problem with my trip." *Especially since they don't know about it. They're probably on a tiger hunt in India right now in blissful ignorance, and I'll be home long before they are.*

The coach bounced hard over a rough section of the road, almost throwing Katherine to her knees on the floor. Catching herself, she pushed back into the seat.

"If I had it to do over, I confess I'd be on a train right now."

Estrada nodded his understanding, and Katherine turned the conversation to the purpose of his own trip. As the first way station of the day came in sight, they fell silent. When the stage continued on with fresh horses, Alfred Hochner made it clear there would be no more opportunity for conversations in Spanish.

"How about talking to us in American for a while, missy," he boomed.

Katherine stiffened and turned an icy glare on the man. As she drew breath to give Hochner the reply he deserved, she heard Estrada's soft Spanish plea. "Please, señorita, do not antagonize these men."

After another deep breath, Katherine took his advice, although she didn't try to keep the frost out of her tone. "I'm so sorry, Mr. Hochner. We never meant to exclude you from our conversation. We merely shared information about our travels. Mr. Estrada is going to take a new position in Santa Fe. I'm returning home to New York."

"You shouldn't be traveling alone," Hochner said, staring rudely.

"You're absolutely right, and I'm never going to do it again." Let the oaf find a way to argue with that.

He didn't argue; he lectured. "A lady like you shouldn't be out here alone. It's bad enough for men like me and Jake here. At least we're armed." He slapped the holster on his hip for emphasis.

Katherine ran a gloved fingertip over the hand-tooled flower design on the leather of her traveling purse, feeling the hard outline of the Remington pistol inside. Carrying a weapon handy in a holster at the waist would be an advantage, but there was something to be said for surprise.

Hochner hadn't stopped talking, and Katherine flinched at his next words. "You may not know it, but we got an Apache problem here in Arizona."

How could she not know? From the time she had first set foot in Arizona Territory, she had heard as much about Apaches as she could stand. Hochner could not, absolutely could not, conjure up a single Apache atrocity she hadn't heard told in varying bloody detail at least three times.

Thank goodness the stories no longer had the power to bring the sour taste of bile to the back of her throat because for her sins she was going to have to listen to Hochner's version today. She briefly considered citing the travel rule posted in the stage depot forbidding passengers to talk of Indian attacks and robberies and abandoned the thought. No rule would divert a blowhard like Hochner.

As he and his son traded stories of one depredation after another, a familiar tone resonated. In Africa her five brothers had never missed an opportunity to tell gleeful tales of man-eating lions. In the Philippines they had made her believe a cannibal hid behind every tree. The Hochners were grown men, but the sly looks on their faces as they glanced at her every so often matched her memory of five boys checking to see if they had scared the girl yet.

Regretting that she was about to break the stage company rule herself and make Señor Estrada very unhappy, Katherine said, "Are you worried about an Apache attack on the stage, Mr. Hochner?"

"I always worry about Apaches, and you should worry more, being a lady and all."

"How often do they attack a stage?"

He looked at his son and smiled. "What do you say, Jake? Pretty much every week?"

Jake pursed his lips as if trying to remember. "Yeah, that's what I'd say all right. At least once a week."

So they considered her a mindless twit. Katherine felt a twinge of temper. "Are you sure? That's not what I heard from John Clum."

The blank look on Hochner's face told her the name rang no bells in his thick skull.

"Mr. Clum is editor of the *Tucson Citizen*," Katherine said, "and he was the agent for the Apache reservation at San Carlos before that. He told me it's been years since an Apache attack on a stage. General Crook has things well in hand, and most of the Apaches are on the reservations now. He told me what I should worry about is a robbery by bandits, that there have been two robberies already this year where everyone was killed."

Hochner flushed a deep red. "So you been talking to a lily-livered Apache lover, and now you're calling me a liar?"

Katherine raised a hand to her throat, widened her eyes and gave a delicate gasp. "Of course not, Mr. Hochner. Never.

I merely wondered about your sources, and the bandits Mr. Clum talked about sound quite as evil as the Apaches, don't they?"

"Nothing's as bad as Apaches. Nothing."

The men treated her to sullen silence after that. Even Estrada shot her a look of disapproval, but Katherine gazed out the window beside her at the empty, dry land passing by and smiled. Maybe those two would think twice the next time they decided to scare the girl.

2

In the early afternoon of the second day after she had insulted the Hochners, Katherine jerked out of her trance-like state of endurance when the coach tilted and started up a steep grade. The driver's yells of encouragement to the straining horses sounded loud inside the vehicle. Maybe he would pull up soon and order them all to get out and walk up the hill.

Hoping for a chance to stretch cramped muscles in fresh air and sunshine, Katherine leaned forward, her face almost out the window, trying to see the road ahead and along the side of the coach.

"Stick your nose out there, and it's liable to get knocked off," Hochner said.

This time the big man was right. The mountain closed in on the coach more tightly with every foot they traveled. Were they headed into a canyon barely wide enough for the stage to pass? Definitely not. On Hochner's side of the coach, the view was of a cascade of rocky canyons falling away in the distance.

The coach canted at a steeper angle. The snap of the driver's whip punctuated his shouts, echoing off the side of the mountain only to be swallowed in the vastness of the canyons. Jake Hochner watched her, enjoying her dismay.

"Scared of heights, are you?"

"No, but I don't like imagining what would happen if one of the horses hiccuped about now. Are you familiar with this road? Does it run on a ledge on the side of the mountain?"

"Yeah, we take this trip every year. With a full coach, we'd be walking already. Even with just the four of us, he'll stop when it flattens out aways up ahead. We'll have to get out there, and it's a rough hike. Last time there was a lady on this route, her husband about had to carry her."

Katherine lifted the hem of her dusty brown linen traveling dress enough to show the feminine, pointed toes of sturdy cowhide walking boots. "I bought them in Tucson just for occasions like this."

He looked so disappointed, she couldn't help but add, "I ruined a pair of good shoes in my first days on the stage and learned my lesson."

The vehicle leveled out and came to a halt with many shouts of "Whoa there" from the driver. As Katherine looped the strap of her purse over her arm and prepared to get out and walk, a shotgun boomed overhead. Gunfire cracked amid cries from the driver and guard. The coach rocked and jolted as the horses started forward, stopped, backed and finally halted.

Cursing sounded in a coarse voice completely unlike that of either the driver or the guard. "God damn it! I told you to stay out of sight until they were all out."

The door on Hochner's side of the coach flew open, and the same voice said, "Out. All of you get out."

Katherine couldn't believe her eyes when neither Hochner nor his son made any move to draw a gun. She grabbed his arm. "Don't do it. We should resist. Remember what Mr. Clum said."

He shook her off and flicked a finger at the cameo broach pinned at her neck. "They're going to take your baubles is all. If they spook the horses, we'll go off the side of the mountain, and they can pick the pockets of our corpses."

The Hochners jumped down from the coach, but Señor Estrada gestured for Katherine to precede him. Clutching her purse against her chest, she shook her head violently. Brown eyes drooping with resignation, he went ahead without her.

As Estrada's back filled the doorway, Katherine tried the door on her side. It hit rocks before opening enough for her to squeeze out.

Undeterred, she squirmed through the window, yanking and ripping her skirt free when it caught in the frame. The mountainside was steep but not an impossible climb. Up, sideways—she clawed her way along any path that led away from the robbers and their guns.

More shots sounded behind her, evenly spaced, one after another, drowning out pleas in English and Spanish. "No, please!" "*Por favor!*"

She slipped, fell back and scrambled up again. Jamming her boots in one foothold after another, Katherine fought her way up through the rocks until she reached one large enough to hide behind. As she crouched there, gulping for air, a tiny hope flared. Maybe they didn't know about her. Maybe they hadn't seen her crazed flight and wouldn't come looking. Maybe....

"Go get that damn fool woman!"

She needed a better defensive position. A cluster of tumbled rocks leaning against each other on a shelf below caught her eye. To get there meant running more than twenty feet exposed to rifle fire.

She ran.

The first shot exploded rock behind her, adding impetus to her mad dash. The second showered her with stinging shards of stone as she jumped down and dove into the shelter of the small granite fort.

She peeled the shredded gloves off her bloody hands, threw the scraps of cloth aside and yanked the Remington out of her purse. Dropping down flat on her stomach, she peered through one space between the rocks after another until she found a spot where she could see without being seen.

If only the pistol in her hand were a rifle. In imagining dangers she might face, Katherine had envisioned pointing the gun at a single man intent on harming her. The enemy was supposed to be close, well within pistol range and impossible to miss.

If she didn't stop wishing for what she didn't have, the enemy *would* be close. What she did have was a pistol with five bullets loaded and another five spare in her purse. She dug the extra bullets out, loaded one into the empty chamber under the hammer, pulled her hat off and settled down, trying to steady her breathing, determined to make every shot count.

One of the men climbed the hill in the open, making no attempt to stay behind cover. The fools would never expect a woman to be armed. The corners of Katherine's mouth pulled straight back and her lips parted just enough to expose her teeth.

She heard her brother Mark's voice. *You're giving yourself away with that smile that isn't a smile, Kate. Anyone who sees that knows you're going to make trouble.* The corners of her mouth turned up, changing the smile to a real one, the memory of Mark's words steadying her.

Surprise was her best weapon. She had to let him get close enough. She had to remember about shooting downhill. She had to keep her nerve. She cocked the pistol and waited.

As the killer closed in, he showed some caution at last. Stopping before he reached the open ground around her, he drew his gun and called to her, his tone friendly.

"Come on out, lady, and we won't hurt you."

"Then go away and leave me alone."

"You know we can't do that. You'd starve or die of thirst out here all by yourself. All we want is your jewelry and your cash. We never would have hurt nobody except they started shooting."

Katherine bent the pin on her broach ripping it off and threw it at him. She followed it with her purse. "That's all I have. Take it and go."

"That's not good enough."

He started toward her again, and she lined her sights up just below where his rotten heart should be. Praying that allowed enough for the slope of the hill, she squeezed the trigger.

The bullet hit him square in the chest, turning him into a boneless rag doll wavering on his feet for a long second before he fell backward. His body rolled downhill until stopped by a clump of scrawny bushes.

"God damn it! She's got a gun. She's got a gun, and she shot Butch."

Katherine squinted down at the stage road through eyes burning from gun smoke. Four men stood there staring up. Not one of them wore a mask. No wonder after killing the driver and guard they had executed the Hochners and Señor Estrada. If the robbers were identified and caught, they would hang.

She studied their faces. If she lived, she would bear witness.

"Yes, I have a gun, and I know how to use it," she shouted. "So you just take what you've got and leave me alone."

Even down in the road, well out of range, two of the men sidled behind the coach. One of the others put his hands on his hips and yelled back.

"You got nothing but a pistol, lady. We're going to dig you out of there, and if you killed Butch, you're going to pay. Butch? Butch!"

In other circumstances, it would be funny. Did that killer think anyone could be stupid enough to believe when this was over a live Butch would mean a live Katherine?

Nine bullets. She had nine bullets, and there were at least four of them, four men who now knew she had a gun and its limitations.

Fighting the urge to do some cursing of her own, Katherine examined the terrain around her. If she could hold out until dark, she might be able to get away, but even this early in spring, night was long hours away. Down below, the brave one waved his arms and pointed high up the mountain. Katherine looked up too, knowing what he must be saying. If a man with a rifle got above her, he could shoot her like an animal in a trap.

Sure enough, another robber started up through the rocks. He kept well out of decent pistol range and used any cover available, but Katherine remembered how the shards of rock had exploded around her from a missed shot. She sat up, steadied the pistol on the rocks and watched until he reached an exposed spot.

Her shot missed but had the effect she hoped for. He dropped from sight with a yell. After a minute, he started back down to the road. To Katherine's regret, he didn't look hurt.

When the climber reached the others, they gathered in a group, gesturing and conferring. No one betrayed any noticeable eagerness to come dig her out. As she watched, one of the men pointed, and all four scattered and ran. They fell and dove behind rocks, shooting wildly in every direction.

Katherine's heart lifted. Anything that terrorized the bandits like that had to be good for her. Lawmen? A cavalry patrol? What could have that effect on so many armed men? Their shouts made no sense until one word sounded clearly and destroyed her hope. *Apache.*

Stretched on her stomach again, peering through the crevice in the rocks, Katherine watched long-haired, darkskinned men close in on the bandits from above and below. Gunfire cracked and echoed, and one after another, the bandits slumped and fell.

For the second time, she prayed that an enemy intent on harm didn't know about her. Still, they had surrounded the bandits, come at them from all sides. What if....

She whirled. The muzzle of a rifle pointed at her nose from less than two feet away. Even half prone at his feet, Katherine could tell he was tall, slender. Black hair held by a red headband brushed his shoulders. A bandolier crossed his chest over an untucked, belted calico shirt. Dark leggings hardly showed under moccasins that reached almost up to his knees and a breechclout that reached almost down to his knees.

"Put the gun down," he said, his English flawless for those few words, his voice soft.

Katherine stared up, her mind racing. She lowered the pistol as if to obey, then flipped it so that the barrel pressed against her breast.

Whatever she expected, it wasn't the flash of amusement that crossed his face and sounded in his voice. "I can take the pistol from you before you can cock it."

"I don't think so." Her tongue felt thick and clumsy with fear, but her voice sounded steady in her own ears.

"You're too young and have too much courage to die today. Put down the gun and come with me. No one will hurt you, I promise."

"That's what the stage robbers said. They lied."

He nodded. "Most white men are liars, but I'm not. Put down the gun and live. You need to decide quickly. There isn't much time."

Ignoring the rifle barrel was almost impossible, but Katherine forced herself to look past it at the man. He was young and not trying to hide his pleasure at catching her unawares. Unpainted bronze skin covered a broad forehead and high cheekbones. The lower part of his face narrowed only slightly. Straight nose, firm-lipped mouth, the face she searched for clues to the man would be handsome no matter what color skin covered it.

The fact he didn't look like the savage of countless horror stories affected her, as did the fact he spoke English better than many of the people she had met in her travels, but in the end what convinced her to take a chance on surviving as an Apache captive was the combination of amusement and sympathy in his dark eyes.

Katherine gave her pistol to the Apache.

3

Gaining possession of the gun didn't transform him into the merciless killer of the endless stories. Katherine let her breath out in a relieved whoosh when his expression sobered but didn't turn ugly. He picked up her extra bullets and jammed them into empty loops on the bandolier. After checking the pistol, he tucked it under his belt, then pointed with his chin.

"Go that way. It will be easier."

Anything had to be easier than the mindless path of her flight from the stage. Obeying his directions had them back on the road in minutes. Katherine barely set her boots on level ground when the stage lurched backward, angled and disappeared over the side of the mountain, crashing and banging its way down to a final resting place. The terrified horses, cut free at the last minute, tried to run, but half a dozen Apaches held them, calmed them, then began cutting the harnesses away.

The bandits and their victims sprawled where they had fallen. She had steeled herself for the sight of scalped and mutilated bodies. Now she stared wide-eyed. Not one body looked disturbed. What kind of Apaches spoke excellent

English, killed highwaymen, didn't scalp them and rescued their victims?

Before she decided whether to ask or how to ask those questions, the savage of nightmares charged down the road on a dark horse. Frozen by the sight, Katherine waited for man and animal to smash into her and trample her into the dust or knock her over the side of the mountain to the same rocky grave as the stagecoach. Rage masked his face better than any war paint. His eyes glittered with fury as he pulled his horse to a sliding stop that sprayed gravel and raised his rifle.

Calm words from the man beside her unlocked her brain and muscles. He took her by the arm and pushed her behind him.

"Stay there."

She didn't want to stay there. She wanted to run. After a single step, commonsense stopped her. Where would she go? Without even the pistol what would she do? The madman on the horse could run her down in seconds.

Rage emanated from the horseman and permeated the words he spoke in a language unlike any she had ever heard. The control in the deep voice made it more menacing. The young Apache shielding her answered calmly. They argued, rage on one side competing with reason on the other, and Katherine knew her life hung in the balance.

At last her Apache said only a few short words in a sharper tone. The two men faced each other for long, tense moments before the horseman spit and wheeled away. Katherine sagged with relief. Pain she hadn't noticed made her open hands clenched in tight fists. Her fingernails had dug into her bloody palms.

"He wants to kill me."

"Yes, but you're mine. Gaetan won't kill you unless you let him. Don't run."

She swallowed hard. "I won't run."

"I'm called Nilchi."

"I'm Katherine. Katherine Grant. I think.... I think, thank you."

He gave a brief nod and pointed toward the horses. Walking past the bodies of the stage passengers, Katherine bent over and picked up Señor Estrada's wide-brimmed hat.

Nilchi grabbed it from her and threw it down. "Don't take from the dead."

He didn't seem angry but determined, and Katherine really needed protection from the sun, at least until she turned as brown as an Indian herself.

"He was a friend," she lied, "and he would want me to have his hat."

Nilchi's frown made her wish she hadn't spoken, but after a moment his expression cleared. "You're not Apache. Take it."

She picked up the hat again and put it on, tightening the cord under her chin as she followed Nilchi toward the horses.

The other men had stripped all but two of the thieves' horses of their saddles and bridles when Nilchi called out. Left to choose between a broad-backed bay and a weedy chestnut, Katherine chose the chestnut, mindful of how long it had been since she rode astride.

Of course she couldn't ride until she got on, and getting on with her stylish, narrow skirt and petticoat stymied her. Nilchi solved the problem by throwing her up onto the horse, but there was no way to sit astride without leaving her legs exposed above where her stockings ended, indeed so high that her drawers showed.

Before she could think of any way to preserve modesty in front of all the savage male eyes, the horse crowhopped forward, as unhappy with the situation as Katherine. She shortened the reins and dug in her heels, glad to be taking control of something and mindful that Nilchi wasn't the only one amused.

Turning the animal in a tight circle to be sure it understood it had to put up with her, she almost smiled herself until Gaetan came into sight. A face carved in stone showed more expression. A snake's eyes held more warmth. Any desire to smile died. She straightened her horse and followed Nilchi down the stage road.

More than a mile from the massacre site, a large herd of horses, cattle and mules grazed under the watchful eye of a single young guard. Most of the mules carried packs. The Apaches ran the extra horses from the stage in with the others, headed them all up and started them moving south. What had seemed like a horde when killing bandits and swarming over the stage turned out to be eleven men.

Maybe only eleven, but ten of them wanted to kill her. Katherine kept close to Nilchi, made sure her horse stayed slightly behind his, kept her mouth shut and her head down. Other women had survived this. If they could do it, so could she.

BY SUNSET EXHAUSTION and screaming muscles had Katherine holding on to the saddle horn in a daze, her only thought to somehow stay on the horse. She understood why the army had so much trouble controlling these people. Under the Apaches' relentless prodding, even the cattle and the mules burdened with packs moved faster than should be possible.

The last purple and orange streaks of the sunset were fading in the western sky by the time the Apaches stopped. Katherine managed to dismount unaided but had to cling to the side of the horse until her shaky legs regained enough strength to support her.

"If you never ride a horse, how did you know what to do?" Nilchi asked.

"They make me.... Ladies don't ride astride. I ride, but I ride sidesaddle."

"Hunh." The single sound expressed disapproval of ladies, sidesaddles and probably women who rode in stagecoaches. Katherine followed him to where the other men sat, talking in low voices. For one wild moment she wondered if as the only woman, they expected her to build a fire and cook in this dry camp.

When Nilchi pointed at the ground and said, "Sit here and wait," she almost thanked him.

Dinner was stale water from a curious water jug woven like a basket but waterproofed by a mysterious glaze and iron-hard dried meat that burst with flavor once saliva softened it enough to chew. Almost hungry enough to eat the fat and gristle she had disdained in the stage stations, Katherine chewed with relish and tried to study Nilchi in the fading light without him noticing. He not only noticed, he studied her back.

"You're very beautiful. We'll marry, and you'll make a good wife. The sun sets your hair on fire."

Something in his expression reminded her of her brothers when they were teasing, so she dared reply in kind.

"My hair is plain brown with occasional reddish highlights. My nose...." How did one describe a nose with what her father euphemized as an aristocratic arch to an Apache? "My nose is not straight. My chin sticks out too much. My eyes are an ordinary blue, and I'm too tall and too...." She searched for an acceptable word. "Lean. Why aren't you courting some beautiful Apache girl who wants to be your wife? Surely many do, and I don't."

"Your nose and chin are strong. A tall woman is strong. Your eyes are like the sky before a storm. You have courage, and you'll make a fine wife." He hesitated then asked, "Do you mourn a husband? Was one of the men on the stage your husband?"

"No, they were strangers until we all boarded the stage in Tucson. The bearded men were unpleasant." Remembering her fib about Señor Estrada, she exaggerated. "The Mexican gentleman and I became friends. He was a good man."

"Do you have a husband waiting for you?"

Katherine considered inventing a husband, decided her marital state would make no difference to him and said, "No, I have no husband."

"Good. We'll marry, and I'll make you very happy."

"We're not going to marry, and I'd make you miserable if we did. I have a bad temper and a worse tongue, and you're too young."

"You don't look like an old woman. I'm twenty-four."

"Twenty-six," Katherine admitted grudgingly. She had thought him much younger, boyish.

Too tired to argue further, Katherine changed the subject. "This dress is not made for riding. I need to fix it, and I need—to be alone for a few minutes." Night had almost closed in around them, but even so.

"Go a little way behind me. No one will see you."

Not seeing wasn't enough. She wanted a solid wall, or a fort with a lock, or better yet to be hundreds of miles away. How far was a little way? Far enough to make the men disappear in the shadows.

With her back to them all, Katherine ripped a wide band of cloth from the bottom of her chemise then unbuttoned the bodice of her dress and let it fall around her waist. She undid her corset laces, yanked the thing off and threw it into the night.

Running the band of torn cloth around her back, she tugged the ends together in front to get enough extra cloth to tie it together and bind her breasts. Maybe if she got out of this mess alive, she'd write Henry Dumont and tell him how small breasts were an advantage in certain situations.

Henry had been so disappointed the first time he saw her unclothed he hadn't tried to hide it. "Oh, well, all I need is a mouthful," he'd said.

The thought of Henry caused her to jerk the knots in the binding so tight undoing them would be difficult.

Feeling better than at any time since the first sound of gunfire, Katherine rebuttoned her dress, lifted her skirt and ripped her petticoat from hem to waist right up the front, then twisted the back to the front and did it again. Wriggling the petticoat back around the right way, she scoured the darkness in all directions before daring to relieve herself.

After only a few steps back toward the Apaches, she slowed and stopped. How could she pick Nilchi out in the dark? What if she stumbled across one of the others? Did she dare call out?

His voice came out of the night, and he was nearby. "Why did you tear your dress?"

Where had he been when she did that and other things? The relief of finding him close and not having to worry about the others kept her from caring.

"I tore my petticoat so it will cover me decently in the saddle tomorrow. At least I hope it will."

"You threw something away as if you're happy to be rid of it."

"I am."

He led the way to blankets spread side by side on the ground. Katherine lay down, trying not to think of the looks on the faces of her father, brothers, aunts and cousins if they could see her here. No matter how good his English, handsome his face or charming his manner, Nilchi was an Apache warrior, and the two of them lay side by side mere inches apart.

Then again, if her father and brothers were close enough to see her, they'd be close enough to attempt a rescue. Six of them, eleven Apaches. Better that they were safely off having great times halfway around the world.

From the smell of the blanket under her, it had spent the day on the back of a horse, and it hardly padded the ground. Still, she had slept on hard ground before, and exhaustion should make sleep come easily. It didn't. She stared at the endless sky and familiar stars overhead, considering and rejecting one impossible plan after another.

Her best chance had to be to convince Nilchi to take her to the outskirts of a town and let her go. Would an Apache be interested in ransom? In spite of the marriage talk, he didn't seem serious, which was why she couldn't stop thinking of him as young, boyish.

Except when standing up to the devil on the dark horse, Nilchi's attitude was one of amusement, at her, at everything. The other men with their impassive faces would fit into all the stories she had heard. And of course Gaetan.... Katherine shuddered.

Nilchi must have grown up on one of the reservations, and the reservation schools must have very good teachers.

As if he could hear the thoughts tumbling in her mind, he said, "You need to sleep."

"I know, but I can't. Too much happened, and there's too much I don't understand. I know you're Apache. This is a war party, isn't it?"

"A raiding party. Your people and the Mexicans call us Apache. They call all our people Apache, but we call ourselves Nde, the people, and we're not all the same. I am—these men are Chiricahua."

The Chiricahua—the most recalcitrant of all the savage Apache bands—had featured prominently in the stories Katherine had been bombarded with for days.

"Were you going to stop the stage but the bandits got there first?"

"No, we raided far to the north, and now we're going home. We never thought about the stage, but when we crossed the trail of the white robbers and saw they were few, we decided to follow and kill them."

The casual way he said it drove the true meaning of all the stories she had heard about the Apaches home as nothing else had. The few renegade bands still on the loose were engaged in all out war with the United States and Mexico. Now she was in the middle of that war, her life depending on the whim of this one young man.

"So I was just lucky that you saw me and got to me before one of the others."

"Some of the others wouldn't kill you and would want to keep you, but maybe they wouldn't stand against Gaetan."

"Probably not," she whispered. Not many would argue with that kind of fury.

A mere sliver in the sky, the moon still gave enough light to see Nilchi turn on his side toward her. She tensed, afraid he'd touch her and unsure what she'd do.

"Where were you going on the stage? Why are you traveling alone with no husband or father for protection?"

Her tension dissolved, and she turned the beginning of a laugh into a cough. Enemies to the death, the one thing that Americans, Mexicans and Apaches all agreed on was Katherine Grant should not be traveling alone on the stage without husband, father, or brother. They were all right too, weren't they? A male protector would have died today, but if she had stayed home, she would be safe and comfortable right now.

"These are secrets you're going to keep?"

Telling him had to be better than staring at the stars and worrying, and maybe an Apache, riding and raiding free across empty land, would understand what civilized men could not.

"No, no secrets. I'm on my way home. I live far to the east near the ocean in a place called New York."

"I remember New York. It's one of the states in the United States. I remember it on the map."

Much as she wanted to know, she couldn't think of a polite way to ask where he'd seen a map or how he'd learned such good English. "My family owns a shipping company. Our ships transport goods from the United States all over the world and bring goods back from all those places."

She hesitated, but he said nothing, asked no questions. "My mother died when I was young—six—and my father couldn't find anyone to take care of us when he was away. I have five brothers, and we were just too many." *And too angry and unwilling and bereft.* "So he took us with him. We sailed all over the world, and when we put into ports and my father did business, we left the ship with him. My brothers took care of me, and I dressed like them and ran after them and did everything they did."

"You grew up that way, always on ships on the ocean?"

"A lot of the time, but not always. In truth, my father could stay in New York and run the business from there, but he has a wanderlust and likes to sail and visit one country after another—and to hunt. I believe my father has killed at least one of every animal over fifty pounds in every country in the world."

"Did you hunt too? Is that how you learned to shoot?"

"Oh, yes. I hunted right alongside Father and the boys for years."

He made a little grunting sound that could have been approval or disapproval.

"As I got older, I had to start wearing dresses and behaving like a girl. My brothers even decided that I should have to take care of girl things, so I was the one who cooked and cleaned, or arranged to have it done."

She fell silent for a moment before deciding to tell him the truth, and all of the truth. "And then one day when we were in home port, my aunt told my father I was a disgrace. She said I was no better than a half-wild animal with no manners and no chance of ever finding a husband and something had to be done with me. So my father and brothers left me with my aunt and told me to learn to behave like a lady and to find a husband, and they sailed away without me."

The quaver in her voice as she related this last embarrassed her. Shouldn't she at least be able to control her voice?

"You ran away from your aunt?"

"Oh, no, that was years ago. I was seventeen when they put me ashore, and I did what my father wanted. I wore the clothes I was supposed to wear and learned never to raise my voice and never to run—at least never where anyone could see—and what to talk about and what never to say. I even almost caught a husband."

"He got away?"

She could hear the amusement in his voice again. "No, I threw him away."

"He wasn't a good husband?"

"We never got that far. We were engaged, promised, and he did something unforgivable, and I broke the engagement and said I wouldn't marry him."

"What did he do?"

The thought of it brought a flash of the old anger and indignation as she told this stranger what she had never told anyone except her father and brothers.

"He hit me."

Nilchi made the same non-committal sound as before. Probably Apaches had no problem with hitting wives. Most men didn't. Ignoring his attitude, whatever it was, she finished the story.

"My father and brothers were home for the wedding. This happened only a week before we were supposed to be married, and they took Henry's side. They believed that I provoked him. They wanted me to apologize and marry Henry anyway. When they couldn't make me agree, they sailed away without ever looking back."

She didn't know that, not for sure. Maybe they looked back, and if they did maybe their faces reflected sorrow or regret instead of the anger with which they had berated her every day since she'd raced home after getting away from Henry. Maybe by now they regretted ignoring her pleas, her *begging* to sail with them again.

"That's when I came West. That's why I was alone. The one country I never saw was this one, and I decided if they could sail around the world, I could travel across this country. I went from the Atlantic Ocean in the East to the Pacific Ocean in the West by train. Every time a place looked interesting, I stopped and stayed there for a few days. I didn't want to see the same places on the way home, and that's why I was on the stage. I wanted to visit different places on the way back to New York."

"And now you're here with me."

"And now I'm here with you."

"I'll be a good husband. I won't hit you."

"You need an Apache wife. I need to go home."

"You'll stay here and be my wife. We'll be good together."

Strange as it might be, nothing in his words or manner felt threatening, and talking to him had relaxed her. She yawned, fatigue tangling her thoughts. Tomorrow she would make him understand he was wrong. Tomorrow she would convince him to take her to a town. Tomorrow.

4

KATHERINE HAD NO opportunity to talk to Nilchi about anything in the morning. The pale gray promise of false dawn had only begun to chase the night when faint sounds of the men rising brought her awake. Nilchi no longer lay beside her. Even the blanket that had served as his bed was gone.

Staying quiet in her own blanket, she turned only her head, observing the shadowy Apaches as they rose and moved around the campsite. Before long the strengthening light let her pick out the tallest two of the men, standing face to face a short distance from the others.

One talked, gestured. The other stood motionless until his head moved in a distinctive way before he turned and stalked off. Even before Nilchi walked back toward her, she knew he was the man who remained. The one who had spit and left could only be Gaetan.

She turned her head as if she hadn't been watching and used stiff, aching arms to push her stiff, aching body to a sitting position. A night on the ground had finished turning her body into a version of the piece of dried meat that served as breakfast. Someday she would tell her brothers how she gritted her teeth, struggled to her feet and crawled back on the chestnut horse without a whimper, and they would applaud. Today the Apaches ignored her.

They drove the herd of mixed livestock south at the same relentless pace as the day before. As her sore muscles slowly loosened and adapted to the saddle, Katherine began to take note of the way the men had organized themselves. Nilchi rode on the left flank of the herd as he had the day before. She obeyed instructions and stayed near him but out of the way. Dust swirled up into her eyes and nose, and the chalky taste filled her mouth. Even so, only the men on point had a better position. She wondered what hierarchy dictated who rode behind, invisible in the choking cloud.

Last night there had been eleven men in the camp. Today only nine drove the herd. A sharp stab of disappointment lanced through her. Maybe the armies of both the United States and Mexico weren't searching for these particular Apaches, but they were in the field looking for hostiles. If the two missing men served as scouts, chances of rescue by gallant cavalrymen were slight.

Except for an occasional shout at an animal that broke from the herd, the men were silent, their faces closed and expressionless. Every man had a rifle slung over his shoulder or tied to his saddle and a knife at his belt. Several carried pistols. While the water jugs and leather canteens tied to their saddles all looked empty or close to it, each one did have a way to carry water. They rode tirelessly as if born on horseback.

Abandoning thoughts of rescue, Katherine considered escape. In contrast to the Apaches, she had no weapons, no way to carry water, no food and no knowledge of the land. Her body would soon adjust to long hours in the saddle, and she would be able to run, climb, ride and hide. If no one watched her more closely than last night, she could get away. Then what? No matter how she examined one idea after another, by midday she had to accept that a successful escape was no more likely than a speedy rescue.

Which left her right back where she had been the night before, plotting the best way to change Nilchi's mind and convince him to take her to a town or at least leave her near one. By early afternoon, Katherine had decided to use what he had said about his people needing the livestock and supplies on the mules.

Her family would forget how unhappy they had been with her once they knew she was missing. They'd be more than willing to give the Apaches many times what they could steal on dozens of raids for her safe return, but would the army let them? What else could she promise as a lure or say to disenchant him?

As she considered possibilities, a change rippled through the animals. The drooping head on her own horse came up, and his steps quickened. The men along the flanks and in the drag rode forward, all positioning themselves so as to hold the herd back. The only thing that would affect the herd like that was water. The animals must smell water.

Katherine followed Nilchi forward and stopped when he did, eying the cattle nervously. Standing between an animal with a four-foot spread of horns and something it wanted didn't strike her as smart.

The two missing Apaches raced from behind the next hill, shouting and gesturing. The faces around her finally showed expressions. Relief, eagerness. She gave Nilchi a questioning look.

"The soldiers set traps for us where there's water. We think this water is known only to us, but sometimes the soldiers surprise us." He gave a small shrug with one shoulder.

"What would happen if soldiers were here?"

"Unless they were very few, we'd go to another place."

None of the animals had had water since she'd been with the Apaches, and none of the men had taken a drink since early this morning. Katherine's own thirst raged. She wasted no time regretting the absence of soldiers who would get no chance to rescue her and shared in the general anticipation of as much water as she wanted.

"Why aren't they letting the animals go to the water if it's safe?"

"The spring is small. Only a few can go at a time."

Even as he spoke, three men cut several mules from the herd and followed them as they took off around the hill at an eager trot. Half a dozen at a time. Including the mules and saddle horses, there had to be more than a hundred animals in total.

"We'll be here until dark," Katherine said. "Will we stay here tonight?"

Nilchi looked toward where Gaetan and another man discussed something intently, their attitudes and occasional gestures signaling strong and conflicting opinions. "Yes. Chishogi won't listen to Gaetan."

"How can he not listen to the leader?"

Nilchi frowned at her for a second before his face cleared. "Gaetan isn't the leader. Chishogi is the leader. The men would never follow Gaetan. We aren't alike in many ways, but we're alike in that way."

"That's Chishogi he's arguing with?"

"Yes."

She had picked Chishogi out of the other men already, not because he struck her as a leader but because he didn't. Flat, thick features made him look dull, and he walked with a swagger. On the ground she doubted the top of Chishogi's head would reach Gaetan's nose. She wondered if that's why the argument was taking place on horseback.

Much as she didn't want any part of the hate-filled devil who wanted to kill her, Gaetan looked as if he should be the leader of these men. Since his furious confrontation with Nilchi the day before, Katherine had never looked directly at Gaetan, not wanting to attract his attention in any way.

Avoiding an accidental glance in Gaetan's direction had been easy because he stood out from the others. His size was part of it, but it wasn't just size. Nilchi was also tall, but Nilchi looked young, slender and lithe. In contrast, Gaetan was mature, lean and powerful.

Every one of the Apaches looked tough to the bone. Imagining them in the stories of terror and killing took no effort, but none of them emanated the dark aura of raw power of Gaetan.

We are not alike in many ways, but we are alike in that way. Gaetan was still arguing with the other man. Katherine dared to study him and saw what she did not want to see. His face was Nilchi's with a dozen years added to it and the charm and amusement replaced by bitterness and anger.

Her mouth felt drier than ever as she swallowed hard. "He's your brother."

Amusement danced in Nilchi's eyes again. "You didn't see? I'm much more handsome, but one of the ways we're alike is our faces."

"I see now. Yesterday all I saw was how much he wanted to kill me. Does he speak English as well as you do?"

"I don't know."

Before she could question that unbelievable statement, Gaetan finished his talk with the other men, rode toward them and pushed his horse between hers and Nilchi's. Katherine kept her head down and didn't move, had to remind herself to breathe. Their voices were different too, one lighter, calm, the other deeper, passionate. When Gaetan turned away, helped cut more mules from the herd and went with the next group to the water, she dared raise her head.

"Is he always so angry?"

"Yes. Gaetan says the white men stole my Apache heart and gave me a weak white one. I say they turned his heart black. Sometimes I think if Gaetan is cut, his blood will spill out black from the poison inside him, but he's my brother, and he tries to protect me."

"Protect you from what?"

"From any danger. He came on this raid only because he thinks there may be trouble because Chishogi is careless. The men believe in Chishogi because he's a good leader and has had many successes, but Gaetan has no respect. He says Chishogi should be more cautious, that he's arrogant and foolish. That's why they argued. Gaetan says to stay here is dangerous, but we'll stay here tonight."

Katherine didn't want to agree with Gaetan about anything. Even so, if the army set traps for the Apaches at water sources, she agreed that lingering around water with a hundred stolen animals was careless. She turned her head to hide a smile. Maybe the chances of rescue were higher than she had calculated.

Night had not yet fallen when men, beasts and woman had all drunk their fill, but the sun hung low in the west. Nilchi's prediction proved true, for the men settled into a camp not far from the spring. They butchered a steer, and in what seemed a matter of minutes, had a fire going and strips of meat cut out and roasting over the open fire. Katherine's mouth watered as the scent filled the air.

She ate her piece of beef, licked her fingers and sucked the bone bare. Thoughts of coffee, fresh bread and butter danced in her head as she did it. And fruit. She pictured a juicy red apple wistfully. If the Apaches subsisted on a diet of meat alone, it would be one more reason to find a way back to civilization as fast as possible, not that she needed another one.

The men sat in groups of two and three, but none approached Nilchi. They had also kept their distance the night before. "Are they avoiding you because of me?"

"No. Because of Gaetan. He's going to argue against Chishogi even more soon. They think Chishogi is right and Gaetan wrong, and they think I'll side with Gaetan."

"What will they argue about?"

"Soon we have to choose our way home. There are several ways we can go. Chishogi will choose the way that's easiest with the horses and cattle, the way that will take the fewest days. Gaetan will argue that way is too dangerous."

"Is it? Is it more dangerous?"

"Maybe."

"So will you support Gaetan against Chishogi ?"

He shrugged one shoulder. "I think not. I want to get home quickly too. The sooner we get home, the sooner you and I will marry."

"If I continue to say no, will you force me?"

"The people don't force women to marry. I'll court you, and you'll say yes soon."

Katherine met dark eyes alive with humor, aware of the handsome face those eyes brought to life, and her heart sank. Not long ago she had let Henry Dumont, a man without one particle of Nilchi's charm, talk her into his bed and all but ruined her own hopes for a decent future.

The slanting rays of the setting sun burnished the young Apache's face, and Katherine swallowed hard, unable to deny the attraction she felt for the uncommonly beautiful young man. Heaven help her. Given enough time, he could talk her into anything. She needed to get away before she did something stupid again.

Unable to remember any of her convincing arguments about why he should let her go, she changed the subject back to their earlier conversation.

"What did you mean when you said you don't know if your brother can speak English? Did he go to a different school than you did?"

He stared vacantly across the camp for so long she thought he wouldn't answer, but then he said, "We were in the same school for many years. Gaetan escaped when he was sixteen, and since that time he has never spoken English or Spanish. He says the words are dirt in his mouth. He still understands, I think, but he won't speak."

His own English must have failed him. No one had to escape from a school. They just stopped going. But how could they have been in school for years together when Nilchi was so much younger?

"Your parents must have been pleased that you stayed in school and learned so well," she said finally.

"The reason we were in the school was that the white men who killed our father and mother took us there."

The matter of fact way he said it disconcerted her. Before she summoned words of sympathy, he continued.

"I was five and Gaetan was nine."

Katherine couldn't believe her ears. How could they be so close in age? Gaetan looked so frightening. *Mature.* So much more mature. She missed some of what Nilchi said while readjusting her preconceived notions then gave him her full attention again.

"Gaetan says we were going to visit my father's family, but I don't remember that. I remember the way four men rode toward us smiling and friendly, and how when they were close, they shot my father and mother and laughed. We couldn't understand them but could tell two of them wanted to kill us. Two of them argued with the others. They laughed at me, threw me in the air and from one to the other. They tried to do the same to Gaetan, but he fought them. He cut the face of one with a stick. He kicked another so hard the man fell down. After that, I think three wanted to kill Gaetan, but one still argued against the others."

"I'm sorry," Katherine whispered when he paused. She remembered the devastation of her mother's death, and she had still had a father and five brothers.

He gave that same indifferent little shrug of one shoulder.

"They tied us up and put us in their wagon. They took us to St. Tilden's Indian Mission School. A man there gave them money for us. The people at the school believe they will go to heaven because they teach Indians to be like white men. Not just Apache. They also had Papago, Pima and Navajo there. We were all the same to them."

For years Katherine had felt sorry for herself because she lost the freedom to run wild with her brothers when she was seventeen. He had lost everything when he was five. She couldn't think of anything to say, and no words would fit past the lump in her throat anyway.

"Don't look so sad. For me the school wasn't so bad. I did what the white men wanted. As you say, my English is very good."

"Were they—were they kind?"

"Not in the beginning. After Gaetan gave in, sometimes."

"Gave in?"

"Gaetan fought them the same way he fought the men who killed our father and mother. They beat him, and they gave him no food, and they shut him in small places, but he fought them, and in the end, I think they knew they would have to kill him. He would never give in."

"But they didn't kill him."

"No, doing those things to him didn't make him obey, but when they did those things to me, Gaetan did what they wanted. He stopped speaking Apache. He spoke English, and he spoke Spanish. He learned the other things they wanted, and he was respectful to them. They gave us stars. We were very good Indians."

She didn't realize she was crying until he reached out and brushed away a tear with his thumb. The thought of him touching her had frightened her only the day before. Now his touch comforted.

"They only hit me a few times. He's my brother. He didn't let them hurt me."

"How did he escape?"

"A teacher took him outside the walls of the school. He told me it was going to happen, and I told him to go. No one blamed me for what he did then."

"Did you graduate? Is that how you got out?"

"When Gaetan became a warrior, he came back for me. I was fifteen."

"He didn't just knock on the front door and ask for you, did he?"

As she'd hoped, Nilchi laughed at that. "He came over the wall with guns and knives, and we left the same way."

Katherine didn't ask what Gaetan had done to any teachers or staff he'd encountered, refused to even think about it. "Were you glad to get away?"

"I was glad to see my brother again. He came to take me back to our own people, and he did. He's wrong that the teachers changed my heart, but they put things in my head. I speak very good English and Spanish, I can read and write, and I can do sums. I know the states of the United States and their capitol cities, and I know the names of the presidents. When I returned to the people I couldn't speak our language and didn't know our customs, but I could do all those other things."

"Oh." He had been dropped into a foreign world where he didn't know the language or customs once at five and then again at fifteen. She couldn't even imagine it.

"That's what you meant when you said the men wouldn't follow Gaetan. It was the same for him."

"Nothing is the same for Gaetan. He threw away everything he learned in the school and honors the customs of our people in all ways, but he believes only what he wants to and sometimes I think that's nothing. He's an unbeliever."

"The way he was arguing with Chishogi, I'd say he believes in himself."

She'd hoped to make Nilchi laugh with the comment, but he didn't. The sun had sunk below the horizon, shadows closing in, but the empty bleakness in his eyes was still too easy to see.

"It's the same for you, isn't it?" she said. "You learned different ways in the school, and then you came back to your people, and it's hard to believe in their ways."

"Yes. Some things the whites taught are so different it's hard to decide what's true." He chased the empty look with a smile. "But I believe you and I will be happy together."

Katherine suppressed a sigh and ignored the marriage subject. "Do you wish Gaetan had left you alone? Did you want to stay at the school?"

"I never thought about it until he came back, but the school does no good. Some who leave when they're old enough go to work for white men, but most become beggars and drunks. Soon the soldiers will kill us or make us live as they say on the reservation, and we'll be beggars and drunks there, but because Gaetan came for me, we have this time to be free."

He gave another indifferent shrug, and she fought an urge to grab him by both shoulders, shake him, and tell him to stop that. Decisions *did* matter. Her decision about Henry had mattered. Her decision not to follow the other passengers out of the stagecoach mattered.

"Maybe living on the reservation wouldn't be so bad," she said. "Maybe you could teach others there."

"I lived at San Carlos and at Tularosa. The reservations are bad. When Victorio decided he would fight before he would go back to San Carlos, we went with him."

Katherine stiffened, staring at him in shock. That name was the one most often cursed in all the stories, the one blamed for the worst murder and torture.

Proud of how steady her voice sounded, she said, "You rode with Victorio?"

"I told you we're Chiricahua. Our band is the Chihinne. The Mexicans call us Mimbreños, and your people call us Warm Springs Apaches. Victorio was our chief. Gaetan and I only went to war with Victorio a little while. Gaetan wants to kill every white and Mexican he can, but he likes to hunt alone. He doesn't want to listen to others, and he says to take captives and to torture is stupid. If you kill an enemy quickly, no one can rescue him. Some say the hate in Victorio was so strong, he went insane at the end. I think someday the poison inside will drive Gaetan insane too."

Jaded cynicism tinged his words. The men around the campsite looked more dangerous than before. She should be thankful Gaetan believed in killing quickly, but he wasn't the leader, and Chishogi's opinions in that regard had just gone on the list of things she didn't want to know. If anything happened to Nilchi, or if he did change his mind about wanting to marry her....

Nilchi left her, went to his brother, crouched down and started talking. After one worried glance, Katherine kept her head down and her eyes on the ground. Behaving sensibly would be easier if she didn't see the devil spitting.

She lay awake on her blanket that night, going over and over what she'd learned. No matter what Nilchi said, she had five brothers and knew how things could be between brothers. She wasn't sure she believed his denial that he would have preferred to stay at the school, and she remembered how much she and her youngest brother had resented the overprotective attitude of the older ones.

She and Tom had spent one whole summer flaunting every restriction imposed, no matter how reasonable. Nilchi admitted by coming on this raid he had forced Gaetan to do something he wouldn't normally do and didn't like doing.

The moon rose, a thin, cold crescent in the sky. A powerful desire to run into the night swept over her, and she dug her nails into her scabbed palms to keep control, stay still. If a younger Apache brother wanted to tweak an older Apache brother who hated whites, what better way than to take a white woman captive and claim to want to marry her? Only Nilchi stood between Katherine and disaster. What if Gaetan was right about one more thing—the consistency of his brother's heart?

5

With heightened awareness of how precarious her situation was, Katherine obeyed instructions, stayed out of the way, and asked no questions for the next two days. Learning that Nilchi had been with Victorio, even for a little while, had shaken her, as had the glimpse of his cynicism about the tragedies in his own life. His charming manner, good looks and excellent English had led her to believe he was different than the other Apaches, civilized, reasonable.

He had shaken her confidence in her original judgment. If convincing him she would never marry him didn't mean being forced, would it mean becoming prey for the other men? Or death from a swift thrust of Gaetan's knife? In that case, she'd sew her own wedding dress.

As they prepared to head out early in the morning of the third day, Gaetan approached for the first time since they'd watered at the small spring. At first his voice was low, persuasive, then increasingly angry until his rage was as powerful as the first time Katherine saw him at the site of the stage robbery. At one point he looked right at her, raked her from head to toe with a contemptuous glare, and said a few words in a tone that made the back of her neck crawl.

Nilchi said little and kept shaking his head until Gaetan whirled and stalked off. Only because she was looking for it, Katherine caught the satisfaction that flitted across Nilchi's face as he watched his brother's back.

She couldn't keep from saying, "Are you really angry enough at him to do something dangerous to get even?"

He looked surprised. "I'm not angry at my brother."

"Resentful then."

For a second she thought she'd gone too far, then he said, "He thinks I'm still five years old and need his protection. He's too...." He couldn't find the word.

"Bossy."

"Yes. He thinks Chishogi isn't careful enough, but Chishogi is a good leader. No one is ever careful enough for Gaetan. He should never have come with us."

"Maybe he won't next time. What did he say about me?"

"He said if I went a different way with him, I could bring you, and he wouldn't kill you."

Anger let Katherine forget any remaining muscle soreness and swing up on her horse as if she had spent hours every day for the last year riding astride. At least if she had to marry Nilchi, the world would be saved from whatever horrors Gaetan would perpetrate in the future. If he didn't die of his own rage at the wedding, his new sister-in-law was going to find a way to augment the poison already in him at the wedding feast.

No more than a few miles passed before Katherine understood the danger of the trail. An ambush from the cliffs above would be easy. Only a few men would be in position to fire at a time, though, and the army would want to bring greater strength to bear.

That afternoon the steep walls of the canyons fell away, and the trail widened. In the narrow canyons, the livestock had strung out into a long, narrow snake. Now the Apaches bunched them into a herd again. Thick clumps of scrub brush leading into steep hills offered too many hiding places for animals determined to break away.

A single gunshot popped, and Katherine stiffened in the saddle. She scanned the Apaches, expecting to see one of them with a rifle raised. Instead she saw the warriors kicking and whipping their mounts to a dead run and ramming their way in among the loose horses. They hung so low in the saddle they all but disappeared, their shrieking yells increasing the panic of the stampeding animals.

A blaze of gunfire erupted as riflemen opened up from concealment in the hills on both sides of the trail. Katherine's vague ideas that she could go toward attackers, that the sight of her dress and sound of her English would make them hold their fire, dissolved in the face of reality.

She tried to stop her half-crazed horse until a bullet spurting dirt into the air only a few feet away brought home the danger. Her hesitation had let the loose animals thunder on by.

Leaning low against his neck, she gave her horse his head, intending to imitate the Apaches and work her way in among the laggards of the herd. Once out of the line of fire, she could stop her spent horse and start shouting.

Getting away from Nilchi or any of the other Apaches posed no problem. Through the roiling clouds of dust, she could see the Apaches ahead of her, racing for their lives in the midst of the herd. Behind her.... She glanced back, saw horses down, saw a lone figure crouched behind one of the big bodies, firing at men emerging from the brush.

A lone man trying to hold off a dozen with a single-shot breech-loading rifle had no chance. As if he heard her thought, Nilchi threw down his rifle and pulled her Remington from his belt.

She reacted instinctively, yanking her horse's head around with all her strength, kicking one side to force him to turn. The gelding fought her, wanted to follow the herd, almost fell, but in the end he turned. Nilchi saw her coming and vaulted up behind her before she stopped. He reached around her, grabbed the reins and urged the horse to turn again.

The pursuers all wore gray, yet they looked more like rabble than soldiers. They had the advantage of fresh horses not carrying double. Katherine twisted around in the shelter of Nilchi's body, peering over his shoulder to see how fast the men were gaining.

A hammer-like blow slammed into the rib under her left breast, knocking her sideways. She grabbed for the saddle horn, fighting to keep her balance as Nilchi slumped over her.

The saddle slipped. The horse's stride roughened. Katherine kicked free of the stirrups, ready for the inevitable fall, when Gaetan charged out of the dust ahead. The saddle slipped another inch.

Even if Gaetan meant to help, he couldn't get his horse turned in time. He couldn't, but he did. As he drew up beside them, he threw his rifle away, grabbed Nilchi by the shoulders and shoved him and Katherine with him back up on the horse.

The reins flapped uselessly around her horse's legs, but it didn't matter. Gaetan drove both horses toward the brush ruthlessly. They hit it at a run, the thick tangle dragging them to a stop as the branches closed behind them.

As fast as the horses stopped, Gaetan was faster. On the ground before they halted, he let Nilchi fall into his arms and moved deeper into the brush, bulling his way through the thick growth as if it didn't exist. Katherine got off her horse and stood there, uncertain what to do.

Blood drenched the bodice of her dress front and back. Nausea rose in her throat at the sweet, metallic smell. Her rib and breast burned liked fire. How could she even stand with a wound like that?

Unbuttoning the top of her dress, she explored the source of the pain. The bullet had grazed a rib and torn a gash several inches long, but so far as she could tell, the wound wasn't deep and was hardly bleeding. The blood that soaked her was not her own.

Coarse voices cursed in Spanish, getting louder as the men drew near. A bullet zinged by her, followed by a shout.

"No! No shooting unless necessary. Take them alive. Position yourselves."

In spite of the reassuring order, another gunshot sounded, making up her mind. She pushed through the clinging branches as fast as she could until she reached the place where Gaetan had broken trail and followed him even faster.

He had laid Nilchi down in a small clearing. Nilchi was alive, talking to Gaetan in gasps through a bubbling pink froth. Katherine slipped close silently, knelt and took the hand Gaetan was not holding in both of hers. Nilchi's eyes slid across her face, and she thought he tried to smile before he spoke again, the Apache words meaningless to her.

Shaking his head, Gaetan uttered a single word she would have no trouble recognizing in any language. *No.* How could he? How could anyone not give a dying brother whatever assurance he needed?

Nilchi spoke again, the gasping effort dreadful to see, the froth on his lips darkening. Gaetan gave in, his face softening as he spoke. Nilchi whispered a few more words. When he stopped, the only sound was of his labored breathing, and then there was nothing. The light left the dark eyes, and the feel of his hand in hers changed. The beautiful young man was gone.

Fighting tears, Katherine looked up into eyes still alive, alive with so much hate and rage she froze in place. When Gaetan pulled his hand free from Nilchi's and went for the knife at his waist, her paralysis broke.

Throwing herself backwards, her heels digging through the layers of leaves and sticks on the ground, she scrambled away like a crab, knowing she had no chance, no chance at all.

The killing attack never came. Gaetan didn't lunge across the body after her. He faded away into the brush, a wild animal stealing away from hunters.

The voices of the men calling back and forth in Spanish sounded nearer. In open country, they could follow the blood trail at a run, but thick growth and caution slowed their pursuit. In spite of how rough they looked and sounded, they must be soldiers of some kind. The shooting had stopped. Once they arrived, she would explain herself, tell her story, and this whole nightmare would be over.

Katherine crawled back to the body. "I'm sorry," she whispered, pressing his eyes closed. "You saved me from the bandits, from your brother and the others, and I didn't save you at all, did I?" She stopped holding back her tears, took Nilchi's hand in hers and wept.

When the Mexicans broke through to the clearing, the first man to reach her pulled Katherine away from the body, held her with her back against his chest and shouted in Spanish.

"I have the woman. We were right. She's a gringo!"

The contact was disgustingly intimate. Katherine forgot her Spanish as she drove an elbow back into his ribs and stomped on his instep.

"Let go of me! Yes, I'm American, and I want to speak to an officer right now. Let go!"

He did let go, then grabbed her by the arm and yanked her back, one hand raised to hit her. An order barked in Spanish stopped him.

"Let her go."

"Commandant, the woman helped the Apache. She was weeping over him."

"I saw what she did. Leave the Apache whore to me."

She needed to calm down, start talking and start talking fast. Katherine took a deep breath, but before she said a word, the man who had just called her a whore spoke to her in English, his manner solicitous.

"Señorita, I apologize. My men have their blood up after the chase. Why are you with these savages? Did they capture you in the north?"

He was thin and sharp faced, barely her own height. He wore clothes the same style and light gray color as the other men, but his were better quality with rows of lace on the sleeves. In spite of his labored, heavily accented English, Katherine didn't answer him in his own language. Instinctively she knew this was not a man who needed to know she spoke Spanish.

"Yes, I was on a stagecoach traveling east from Tucson. I know the Apaches are your enemies, but this man rescued me from stagecoach robbers who were going to kill me. The other Apaches would have killed me too, but this was a good man. He didn't hurt me, and he was kind. My name is Katherine Grant, and my family will be most grateful to you and your men."

A hint of a possible reward for her safe return could do no harm.

"I am Commandant Eleazar Hierra Vargas—Commandant Hierra—of the Rurales," he said with a trace of a bow. "We are charged with keeping the countryside safe from the likes of that."

He gestured toward the body, and the motion drew her gaze there. She saw one of the men with a knife pulling Nilchi's hair back and cutting, cutting.

Katherine threw herself at the man, knocking the knife from his hand.

"Stop that! Stop it! Make him stop. Make him stop!"

Hard hands clamped on her shoulders and pulled her away. Hierra stepped in front of her.

"Señorita Grant, control yourself. Every man here has lost family and friends to the Apaches. They are inhuman savages, and my men are entitled to a small measure of revenge. For now I will accompany you to where we will spend the night. After you have rested and feel more like yourself, we will discuss how to return you to your family."

In Spanish he said to the men, "*We'll bivouac near the water tonight. After I make the whore wash the Apache stink off her, I'll decide what to do with her. Bring me the scalps.*"

"*The others fell under the running horses, Commandant. They'll be torn up badly.*"

"*If you want your share of the bounties, find me enough hair to collect on. Do it.*"

"*Yes, sir.*"

As Hierra had advised, Katherine had regained control of herself. When he switched his attitude back to concerned and his language to English, she didn't spit at him or call him a liar, but smiled with what she hoped was a better imitation of sincerity than his.

"Come, Señorita Grant. My men will have camp set up very shortly. I'll arrange for you to bathe and have a hot meal. After a night's sleep, you'll be able to forget this unpleasantness."

Katherine didn't want to bathe, eat, or sleep around Hierra and his men. And she didn't want to forget. "Of course, Commandant," she murmured as she headed back the way he indicated.

The chestnut gelding stood with his head sagging, sweat drying white on his neck. One of the Rurales had already repositioned the saddle. Katherine gave the horse a sympathetic pat and climbed aboard.

Hierra was still issuing orders when one of his men galloped up, waving with excitement.

"*We caught him, Commandant. You were right. He had no gun and the cordon worked. We have ropes on him!*"

Hierra's eyes lit with triumph. "*Take the woman to the camp,*" he ordered the others. "*No one touches her, but make sure she washes and get those clothes from her and burn them.*"

He took off with his messenger, and Katherine watched them go. Maybe the world would be a better place without Gaetan in it, but she regretted he had been captured by men like these because he wouldn't leave his brother to die alone.

One of the Rurales took the reins of her horse and led her toward the hills. She made no objection.

6

Hours later Katherine stood in the middle of the small tent Commandant Hierra usually occupied and examined every support, every square inch of canvas and the few sparse furnishings.

A locked trunk sat against one wall. She knew it was locked because she had tried to open it. An oil lamp hung near a blanket-covered cot set against the opposite wall, and a small table with one drawer stood across from the closed fly of the tent. The drawer contained a few sheets of paper, a pen and a pot of ink.

Hierra's accommodations were the height of luxury in a camp like this, and all she could think of were the hunts she had come to hate, the ones that trapped the prey in net or pit. Of course, she was not like a trapped tiger. She was like a fatted calf.

The Rurales had indeed taken her to the stream that ran close to where they bivouacked and given her dubious privacy to bathe. At least she had been able to scrub the wound under her breast with soap.

The only battle she won was to keep her boots, perhaps because Hierra's order had only mentioned burning her clothes. So far the shadows under the cot had concealed the boots from notice. A spare shirt from one of the men was the only dress Hierra had allowed. It barely covered her knees, but at least it was clean.

The Rurales had also given her the blanket she clutched over the shirt. Now, as she listened to the men talking outside, they gave her information she desperately needed.

"*Carlos says he heard the woman talking to the Commandant when they ate. She's a rich American, and her family would pay a big ransom to have her back.*"

"*You know it will make no difference to the Commandant. Apaches killed his wife and son. Do you think he'll send a woman who whored for an Apache and wept over his body home for money?*"

"*He should. He should think of us. His family is rich, and he doesn't need the money, but we're entitled to a share of the ransom, just like the scalps. We should have a say in what he does with the woman.*"

"*Tell him that then. Here he comes.*"

Katherine already knew telling Hierra anything was a waste of breath. He had given her no choice except to share a meal with him, barefoot and dressed in a shirt and blanket. In spite of the pretense of concern for her well being, not one word of her explanation of how she had come to be with the Apaches or what happened afterwards had changed his contemptuous asides to his men in Spanish.

Maybe if she could get one of the greedy ones alone long enough to have a talk with him....

The fly on the tent opened, and Hierra stepped in, followed by another officer. "I hope you feel better now, señorita."

"Yes, thank you, I do. The bath and hot meal made a great difference."

"Good. I have one more thing for you, a little aid to help you sleep tonight. I know ladies such as yourself do not drink brandy, but in circumstances such as these, it is medicinal."

Refusing had not been an option with the bath or food, and she knew it wasn't an option now. As she took the tin cup, a voice in her head that sounded remarkably like her oldest brother warned that drinking the contents would be a terrible mistake. She believed the warning. Spilling the cup's contents would only mean a brief respite, but she couldn't think what else to do.

"Commandant."

At the sound of the voice, Hierra and his officer both turned toward the tent entrance. Katherine spilled all but a swallow of the brandy into the folds of the blanket around her. The liquid soaked through to the skin at her waist and started to run down. She let the blanket sag around her feet.

One of the men entered the tent, a leather pouch in his hand. *"The scalps, Commandant."*

"Are they wrapped well?"

"Yes, sir. I wrapped them in oilskin first myself."

Katherine knew she should pretend indifference and wasn't able. She stared as Hierra took a small key from his pocket, opened the trunk, and tucked the pouch inside. After refastening the lock, he pocketed the key and turned back to her.

"Have you finished the brandy?"

She swallowed the last liquid in the cup and didn't have to fake a shudder as it burned its way to her stomach. "Yes, Commandant. I'm sure it will make sleep come more quickly. Thank you."

"We leave you to your dreams then." He gave the smallest of bows and led the way outside, speaking to the other officer as they went. *"How much did you put in?"*

"More than enough. You'll have to shake her awake in the morning."

"I hope not too much. I want her awake to weep over the big Apache. When she sees how I kill him, she'll be very cooperative, no matter what I decide to do with her."

"The men could use a laundress."

"And a whore. Maybe the Apaches taught her interesting things."

The two men walked out of the tent laughing, and Katherine listened as Hierra assigned guards. Once they were sure she was asleep, only one had to stay the night. That meant they were going to check. She had to stop the panicked panting, stop shaking and feign sleep believably.

The only thing in the tent with a point of any kind was the pen in the drawer of the table, not exactly a formidable weapon. Katherine cocooned the blanket tightly around her body to discourage casual groping, clutched the pen in her hand and stretched out on the cot.

Her eyes closed against her will. If one swallow of the brandy had this effect, how much laudanum or other sleeping potion had been mixed in? Maybe Hierra's lieutenant had been trying to do her a favor and poison her.

She played mind games, recited favorite poems in her head, pinched herself regularly and she fell asleep.

The sound of male voices brought Katherine awake in time to keep from reacting when a callused hand touched her face and ran down across her swaddled body.

"Bah, she's wrapped herself so I can't feel anything."

"All we need to know is she's asleep. If you do more, the Commandant will string you up beside the Apache."

"He'll never know."

"If she wakes up and starts screaming, everyone will know. She's asleep. Let's get out of here."

"I'll keep watch now."

"Don't do anything foolish, Ramon. There's no way you can have her without leaving sign. No woman is worth dying for."

The men left, Ramon still cursing and mumbling under his breath. Katherine pushed off the cot and unwrapped the blanket. How long had she slept? How long did she have before Ramon worked up courage to attack a drugged woman? Maybe screaming would take care of the guard and his lust tonight but it wouldn't save her from Hierra's plans tomorrow. She needed a real weapon, and she needed to get away.

The blackness inside the tent was total now. The only thing inside with her that she hadn't explored was the trunk. Reaching out with each bare foot carefully before trusting her weight to it, she groped her way to the trunk.

The point of the pen fit in the lock, but no amount of twisting or pressing had any effect. Thwarted, she stabbed the point into the keyhole in frustration. The lock popped open with a click that sounded so loud she froze, waiting for the guard to come running.

After long seconds of silence, Katherine opened the lid an inch at a time and reached in. The leather pouch she had seen Hierra put inside was on top. She set that aside to take with her. If she had to toss it on the first campfire she came to after leaving here she would. Whatever else happened, the Commandant wasn't going to get a penny from those scalps.

After that she began pulling out clothing. She separated things by feel. Underclothing of soft cotton, stockings of wool and silk, wool trousers, linen shirt.

Much as she hated wearing Hierra's clothes, they smelled of soap, clean, and he was about her size. She added to her list of things to write Henry about someday. The less than voluptuous figure he had disparaged once again proved to be an advantage. Hierra's drawers and trousers fit snugly over her hips, but they fit.

Dressing in trousers brought back memories of running over ship decks after her brothers, of some of the best times in her life, and she felt stronger and less vulnerable as she returned to her exploration. The last items of clothing in the trunk were wrapped around hard shapes. A crucifix, a carved frame as for a photograph, a book. Across the bottom of the trunk, Katherine found what she had been praying for.

The scabbard was too long for a knife, decorated and tassled. The short sword it sheathed slid free easily, and the blade cut her thumb at a touch. Katherine knelt there unmoving a moment, shaky with relief. The sword would be clumsy, but it gave her a chance.

Fully dressed, boots laced over Hierra's fancy stockings, Katherine sat on the trunk lid with the sword in one hand, the leather pouch in the other and the folded blanket over an arm as she considered her next step. Should she wait for Ramon to come back inside after her or walk outside and take him by surprise? Go after him, she decided. She had no idea how much of the night was already gone, how long she had slept.

Once she escaped, she could work her way around the camp to where the horses were picketed, take one and escape. And then what? She had to face the fact she was now in the same position she had been in when thinking about an escape from the Apaches.

She tried to picture herself slipping off into the night on a horse and successfully escaping Hierra's pursuit, finding enough food and water for herself and the horse, or even for herself. If she made it to a town and asked for help, could anyone help her before Hierra tracked her down? She had no money for bribes, telegrams, or even food. Could she make it far enough north to be safe in Arizona or New Mexico?

Her mind skittered away from the one possibility that kept creeping in.

Ramon saved her from wasting time in further fruitless speculation. The canvas ties that held the tent closed whispered as he released one after another. She dropped the blanket and scalps and moved to a position near the opening as he muttered his self-justification.

"No one will know. The woman won't remember, and Commandant will never know."

Enough light followed the guard into the tent for Katherine to see his outline. She drove the sword into him the way she had heard Mark describe years ago, from below the rib cage at an angle toward the heart. When the hilt hit flesh, she wrenched it to the left, then the right. He fell with a grunt of surprise and pain, thrashing and groaning loudly several times before he stopped moving and fell silent.

Katherine grabbed the pistol from its holster at the dead man's waist and crouched over the body, hands shaking, waiting to see if anyone had heard him. The night stayed quiet. The coppery scent of blood brought bile to the back of her throat again. Swallowing it down, she ran her hands over Ramon's belt. He had carried both a pistol and a knife. Draping the gun belt around her chest like a bandolier, she retrieved the leather pouch and blanket and stepped outside.

After the blackness and close air of the tent, the light of the quarter moon and stars made her blink. She sucked in deep breaths of fresh air, savoring freedom, determined to keep it and more aware than ever that she had no time to waste. The positions of the moon and stars told her the night was more than half gone.

Ramon's rifle leaned against a wooden crate. His hat sat on top. Grimacing with distaste, Katherine twisted her hair on top of her head and jammed the hat down over it. With luck any guard or light sleeper who spotted her now would see only a fellow Rurale walking to the edge of the camp to relieve himself.

By Katherine's best guess, there had been more than sixty Rurales in the troop even before the wagons with equipment and supplies pulled into place late in the afternoon. Tents for

Hierra and the officers were on one side of the camp, soldiers slept on the ground opposite. The picketed horses and the wagons formed the other two sides of a rough square. Reminding herself to walk like a man who had every right to stroll through the camp in the middle of the night, Katherine set out.

A fire with flames still leaping from fresh fuel burned near the wagons. Voices came from that direction. She approached carefully, crouched behind a stack of equipment and crawled closer before peering out. The scene before her stopped her breath.

Two Rurales moved back and forth between the fire and the wagon, their shadows falling across Gaetan's contorted, naked body where it stretched across one of the big wagon wheels. A leather thong bit into his neck, holding his head back over the wheel rim and exposing his throat as if for sacrifice.

His chest heaved with the effort of each breath. Every muscle and tendon bunched and strained against the pressure of the way his arms and legs had been stretched and tied. Sweat-sheened bronze skin glowed in the firelight. She slapped a hand over her mouth to keep a moan inside.

As she watched in horror, one of the men picked up a rifle with bayonet fixed and walked over to Gaetan. As he ran the bayonet up the inside of a leg, a black line followed the tip of the blade. Katherine's vision blurred.

This time the voice in her head was Nilchi's. *Sometimes I think if Gaetan is cut, his blood will spill out black from the poison inside him.* She shook her head and made herself look again. More black lines crossed his chest and stomach. The blood simply looked black in the firelight. That was all. That had to be all.

She had come looking for him thinking to make a deal with the devil, and now her nerve failed. If she could find a way to cut him loose and he could still move at all, he would surely kill her first and then go berserk through the Mexican camp. She thought of trying to escape alone. She thought of leaving him here knowing if not exactly what Hierra planned, the kind of thing he planned.

In the end, Katherine ignored the shivers of fear running up and down her spine, wrapped the dark blanket over her light gray clothes, and worked her way behind the wagons. If Gaetan repaid her by killing her, not only would she escape Hierra, she would die with the satisfaction of knowing she had loosed a madman in the Mexican camp.

She hid in the shadows of the wagons and listened to the Rurales while she decided on the best way to get close to Gaetan. One man pulled the other back toward the fire as they argued.

"The Commandant said we could toy with him a little. If you do more, we'll be beside him tomorrow."

"Look at the size of him. Cutting deeper won't weaken him."

"Your opinion doesn't matter, only Commandant Hierra's, and he said he wants him strong. He should last days."

Their argument continued. Katherine stopped listening to the words and kept an ear open only for their tone and volume so as to be warned if they turned back to Gaetan. The way to get close enough for him to hear her was to get in the wagon. The Rurales were insulting each other now. With luck they would come to blows.

Barrels filled the wagon but there was a small space between the last ones and the hanging wagon gate. She eased up into the wagon bed so slowly the only sound she heard was her own blood pounding in her ears. Stretched on her stomach, she squirmed until she was behind the rear wheel, behind Gaetan.

Praying Nilchi had been right that after a dozen years Gaetan would still understand enough English or Spanish to know what she was saying, she began in a low voice. "This is Katherine. I'm going to cut you loose. If you wait after I do that, I'll go around and distract those men for you."

As she spoke, she reached out over the edge of the wagon and cut the rawhide thong around his throat. He didn't move, but his breathing eased. She repeated her words in Spanish as she reached out in the same way and cut the rawhide from first one wrist and then the other.

"I ask that you let me follow you away from this place and help me escape these men," she said as she finished. She repeated her request in Spanish, reached out a last time and put the haft of the knife in his right hand. His hand closed around the knife, and he still didn't move.

Katherine climbed down as fast as she could. No longer worried about hiding her movements, she ran around the wagon to the fire. As she stepped into the firelight, the men looked up in surprise. She dropped the blanket, took off the hat and shook her hair free.

"*Sergeant, oh, Sergeant, please help me,*" she said, knowing her imitation of flirtatious friends would have her brothers howling with laughter but not caring so long as these two kept staring at her in wonder.

Behind them, she saw Gaetan lean down and slash the bonds on his ankles. She raised her hands as if in supplication and took a step forward to hold the Rurales' attention. Gaetan stumbled as he came off the wheel, caught himself and reached the man closest to him in three strides.

Before the first Rurale's body hit the ground, Gaetan's arm closed around the head of the second. He slit the man's throat with a single swipe of the knife. Katherine backed away.

Knowing in her mind what she was releasing had been one thing. Facing that ferocity alone in the night was something else. She made herself stand still. Her die was cast, and she would not run. She waited, fighting a foolish instinct to cover her throat with an arm, but Gaetan never looked her way.

He ripped a cartridge belt off a body, grabbed one of the rifles and disappeared into the night at a speed that belied any injury. Katherine crammed the hat back on and picked up the blanket, rifle and leather pouch. A canteen on the ground near the fire caught her eye. She swung the strap over her shoulder and ran after Gaetan.

She only found him in the dark because he stopped at the water to drink. Emptying the canteen, she sloshed fresh water over it and refilled it, glad to rinse away any trace of the pigs by the fire. She fumbled to close the lid and sling the strap back over her head and shoulder as she jogged after Gaetan when he took off. Unless he stopped her with the knife, she wasn't letting him out of sight again.

In minutes Katherine felt a bitter gratitude toward the Rurales. If Gaetan could move at this pace after hours with muscles contorted and straining on the wheel, keeping up with him when he wasn't hurt would be beyond her. Her breath rasped in her ears, her heart pounded, and pain stabbed in her side as she pursued the shadow moving steadily through the night.

Before long she reluctantly dropped the rifle, unable to keep carrying the weight of it. The canteen would have to go next. She was *not* going to be out in this wild land running from Hierra and his men unarmed; no matter what, the pistol would stay.

Gaetan slowed before she had to abandon anything else. Finally able to do more than force one foot after another, Katherine caught her breath and looked around. The eastern sky held the first hint of dawn. In the remaining shadows, she could see that they were back in the area of the ambush. That made sense. It would still be the shortest route to the Apache village. Except that wasn't where she wanted to go.

He disappeared into thick brush before her eyes. Katherine hurried after him, yelping as branches he pushed aside snapped back, stinging her like whips. The clinging, snapping branches, following Gaetan through them—the familiarity brought understanding of where he was going and why.

Would he really risk recapture by Hierra's men to get to Nilchi's body? No, he wouldn't. He'd been unarmed except for a knife when the Rurales captured him. Now that he had a rifle they wouldn't take him again. She touched the pistol where it hung across her chest and ran her fingers over the tops of the bullets in the belt. They wouldn't capture her either, not alive.

Pushing through the brush must be miserable naked and with a body laced with fresh wounds. As Katherine yanked her shirt free from a snag, another branch whipped back across her cheek, and her sympathy dissolved. Too bad she had no salt to throw in those wounds. If he had some idea stinging branches were going to make her drop back so that he could disappear on her he had another think coming.

Weak light and deep shadows hid the details of what the Rurales had done to Nilchi. As she halted at the edge of the clearing where he lay, fresh grief and anger swept through her. She expected a stronger display of the same feelings from Gaetan. He showed no emotion at all as he stripped the breechclout, leggings and moccasins from the body and put them on.

The contempt that flared in Katherine receded just as swiftly. He needed the protection of the clothing. Maybe the Apache taboo on taking items from the dead didn't apply in situations like this. More likely this kind of thing was what Nilchi had meant when he called his brother an unbeliever.

Gaetan walked toward her, and Katherine only just managed to keep from cringing away. He pulled the gun belt over her head, unbuckled it and swung it around his waist.

Indignation banished her caution, and she tried to grab the belt back.

"Wait a minute. I'm the one who brought that. You have the rifle. Give that back."

He ignored her and shoved the knife into its sheath. Taking Nilchi by the arms, Gaetan pulled the body up, hoisted it over his shoulder and moved off into the brush. A ray of the rising sun showed a splash of red in the grass, Nilchi's headband. Katherine picked it up and followed Gaetan.

7

Katherine argued with herself as she followed Gaetan north toward the canyons. She had the canteen, she could take off on her own. Hierra and his men would track them and keep after Gaetan if her tracks branched off in another direction, wouldn't they?

No, she realized. With so many men, some would stay on Gaetan's trail and some would follow her. She had thought of her die as cast, and it truly was. If Gaetan meant to fight over his brother's body, all she could do was fight with him—if she could get the pistol back from the hateful ingrate.

Gaetan laid Nilchi's body down in a grassy area before they got to the canyons. The hills had steepened but were not yet cliffs, and small ravines raked the land. He straightened Nilchi's head, arms and legs, got up and walked away. Katherine watched him go, certain after so much effort to get to the body, he wouldn't leave it like that and would be back.

At first she couldn't bring herself to look closely at the mutilated body, so reduced by death, but after a while she became accustomed. Hesitantly, she got down on her knees beside what was left of the beautiful young man. Sometime ago she had tied the string of the leather pouch to her waist. Now she opened it, unwrapped the scalps and picked Nilchi's from the three. The scent of death rose all around her. Katherine breathed through her mouth and distracted herself by talking.

"I suppose you know that your brother hasn't killed me yet. I think he's going to, if not straight out with a knife or gun then by lingering around here instead of putting as much distance between us and the Rurales as possible. Not that I don't think you should have a proper burial, I do. But I don't see how that's possible. We have nothing to bury you with, and the Rurales can't be far behind us."

She fit the scalp into place as best she could and began braiding the hair into the hair around it as a way to hold it in place.

"Getting away from Commandant Hierra and his men was no picnic. You'd be proud of me for it."

She described how it had been to the spirit she thought might be listening if spirits really were able to do such a thing. With the scalp fixed in place, she tied the red headband over her handiwork.

"I'm sorry. It only makes things a little better, doesn't it? But it is a little better."

Wetting a corner of the blanket with canteen water, she cleaned the dried blood from his face as best she could.

"I jumped from the frying pan into the fire, didn't I? Before long I'll be dancing on the coals. Maybe my real mistake was not following the other stage passengers out the door, but I just couldn't do that. I'm not ready to give up now, but your black-hearted brother took the pistol away."

The tails of the blood-encrusted shirt hung low enough to cover his nakedness, but the stripped lower body bothered her. Katherine picked up the blanket, measured what she thought was the right width and used her teeth on the edge until she tore through. Once she had a long, wide strip, she tore a narrow one for a belt and fashioned a breechclout out of the pieces of blanket.

"I wish that bullet missed," she said softly. "I wish we went the other way with Gaetan. I wish the bullet hit him instead of us."

A shadow fell across her, and she looked up defiantly. Gaetan ignored her and lifted Nilchi's upper body enough to smooth what was left of the blanket under the head and shoulders. He folded the blanket over in a kind of shortened shroud.

Cradling the body in his arms, he carried it in the same direction he'd gone before. Katherine picked up the canteen, shoved the remaining scalps back in the pouch and walked along behind.

Her nerves were screaming in anticipation of the blow of another bullet or the sound of the Rurales' pursuit when Gaetan disappeared over the side of one of the gullies. Hurrying to the edge, Katherine watched the muscles in his bare arms and back bunch and strain as he negotiated the steep bank while carrying the body of a man his own size, but he never lost his balance. With no illusions that she could descend the bank on her feet, Katherine slid down on her bottom, holding onto any scrap of shrub or rock she could on the way.

Brush choked the floor of the small ravine. The water that had dug out this cleft had long ago found another channel. Gaetan laid Nilchi's body down and began tearing out bushes and piling them over the body. If he wanted to build a funeral pyre, she could help, but how was he going to start a fire? She placed the other scalps beside the body and started adding to the pyre, wishing she had checked to see if the lantern in Hierra's tent held matches.

Except a fire didn't seem to be his intent. After adding a few last branches to the pile, Gaetan left the body and climbed out of the ravine. Brush covered the body high on top, but not well at all on the sides.

Katherine placed the sticks in her hand along one side, reluctant to leave with the job half done. Still, what if this was Gaetan's idea of a sufficient burial? She better not let him get out of sight again.

Crawling up the steep bank was harder than sliding down. Searching for Gaetan after she got to her feet on flat ground, she spotted him far up the hillside that towered over the narrow ledge where she stood. As she watched, she saw him at the base of the largest boulder on the slope, saw what he was doing there—and ran.

When she was sure she had run far enough back the way they had come, Katherine attacked the big hill from the side with determination spurred by fury. Gaetan was out of sight, but she knew where he was—behind that rock.

Katherine's father had convinced her at an early age that vulgar language was proof of poor breeding and a lack of both education and imagination. After reaching the rock and catching her breath enough to speak, Katherine said loudly and clearly in one language after another, "You ungrateful bastard."

If he understood, he gave no sign. Having dug around the base of the boulder on the downhill side, he now had his shoulder against it on the uphill side, shoving hard, trying to rock it out of position.

Katherine looked down. They were so high that the place where Nilchi lay looked small in the distance. More large boulders and rocks covered the slope below, though none so large as the one Gaetan worked on displacing. If he succeeded, a good part of this hill would fill the small ravine.

Still angry that he had let her figure it out herself and planned to bury her alive if she didn't, Katherine grudgingly conceded if Gaetan could dislodge the boulder, no one would ever disturb Nilchi's grave.

"Move over."

She squeezed in beside him, put her own shoulder to the rough stone and helped him push. After half a dozen straining shoves, budging the massive stone seemed hopeless, but then she felt it, the first yielding.

Katherine renewed her efforts, heard a low grunt from Gaetan as he did the same, and the boulder gave way. She watched in awe as it hung in the air for a moment, tumbled over slowly, then rolled faster, bouncing and smashing everything in its path. And everything it smashed into started down the hill and smashed into everything else until the whole hillside moved like a living thing.

She couldn't take her eyes off the destructive power of the landslide, aware Gaetan also watched as the ravine filled, the extra earth mounded over it and the dust settled.

Her eyes watered, and not from the dust. *Rest in peace. And thank you.*

Gaetan reached out and pulled the canteen over her head, ignoring her efforts to stop him. Settling it over his own head and shoulder, he started uphill. Katherine scrambled after him, moving more easily without the canteen flapping against her and without the extra weight but unwilling to admit it.

"I'm going to get the pistol back, and I'm going to kill him," she muttered. After a minute she added, "But not until I'm sure they can't catch us."

Gaetan no longer moved so fast she had trouble keeping up. In fact, so far as Katherine could tell, she was the only one worried about pursuit. He moved at a steady pace, but he kept stopping, disappearing over the edge of one ravine after another and then climbing back out before she mustered the nerve to slide down. After the second time, she stopped trying to follow him on these eccentric side trips. After the sixth time, she was almost beside herself.

"You know they're coming after us don't you? We killed Hierra's men. They didn't sit down to a leisurely breakfast before starting after us. They got up, found the bodies and poured out of that camp liked bees out of a smashed hive. The least you could do is let me have the pistol. You can't fire two guns at once, and I *need* that pistol. I'm the one who stole it in the first place. It's mine, and I need it."

The second time she said it—in Spanish—got no more reaction than the first. She tried again, this time with a deliberate barb. "How do you see yourself as some big, brave warrior if you're afraid to let a woman who's on your side have a gun?"

Still nothing. She started searching for stones the right size. Maybe he would ignore her so thoroughly she could hit him, stun him long enough to get the pistol back. Once she had it....

He stopped again. Nothing looked any different to Katherine than any of the other times. The sides of the gully were steep and high. Maybe it wound on farther than the others. Maybe the bottom was sandier.

Gaetan saw some difference she could not because this time he didn't jump down and climb right back up. She leaned over the edge, and when she couldn't see him, slid down after him as fast as she could. She ran, following his tracks in soft sand, too out of breath to say what she thought when she caught up.

She stayed out of breath as she followed him over and around what turned out to be a web of deep cuts in the land. One gully branched off another. When they hit a dead end, they climbed out, then back down in another place.

Exhausted and desperate, Katherine couldn't believe her eyes when she saw her own boot prints in the sand ahead. She looked up at the edge of the gully, wondering how long it would be before Hierra sat there laughing as his prey chased their own tails in circles.

No more did she think that than Gaetan turned down another of the many side gullies. She trotted after him, determined to draw in enough breath to give him another stringent dose of her opinion. Before she could do that, he stopped and shoved her through the growth of tall grass, rushes and brush until her back hit the dirt bank. He made a gesture that reminded her of the signals her brother Peter used on his hunting dogs.

Stay!

"I'm not staying here while you...."

He pulled the knife and laid the flat of the blade across her mouth, daring her to say another word with an unblinking, narrow-eyed stare. She shut up and leaned back against the bank, fuming. Her heart raced as he moved out of sight and slowed when she saw him again, but then she realized what he was doing and bit back a shout.

He backed toward her, sweeping a piece of brush across their tracks, removing footprints and leaving brush prints. She could barely contain herself. What good would that do? Did he think the Rurales would ignore such a clumsy attempt to erase tracks?

As she watched, a small dust devil of the breeze that swirled through the maze of gullies skipped on by, picking up sand, playing with it and spinning it back down, smoothing out a large swath of the brushed sand. Katherine sat down and wrapped her arms around her legs.

The Apaches have been doing this kind of thing for centuries. I will calm down, keep quiet and help if I can. She rested her head on her knees, remembering the feel of the knife on her mouth, the menace in the black eyes. Maybe he wouldn't speak to her, but, oh, did he know how to give orders.

He backed right to where she sat. Katherine understood they were going to hide, not run, but she couldn't see how. The undergrowth along the base of the bank was thick, but not much more than thigh high.

Gaetan got down on his knees and hacked into the dirt with the knife, loosening the sandy soil, then scooping it out. She watched for a while, then began helping. In minutes they had a silent partnership going. He dug. She scooped.

Working together, they had dug a coffin-shaped hole more than a foot deep when Gaetan stilled. Katherine patted the dirt in her hands into place on the small berm around the hole, watched him and listened. Voices. Hierra and the Rurales had arrived.

Gaetan tipped his head at the hole, and she got in, unsure how to position herself. He set the rifle, pistol and knife along the front edge of the hole, pushed her against the back edge on her side and fit himself in front of her, crushing her against the dirt. Only a few times in her life had Katherine felt fragile. This was one. Her shoulders barely cleared the level of the gully floor. His dwarfed her.

In the stagecoach with a full load of passengers, she had hated the enforced intimacy of the male bodies around her. None of those men ever pressed into her the way Gaetan did now. Every breath he took crushed her chest. The hard wall of his naked back pinned her in place. The curve of his rear pressed into a place she didn't want to think about.

She didn't dare so much as wiggle. If she fussed, there was the knife, and he would probably prefer to hide with her corpse rather than a fussy woman.

She could see almost nothing. None too clean black hair tickled her nose, and the scent of unwashed male overwhelmed the musty smell of freshly dug dirt.

Hysteria threatened to break from the back of her throat. This time the voice that advised her was her brother Lewis's, "You're the best of us all at seeking, Katherine, but you need to practice hiding a lot more."

I'm practicing, Lew. I'm practicing hard, and I'll tell you all about it someday.

Something pattered on her legs. She risked turning her head and looked toward her feet. Gaetan threw more loose dirt over their legs. Her right arm rested free along her side. She grabbed a handful of dirt and threw it. Soon the banks of loose soil around them were gone, and they lay under a spotty covering of clumps of sandy soil. How well did they blend in, she wondered. How soon would they find out?

Katherine had relived a fox hunt in England, a lion hunt in Africa, and was in the middle of a tiger hunt in India when she heard a strange, rhythmic noise. Swish, thump. Swish, thump.

"If Commandant sees you cheating like that, you'll wish you hadn't." Swish, thump.

"Ah. What does it matter. They aren't here." Swish, thump.

"You lean over like you should and put your back into it." Swish, thump.

Katherine closed her eyes and pressed her forehead against the back of Gaetan's neck, trying to make herself smaller. They were poking bayonets through the grass, weeds and bushes into the bank of the gully. How low? How far apart?

A blade bit into the dirt near her head. She flinched but kept the sound of fear trapped behind lips she clenched between her teeth. The blade came again, over shoulders, waists, knees and feet, and then they were past.

She opened her eyes, raised her head and saw blood. Red blood, bright and running from the top of Gaetan's arm down between them. She closed her eyes again, trying to deny a strange relief. She had never believed his blood would be black. She hadn't. She really hadn't. But he never moved. What kind of man didn't move when a bayonet went through his arm?

The Rurales were gone now, or at least far enough along the gully that they couldn't be heard. She moved her arm the little distance necessary to put the cuff of her shirt over the wound and pressed, her fingers curving over his warm, bare skin. She wanted to say something, wanted to move her cramped and aching body. Instead she closed her eyes and went back to the tiger hunt.

By late afternoon, rising heat and the crushing force on her chest overwhelmed Katherine. As night fell, she passed into a half-sleeping, half-conscious state. When Gaetan sat up, she stayed unmoving, dragging in one glorious deep breath after another of the cooler night air.

Reviving enough to move, she left her legs in the hole and sat on the edge, flexing her left arm and fingers to get the circulation going.

The slight sound of the cap of the canteen coming off reached her, and she saw Gaetan's shadow, head back, drinking. He lowered the canteen and replaced the cap. She grabbed. He held on.

"Who brought this?" she whispered.

He let go, whether because her words hit home or to keep her quiet she neither knew nor cared. The water sluiced down her throat, better than any iced beverage back in the civilized world. She wanted to drink every drop, but lowered the canteen after half a dozen swallows and replaced the cap. She didn't waste effort resisting when Gaetan pulled the canteen out of her hands.

When they left, he slid so slowly through the shadows of the gully, Katherine had no trouble staying close and concentrating on putting each foot down as quietly as he did in spite of her hard-soled boots. They had gone no more than a hundred feet when a slight cough sounded from above.

Another cordon. If Hierra had every one of his men cordoning off this tangle of gullies could they surround them all? How far apart would the sentries be?

The floods that had formed the gully had not cut as deep here. The banks no longer loomed above their heads. Gaetan bent double, and Katherine imitated him. When he dropped lower, she crawled too, trying to ignore the small stabs of thorns and sharp stones on her hands and knees.

Before long she inched on her stomach, her nose all but touching his moccasins. Climbing out of here would be easy—if they could just slither between sentries. The moonlight showed the gully coming to a dead end, the low banks curving in a semi-circle.

Gaetan stopped, and Katherine waited, listening hard. Each minute lasted forever, but she knew not much time had really passed when a tiny spot of flame flared in the dark. The scent of tobacco drifted through the night air.

Katherine pulled her lips back in the smile that wasn't a smile. If Hierra even suspected one of his men of giving in to the urge for a cigarette while stationed out here, the Commandant would be apoplectic.

Gaetan drew the knife and gave Katherine the dog signal again. *Stay.* She lay quiet and counted to three hundred, straining to hear any sign. Her fear of being left conquered her fear of what Gaetan would do to a disobedient white woman.

She crawled forward and made it halfway up the bank before her left foot knocked down loose dirt. A man loomed out of the night, the muzzle of his rifle in her face, his voice high and nervous.

"You. Raise your hands and get up here. Get up here."

"I can't get up there with my hands raised."

He reached down and pulled her up by the shirt. *"Stay there. Stay on your knees and put your hands on your head. Where's the Apache? Where is he?"*

The Apache was behind him, using the knife with brutal efficiency. Then the Apache was gone into the night, the disobedient white woman right behind him.

8

For the first mile after breaking through the Rurales' cordon, Katherine had no trouble keeping up with Gaetan. He moved cautiously, stopping to listen often. When he picked up the pace, she rejoiced in spite of the difficulty. From the moment she had escaped from Hierra's tent, all her instincts urged putting as much distance between herself and the Mexicans as possible, and finally that's what they were doing.

Expecting Gaetan to head south toward the Apache village in Mexico that Nilchi had described, Katherine never thought to check the direction of their travel. Instead, all through the night she wrestled with thoughts of how and when to start north to United States territories on her own, which of course came down to how to get a weapon from Gaetan. If he knew she'd strike out on her own if he gave her the pistol back, maybe he'd consider it a cheap price to be rid of her.

The sight of the sun rising to her right changed Katherine's plans. They were traveling north, whether to lose the Rurales by returning across the border or for some other unknown Apache reason, Katherine didn't care. Once across the border she could find help in any town or from any travelers she came across—most travelers she amended, remembering the stage robbers.

As the day wore on, the country they crossed became stonier, even more dry and desolate. Katherine watched the way Gaetan picked his way over the flinty ground and felt smug about the hard soles of her boots. Nothing grew here except an occasional cactus or scrawny bush. In the days of travel with Nilchi, they had covered some barren country, but nothing this bad. Worn out, hungry and thirsty, she stumbled up the side of a small butte after Gaetan and collapsed near him when he sat in the shade of a few rocks near the southern rim.

He shrugged the canteen off his shoulder and drank. She counted swallows and waited. He put the canteen down on the ground and ignored it and her. Katherine drank exactly the same number of swallows and returned the canteen to where he had left it.

Her thirst was nowhere near quenched. Her stomach was growling, and if she didn't sleep, she'd soon fall over in her tracks. He leaned back and closed his eyes, and Katherine risked a close examination of his face.

He and Nilchi had not been twins. The forehead was the same, and the arch of the brow. Like Nilchi, and unlike the other Apaches, he had eyebrows, not very thick brows for a man with hair as black as a crow's wing, but distinct. His nose was narrower, his cheekbones sharper, the bow in his upper lip more distinct, but the width of his mouth, and the strength of the almost square jaw matched her memory of Nilchi in every way.

Even with faces so much the same, the fact remained that Nilchi was handsome, and Gaetan was—not. A face always taut with fury and eyes either cold and flat with dislike or glittering with anger did not add up to handsome. Nilchi's eyes had shone with amusement more often than not. What shone from Gaetan's eyes brought to mind dark and dangerous things that made men huddle close to their fires in the night. If most Apaches were like him, she understood the stories that made them sound on the one hand possessed of supernatural powers and on the other less than human.

Years after she had been put ashore, Katherine had overheard her aunt telling a friend that one reason she had insisted that Katherine stay home was to get her out of an environment where she was constantly exposed to "half-naked savages."

In truth Katherine had seen her share of men of all races, sizes and shapes without shirts and sometimes wearing nothing but a loincloth. Many of them had been well muscled from physical labor. Some had probably had muscling as distinct as Gaetan's, but she didn't remember any.

Her own brothers were tall, well built men, but if they sat leaning back like that, with legs slightly bent in front of them, would the legs look as long? Did shoulders that broad usually taper so much to the waist and—rear?

The thong that had held his head back so unnaturally had bitten into his neck, leaving a red line with purple bruises on either side. Bruises and bayonet cuts covered his chest and arms. All the injuries had scabbed over and looked as they should except for a few places where the cartridge belt and canteen strap rubbed and kept the cuts red and raw. His moccasins and clothes must be doing the same to the wounds on his stomach and legs. Would the pain be the same as what she felt from her single wound?

Ignoring the throbbing pain under her breast was becoming harder and harder, and her wound was no more than a graze. The bayonet had sliced into Gaetan's arm muscle just below the shoulder. A thick, shiny scab covered the cut, as if it had bled again recently. On her father's ships a wound like that would mean a trip to the surgeon and stitches. How had he remained as still as death when the blade hit?

She had dined with Hierra almost ten hours after Gaetan last ate, yet his stomach wasn't the one complaining loudly. He didn't look light-headed either, and she had been feeling that way off and on for hours.

Since he hadn't killed her yet, he probably wasn't going to unless she really provoked him, but feeling afraid of him and dependent on him at the same time made her *want* to provoke him. *Pride goeth before a fall, Katherine.*

The words echoing in her head this time were her father's, and she cringed from the thought of him. Thinking about her father meant thinking about what he had said in their arguments about Henry—and what she had said. When she saw her father again she was going to fall in his arms, apologize and pretend she thought he was right.

One thing about trekking all over the Southwest in the company of Apaches—Commandant Hierra wouldn't be the only one to make assumptions about how she survived. Whatever shreds of her reputation she hadn't destroyed being stupid over Henry Dumont were now lost forever somewhere in Northern Mexico.

A slit of dark eye gleamed at her from between Gaetan's lids. Katherine shifted, turning her attention to the vista of empty land before her, her heart pounding. Goodness knew what he'd consider proper treatment of a woman caught staring at him while he slept. There was probably some taboo against it, and that would be one he'd believe in.

After a moment, she lay down a cautious distance away. Aunt Meg would be appalled, but Katherine wished she could tie a string to this particular half-naked savage so he couldn't sneak away while she slept. If Gaetan would just tolerate her long enough, she could get back to civilization and home, her father and brothers would have to admit marriage was no longer a remote possibility, and she could make a productive life for herself in better ways. She could nurse. She could teach. She could....

By the time Katherine woke the next morning, the sun was well up. Gaetan lay stretched on his stomach at the edge of the butte staring to the south. One look told Katherine what he must be watching. She crawled to his side and stretched out the same way, telling herself the pain under her breast was no worse than the day before.

In the distance, the Rurales looked like toy soldiers. A single man walked ahead leading his horse. The main body followed in loose formation, and Katherine thought she recognized Hierra.

"I'd give anything for a rifle with a 'scope right now," she said.

Gaetan ignored her and continued to focus on the Mexicans, but she felt the same commonality of purpose with him they had achieved when digging in the gully. She wondered if they needed to start running soon and hoped not. In spite of the hours of sleep, she didn't feel much like running this morning.

As they watched, the man leading his horse halted, mounted and returned to the others. Toy arms waved on toy men, and the entire column turned and headed back south.

"They lost our tracks on that stony ground, didn't they? Or maybe we're too close to the border. Once we're out of Mexico, you could give me the pistol and point me at a town and be rid of me forever, you know."

She considered repeating all that in Spanish and decided not to bother. Staying low until she was off the crest of the butte, she went down the hill a distance to attend to private needs. When she finished, she pulled her shirt out of her trousers and lifted it high enough to take a good look at the bullet wound.

The sight of the swollen, angry red flesh ended her denial. Instead of healing, the wound was suppurating. In the next few days, either her body would overcome the inflammation, or she would die of blood poisoning. Even back home where a doctor could clean the wound and dress it, she knew the likely outcome. Out here.... She dropped the shirt, tucked it back in and went back up the hill, expecting Gaetan to be gone and to have to track him down.

The canteen sat with its cap off where she had slept and Gaetan sat nearby, cleaning his fingernails with the knife. A few eager swallows finished the last of the water. She screwed the cap back on and held it out. "Unless I can have it now that it's empty."

He took the canteen from her, got up and walked away. Katherine pushed to her feet. When the pain and fever got bad enough, all she had to do was figure a way to make him use the knife. Hitting him with a rock still held a lot of appeal, but devising better and more imaginative ways helped pass the time.

By late afternoon, Katherine knew she would trade a 'scoped rifle for a swallow of water. Her hope rose as they climbed an odd rock formation that had healthy looking bushes growing in every crevice. Maybe there was a spring somewhere close by. *Please let there be water somewhere near.*

Exhausted and fighting fear—fear of being left, fear of not being able to make him kill her quickly, fear of dying alone—Katherine concentrated on keeping her footing on the rocky ground at the base of a cliff no more than head high. She looked up in time to keep from bumping into Gaetan when he halted and gave the dog signal. *Stay.*

He turned to leave, and Katherine's fear exploded. She balled her fists and shook them at him, dancing in place like a prizefighter, ready to launch at him swinging.

"Stop that! You stop with those dog signals right now! I'm through being scared of you. I'm tired of being hungry and thirsty, and I'm tired of you. If I want to follow you wherever you're going, I'll follow you! Nilchi was right about you, you're an overbearing, arrogant, black-hearted, ungrateful...."

He walked into her, hooked a leg behind hers and bounced her down on her bottom. Her furious rant died as her breath thumped out. She sat on the ground sputtering, feeling the effects of the hard landing for long seconds. When she jumped back to her feet, still full of fight, he was gone. The anger drained away as suddenly as it had arisen. She sat back down, fighting tears.

So much time passed, she accepted he had left her, not that it mattered. When he reappeared as if by magic through a crack in the rockface, she looked up at him dully—until she saw the canteen in his hand, water dripping off it. He set the canteen beside her and walked away.

Katherine couldn't unscrew the cap fast enough. She tipped it so high, rivulets of water ran down her neck as she swallowed. After the first greedy gulps, she stopped long enough to pour a little water into her hand and rub it over her face and the back of her neck. There was barely a slosh in the bottom of the canteen when she refastened the cap and set it back down.

"I'm sorry," she said. In two languages.

She didn't move when he picked up the canteen and disappeared again. And she didn't say anything when he returned with it refilled and led the way north.

Two days later, Katherine labored to keep moving for no reason other than a stubborn refusal to give up. Hunger no longer bothered her. The day before Gaetan had knocked half a dozen fruits off an ugly cactus, rolled them in the dirt to get rid of the spines, peeled them and eaten them. When he left the knife in the dirt at her feet, she forced herself to pick it up and do the same with another couple of the bland, fibrous things, hoping she would feel better for it. She didn't.

Fever from the festering wound burned through her entire body. Keeping up with Gaetan was no longer possible. When he stopped, she caught up. When he walked on, she fell farther and farther behind, and she no longer cared.

The sun had set and dusk fallen sometime ago, but Gaetan kept going. If he didn't stop soon, she would stop without him. She wanted rest, sleep. Some part of her knew if she lay down she would never get up again. Her father and brothers talked to her off and on, each telling her in his own way not to give up, but she didn't want to listen any more.

Ahead of her she could barely make out Gaetan's form. He had stopped just short of the crest of a hill and stretched out in that way he had when he wanted to see without being seen. She trudged right up the hill beside him and stood there, swaying on her feet.

Surprise cut through the feverish haze. The ground fell away steeply before her, and a grove of cottonwoods hinted at water beyond the fire that blazed at the bottom of the hill. A male voice shouted something about coffee in English.

Before she took in more of the camp spread out below, Gaetan grabbed her. He pulled her down and shoved her. She rolled down the hill—faster and faster. Katherine landed at the bottom with a moan and sat up to see three bearded men running toward her. A rush of nervous excitement cleared away the last of her lethargy.

"Are you Americans?" she asked the barrel-chested man who arrived first.

"We sure are, darling. Who, or what, are you?"

"My name is Katherine Grant. I've been hoping to find someone like you for days. Maybe it's too late, but I hope.... I need help."

"Where did you come from? Where's your people?"

"I'm—I'm alone. I was on a stage that was robbed, and then...."

Admitting to being alone was a mistake. The big man grabbed her hand and pulled her to her feet so hard her chest smacked into his. Her cry of pain had no effect on him. Wrapping a fist in her hair, he forced her head back and closed his mouth over hers in a bruising kiss. She kicked at his shin hard, only to hit the leather of his boot.

He laughed at her. "You want help from us, you're going to have to be a lot more cooperative."

Before she could tell him what she thought of that—and of him—one of the other men said. "Come on, Cal. The lady needs help. Stop scaring her."

"Lady." The big man made a sound of contempt. "You ever seen a lady with pants stretched over her ass like that? If you don't want any of what she's peddling, I do."

He squeezed one cheek of the body part he referred to as he talked. Katherine kicked at him again, aiming higher, but she was slow, and he avoided her easily. Gripping her left arm hard, he twisted it behind her back. For a moment she floated on the wave of pain. When her vision cleared, she saw more men joining the crowd around her.

"I mean it," the second man said. "There's no reason to hurt her. Let her go."

"I ain't gonna hurt her. She needs help. That means giving her food we paid for, letting her be extra weight on one of our horses. You going to be a Nancy boy and just give her what we scraped to pay for? I'm saying she has to pay her way is all. That's fair."

The men exchanged wary looks. Some of them sidled closer to Cal, some to the other man, but the way the men opposing Cal wouldn't look directly at him told her Cal would get his way in the end. If she weren't so tired, she could organize her thoughts, could tell them about ransom, could....

A ululating scream split the night. The sound scraped across Katherine's nerves and down her spine as did another and another. The thunder of horses stampeding sounded with the last ungodly shriek.

"The horses! Damn it, you stupid sons of bitches, you left the horses!"

Cal let her go, yelling and cursing as he charged across the campsite. A few men followed him. Most of them looked too scared to move. "What the hell was that?"

"Apaches," Katherine said, and she turned and ran.

She ran in the direction the horses had gone, even as the sound of them faded in the night. Stumbling over rocks and crashing into brush and cactus, she ran until she fell to her knees.

"Gaetan!"

Rifle fire sounded behind her. She should pray for a bullet to the heart. Instead she lurched to her feet and ran again, her blood pounding in her ears, a knife tearing at her side, her lungs burning. She fell and rolled.

"Gaetan!"

Staggering up, still she ran, but slower now. When she fell, she screamed a last time.

"Gaetan!"

Or maybe it wasn't a scream. Maybe it was only a weak cry. She huddled on her knees in the dirt, sobbing as she gasped for breath.

The quality of the air around her changed. The ground gave off the faintest tremble. She held one heaving breath long enough to listen. The tremble swelled until the night vibrated with the drumbeat of galloping hooves. She made it to her feet, waved her arms hoping he'd see the light-colored shirt, and waited until a large shadow separated from the darkness, racing toward her.

"Gaetan. Gaetan!"

She stumbled a few steps forward. His outstretched arm hit her middle like a blow. She hung there against his leg and the side of the running horse until they were far from the camp, from the men and their guns.

As Gaetan pulled the horse to a halt, Katherine didn't wait for him to drop her. Whatever his intention, she wasn't letting go. She kept a death grip on his arm and flailed until she got a foot on top of the stirrup and crawled onto the horse behind him. Wrapping her arms around his waist, she locked her hands together. He could pry her off or cut her off, but that was the only way he was going to get rid of her.

Afraid he might do just that, she didn't relax until the horse started forward, slow now. The steady clop of hooves and the rolling easy gait soothed her hammering heart and heaving lungs. Her arms and legs stopped quivering.

Close to full now, the moon showed grass, brush and rocks in otherworldly relief, black, charcoal and silver shadows passing in the night. Cool air whispered like silk across her fevered face. The sharp scent of horse sweat rose so thick in the air, she tasted salt on her tongue. Or maybe she tasted tears.

She sat erect, touching Gaetan only where her arms clutched his waist so desperately, but her hands rested against his stomach, bare skin against bare skin, and against all reason she took comfort from the size of him, from the muscular feel of him, warm and *alive*. He had used her to get the horses and never intended to come back for her. She knew it and decided her ghost should haunt him for it, but only for a little while. All that mattered was that he did come back.

Running like that had probably pumped the poison through her body faster, but it would make no difference in the end. She fought to keep her eyes open, fought the returning fog of fever, wanting to hold on to awareness, to the soft caress of the night, but she lost the battle. Her eyes closed; her head drooped. She sagged against Gaetan's back, her cheek on his shoulder.

9

Gaetan barely remembered a time when anger hadn't burned in his heart and belly. Sometimes it subsided to embers and lay quiet for a while. Sometimes it burned so hot it threatened to consume him, but it never died. The anger fed on his hate for the Americans and Mexicans who had his people trapped between them.

He had been angry at himself before, for mistakes, for missed chances to kill the enemy, but never for weakness. Fury at his own weakness and the price he would pay for it ate at him as he rode back to where he had abandoned the white men's other horses and mules.

Only a white man would use his own death to extract an unwilling promise the way Nilchi had done, but the school had turned Nilchi's heart pale and weak, turned him white inside. For the first time, Gaetan considered that maybe the school had weakened him also, yet how could any man continue to say no while watching blood froth on his brother's lips and hearing him struggle to speak? In the end, he gave the promise.

"Promise me. Promise not to kill the woman or hurt her. Promise to give her back to her own people."

"I promise."

He hadn't killed her. He hadn't hurt her. Tonight he had given her back to her own people, but then he had been weak once more. He had gone back for her. It didn't matter if the white men at the water were like the stagecoach robbers. In giving the woman to white men he had fulfilled the promise. Going back for her because she screamed his name was weakness.

Some of his people believed that when a person used your name three times in asking a favor, the favor should be granted. He believed no such thing. A white woman screaming his name a hundred times meant nothing.

After careful thought, he had decided he owed the woman nothing for freeing him from the Mexicans. She had freed him only to save herself. The debt came because she went back for Nilchi when she saw him on foot and the Mexicans closing in. Gaetan had not seen Nilchi's horse go down. He had turned only because he saw the woman turn and thought to kill her before she could reach the soldiers. Because of the woman, the Mexicans had not captured Nilchi alive.

The way she had honored Nilchi in death added to the debt. She made his body whole for burial, and if their people were right, for the afterlife. Gaetan couldn't forget the way she knelt and washed the blood from Nilchi's face. When he had returned from scouting out a burial place, he had watched as the woman braided the scalp into place and covered Nilchi's nakedness. He had listened to her tell his brother's spirit how she escaped the Rurales.

He shook his head. Letting her live would have repaid any debt, but the promise bound him to more. He had traveled north, intending to cross the border, take her close to a town and leave her. Now he couldn't do that. Chishogi's raid should have brought their small band of refugees supplies they needed after the long winter. By now Chishogi had returned, bringing nothing but grief, and the need would be greater.

The horses and mules hadn't run far after he left them but scattered and started grazing. He counted as he rounded them up and started them moving—eight horses, half still saddled, and six mules, their outlines distorted by the packs they bore.

They weren't much compared to what Chishogi had lost, but the packs would contain enough food to keep the white men fat for many months while they scratched in the earth for gold or silver. That much food would supply his people for a while, and he dared not risk losing it by taking the woman further north. The white men were fouling the water he had thought to use, but there was another place he could reach by morning, a better place, where he could lay up and rest for a few days.

The presence of the woman behind him intruded on his thoughts. In the years he had spent imprisoned at the school, he had seen many white women. They came there as teachers, cooks and housekeepers. None of them had been anything like this one. Nilchi thought the woman's courage commended her, but killing an enemy woman this strong was more important than killing a weak woman. The sons of this one would be formidable enemies, and because of the promise, she would live to bear them.

Nilchi's eyes had turned as white as his heart to think the woman was beautiful, although she was not as ugly as most whites. Her hair was dark, not the color of weeds in winter. Her eyes were blue, but not ghostly pale, and her skin had not turned red from the sun, but browned to where she looked almost human. The bones of her face were strong and distinctive, unlike most white women, whose overabundant flesh hid their bones, making it almost impossible to tell them apart. She had a woman's shape without big soft lumps of breasts and rear end sticking out all over, but no white woman could be beautiful.

Nilchi had teased him by repeating everything the woman confided. Gaetan knew she claimed to have no husband and said the one she thought to marry had abused her. He felt a mild twinge of curiosity over the story.

A man who hit this woman would be foolish to ever turn his back or close his eyes in her presence. Probably the white man hit her and ran away.

She had the temper and pride of a man. As she slumped against his back and fell asleep, head on his shoulder, he added arrogance to her faults. When she first pulled herself behind him and locked her arms around his waist he should have knocked her right off the horse. *Promise not to kill her or hurt her.*

The heat of her was offensive, raising sweat on his back, and the effect her body was having on his own infuriated him. Hunger and lack of sleep had weakened her throughout the day, but now all she had to do was sit on the horse. She could wait to sleep.

He shrugged his shoulder. Her head bounced a little, but she didn't wake. Incensed, he jammed an elbow back into her side. She moaned softly, and her head fell off his shoulder, hanging lifelessly to one side. She wasn't asleep.

He touched her hands where they locked together in front of him, felt the heat and reached back to touch her face. No wonder the feel of her made his back sweat. Her fever was the kind that killed. He relaxed, the anger dying back down. Maybe he'd be free of the promise soon after all.

PAIN SO TERRIBLE it pierced the fever and blackness tore across Katherine's rib and into her breast. She writhed against the weight pinning her to the ground, opened her eyes and saw Gaetan looming above her. He was astride her, sitting on her hips. His weight on her lower body and one hand on her breastbone immobilized her. The blade of the knife in his other hand glinted in the sunlight.

Katherine abandoned her feeble efforts to dislodge him, transfixed by the sight of blood running along the edge of the blade and forming a bead at the point. The ruby red drop grew larger, elongated and fell onto her bare breast.

She tore her gaze away from the knife and the blood and looked into eyes as flat and empty as the first time she'd seen them, but she was beyond fear. Raising a hand, she touched his cheek.

"Poor Gaetan," she whispered, "you can't even kill me. The Rurales did that days ago."

Her hand fell away. The knife flashed, and pain drove her back into the same blackness it had pulled her from.

KATHERINE WOKE CONFUSED and feeling dreadful. Little by little, she remembered running, Gaetan, the knife. Why was she alive? Was she alive? She lay in the shade of a cottonwood, her head pounding, chest aching and throat so dry swallowing hurt.

Deciding she was most definitely still alive, she pushed herself up by the arms, and her shirt fell off—the remnants of the shirt, she saw with horror. Most of the cloth had been wrapped tight around her rib cage, reaching up under her breasts, pushing them up in an absolutely indecent way.

Her trousers were still on, as were her boots. She plucked at the edge of the wrapping, her fingers coming away covered with something sticky. What had he *done* to her? She stared down at herself, slowly putting it all together.

The fever was gone. The throbbing, fiery pain that had started along her rib and begun to move deep into her breast was gone too, replaced by a quiet soreness. The knife—he had cut deep into the wound and drained the purulence. The wrapping was a bandage, the sticky substance a poultice.

And then he left her here half naked! She tried to scramble to her feet, fell back on a wave of dizziness and settled for making it to her knees. The packs from the mules and saddles from the horses sat in a careless heap a little distance away. At the sight of them, her panic subsided. Gaetan would leave her here alone in a heartbeat, but he wouldn't leave the spoils he had used her to steal.

She crawled to the nearest bushes and took care of her most pressing need, then lurched to the supplies. There had to be canteens on some of those saddles. There were canteens; they even contained some water.

Feeling better, she pawed through the pile of goods and found a treasure trove. Not that she'd use the comb she found in the saddlebags before boiling it, or ever use any of the toothbrushes, but rubbing the fuzz off her teeth not just with a bit of cloth but with a bit of cloth and the help of some tooth powder felt good. She found a spare shirt, huge, but it covered her. Two knives. A well oiled gun belt with a Colt in the holster. She strapped the gun on, almost crowing in triumph.

The sight of the foodstuffs that had come off the mules awakened her hunger with a vengeance. Flour and cornmeal, sugar and coffee, bacon and beans. There were also shovels, picks and equipment she didn't recognize.

The men must have come to Mexico looking for gold or silver. Feeling benevolent toward them, she hoped they got out alive. Well, all of them except Cal. And canned goods. Peaches! She pried open a can with one of the knives and ate the juicy fruit with joy, savoring the flavor.

When she was done, she pillowed her head on one of the bedrolls, curled up on her side and went back to sleep.

KATHERINE WOKE AGAIN in late afternoon, clear-headed enough to realize if Gaetan was keeping the livestock here, there must be a source of water nearby. She staggered to her feet and wove through the trees. Sure enough, a short distance away a shallow stream ran through dapples of sunlight and shade. She knelt and drank her fill, splashing water on her face when she was done, reveling in the feel on her skin. There were a lot of goodies in those saddlebags....

Moments later she returned to the stream with blankets in her arms and a bar of soap clutched in her hands. Nervously, she stripped off her clothes, wrapped herself in a blanket and scrubbed Hierra's clothes and the miner's shirt. She took the wet clothing back out into the sunshine to dry and returned to the stream. Bathing her lower body presented no problems. She sat in the water.

The bandage made washing higher problematic. She felt fine, but she had felt fine for days after the bullet hit, and she had washed the wound in Hierra's camp. Unwilling to remove the bandage or get it wet, she settled for a much less thorough cleaning of everything from the bandage up and unhappily abandoned thoughts of washing her hair.

Drying herself off with a blanket, Katherine yawned. She really should go get what she needed out of those packs and prepare a decent meal. Gaetan had to be close, didn't he? Maybe he'd show up if the smell of coffee or bacon reached wherever he was lurking. She just needed to rest a minute first. Here in the shade of the suckers that had sprung up around the base of this tree....

Sensing the presence of another, she woke and lay still, trying to assess the danger. Nothing happened. A bird sang nearby. She sat up slowly, eyes and ears straining, then huddled back down in her blanket. Gaetan.

She watched as he leaned his rifle against a rock, dropped the bandolier next to it and took off his moccasins. He pulled a blue plaid shirt off over his head. Evidently he had been into the miners' supplies also. The gun belt dropped onto the shirt, and then leggings and breechclout all came off at once. He stretched, muscles rippling under bronze skin, turned his back to her and moved the shirt and gun belt closer to the edge of the water.

Katherine's mouth went dry. She shouldn't be spying on him. But if she tried to leave, he'd see her. She closed her eyes. They popped back open.

What was the matter with her? She'd seen him naked in the Mexicans' camp. She'd been crushed against his bare back hiding from Hierra's men and studied him carefully when he slept on the butte. Her bare hands had been against his bare stomach and her chest against his back riding through the night on the horse.

In the Mexican camp she had seen only a nightmare, some crazed artist's vision of hell, complete with demons dancing around the tortured soul. Traveling with him, what had mattered was the size and strength that made him dangerous. He was a man who wanted an excuse to kill her. A man. Male.

Her breathing quickened. She recognized the hollow, dropping sensation low in her stomach and the feel of her own flesh swelling between her legs. And moisture! Henry, who prided his expertise in carnal matters, had kissed her and touched her in intimate ways in order to get her body to respond the way it was now to a man many feet away seen through a screen of leaves and branches.

That wasn't true. Nothing Henry did ever achieved this kind of reaction. Sweat broke out and prickled along her spine. The amount of moisture between her legs would be embarrassing back home, but then back home men were like Henry.

She pressed her lips together to keep from laughing at the thought of Henry Dumont, his narrow chest covered with a thin carpet of graying hair, his pale white stomach protruding slightly over male organs almost invisible in a nest of more hair.

Nothing about Gaetan was narrow or invisible. She could see bone, muscle and sinew in arms and legs, back and chest, belly and rear. She could see male. A small sound reverberated in her throat. She pressed her lips together and bit them between her teeth to make sure it didn't happen again.

Something had to be wrong with her. Maybe this was a symptom of the other problem. She knew, everyone knew, that men were easily aroused, but women were not.

He moved into the water and sat down, and she almost wept with relief. His bare chest and arms were familiar. If that was all she could see, she could regain control. Except nothing looked familiar any more.

How exactly had she come to the conclusion that he wasn't handsome? He wasn't, she realized. Handsome was too civilized a word. Beautiful had fit Nilchi with his amused charm, but she couldn't think of a word in any language that defined Gaetan.

He wasn't using soap but rubbing himself with sand from the streambed. Goosebumps rose on her arms and her nipples ruched tighter as if sand rubbed her skin also. He lay back in the water, his hair floating on the current and water droplets sparkling on his chest. Her throat vibrated again. She scrunched her eyes shut and buried her face against her arm. Until she heard a splash and couldn't stand it.

He was on his feet, moving back to the stream bank. He sat on a flat rock there, his legs bent and crossed at the ankle, his arms around his knees. She closed her eyes and buried her head again, afraid the weight of her gaze would give her away. The *heat* of her gaze. How long would it take him to dry off enough to leave?

She looked again, watched him dress, and then he was gone. She thought of George, the scholar in her family and the prissiest of her brothers. George spent a lot of time justifying the family's wandering ways. *Everyone should travel. Travel expands one's horizons.*

Katherine hugged her arms to her stomach and began to giggle, rocked back and forth and laughed. If Dr. Whitman could see her now, he would diagnose hysteria brought on by the imbalance in her system and prescribe some foul-tasting tincture full of opium she'd only pretend to take. She laughed until she cried. When she was all cried out, she went and got dressed.

10

By sunset, Katherine had a fire going, coffee made and biscuits ready to bake. The miners had thoughtfully provided every utensil Katherine would have packed herself if given the opportunity, including a Dutch oven. She unwrapped the slab of bacon and started slicing. Beans soaked in another pot. If Gaetan didn't pack up and head out in the morning, they'd be ready to cook tomorrow.

As she tossed another slice of bacon into the big frying pan, a rabbit's body dropped down next to her. She jumped and darted a hand for the pistol hidden under the oversized shirt but relaxed as Gaetan sat across the fire. Katherine kept her head down, all too aware the heat scorching across her cheeks must be visible. Maybe if he noticed at all, he'd think her high color came from being close to the fire.

She filled a coffee cup, stuck a spoon in a cup of sugar, and sat both cups on the ground beside him. Returning to her place by the fire, she watched him stir three heaping spoonfuls of sugar into the coffee and couldn't keep quiet.

"That's not good for you, you know. Maybe you don't have to worry about getting fat, but that much sugar will rot your teeth."

He stirred in a fourth spoonful. "They're your teeth," she muttered. "Or at least they will be until they fall out."

She started the bacon frying while she cut up the rabbit. When the bacon turned crispy, she set the slices aside and eased the rabbit into the fat.

Memories of Africa and the last time she cooked over an open fire came back to Katherine as she worked. Life had seemed free and uncomplicated then. Even knowing it was an illusion, the same feeling lifted her spirits once more. Right now, right this moment, she felt happier than she could remember feeling for years.

The meat would take a while to cook and the biscuits to bake. Gaetan sat still the way she had seen the Apaches do when she was first with them days ago, quiet, with no need to fuss over anything or fill the space between them with words.

There were things she needed to say, however. "Thank you." She looked right at him, even though he didn't look back. "I didn't think there was anything that could be done to stop the blood poisoning and it was only a matter of how long it would take to kill me. It was the same bullet that killed Nilchi, you know. I twisted around in the saddle to look back, and that's when we were hit."

He did look at her when she said Nilchi's name, a speaking look that warned and made her hesitate before going on. Maybe the Apaches were like some other tribal people and didn't speak the names of the dead. She repeated herself in Spanish but didn't say the name again.

"I apologize for what I said when I woke up and you were—doing whatever you did. Your brother told me how you feel about whites, how you don't believe in taking captives. I know you'd rather kill me than put up with me, but I'm sorry I assumed the worst, and I'm grateful."

She picked up the coffee pot, walked over and refilled his cup as she repeated her words, then sat back down and refilled her own cup.

"Maybe it doesn't make any difference once you're dead. I'm not sure what I believe about that, but I know I'd rather die sooner with my spirit whole than live a little longer and be broken. Even when I still thought I'd die that night, I was grateful that you came back for me because—because that's how I feel and those men weren't much better than the Rurales."

Embarrassed to have said more than what was necessary to thank him and apologize, Katherine didn't repeat her last words in Spanish. She changed the subject.

"I don't suppose you'd be willing to tell me how soon I can take this bandage off? I cleaned up as much as I could today, but I'm afraid to get it wet. Dog signals won't work, but maybe you could just hold up the right number of fingers? One for tomorrow? A fist for right now?"

She demonstrated, waving fingers at him.

He drank coffee and studied the outline of the hills in the distance, which she expected, but still.... She sighed and busied herself with the food. When the meat was done, she piled most of it on one of the tin plates, opened three fat biscuits and drizzled honey inside. Carrying the plate across the way, she put it on the ground beside Gaetan.

As she filled a plate for herself, she watched him start eating. He chewed with his mouth closed. Maybe that school he was in wasn't all bad.

He went still, staring at her cold-eyed as she picked up a biscuit. Probably Apaches believed women were supposed to cook the food, hide until the men finished eating and eat the scraps. And that would be a belief he subscribed to. This time she ignored whatever message he was sending. She wasn't Apache, and she was hungry. She smiled at him around a mouthful of biscuit, chewed and swallowed.

"You know, now that we have the horses and supplies, you can be rid of me any time. A horse, a canteen, a few supplies, and I can keep going north on my own. A map would be nice. I don't suppose you could bring yourself to scratch something out in the dirt, sort of give me a hint as a goodbye present?"

Nothing. She stopped trying to provoke a reaction and finished eating in silence. Then she plopped a couple of peach halves from an open can on her plate and took the rest to Gaetan.

"They're wonderful. Say what you want about those miners, they knew how to pack a mule."

She finished her peaches and was debating whether to fill his cup again when he rose and crossed to her in a few strides. She struggled and tried to get away in vain as he lifted her by the back of the trousers, pushed the big shirt up her back and sawed through the bandage with his knife. She hung there as he reached around and unbuckled the gun belt.

When he dropped her on her knees and walked away, the belt swinging from his hand, she yelled at his retreating back. "If you won't let me have a gun, you're going to be stuck with me."

Grabbing the frying pan, she lofted it over her head, ready to throw, but caught herself. He disappeared too quickly for her to have a chance to hit him anyway. And after all, he *had* answered her question about the bandage.

OVER THE NEXT two days Katherine explored the small valley where the horses and mules grazed and made friends with some of the animals. She went through every single item in the packs. One of the miners had been a fan of Beadle's dime novels, but neither *Sonora Ben* nor *Tippy the Texan* held her interest for long.

Gaetan showed up morning and evening for meals. She didn't see him bathe again, not that she looked, and she explored both banks of the creek for a considerable distance in each direction before disrobing for her own bath. Her wound stayed a healthy pink and no longer bothered her except when she poked at it and examined the healing surface.

She spent a lot of time gazing at the sky, trying to analyze her own situation and what to do about it. If only she knew why Gaetan had gone north to start with, she might know if he would continue, but she didn't dare count on it. She thought they were still in Mexico, but wasn't sure of that either. What should she do if he started south again when he left here? Even without a gun, with a horse and supplies, she could head north on her own. Would he let her have even that much?

Every time she tried to plan and make decisions, she ended up more frustrated. There had to be some way to make Gaetan cooperate. As evening of the second day approached, she sat on a comfortable pad of folded blankets, leaning back against a saddle and composing persuasive speeches in her mind when the sound of horses caught her attention.

The loose horses had not come to visit. Five Apaches reined their gaunt mounts to a halt only a few feet away, studying her with impassive dark faces. They didn't look any better than their horses, much dirtier and more ragged than any of Chishogi's men.

Swallowing hard even as her stomach tightened and heart raced, Katherine smiled at the wizened, gray-haired man closest to her. "Good afternoon. Do you speak Spanish? Or English?"

"I speak Spanish. Where is your man?"

How did she answer that? Truthfully, she decided. "I don't exactly have a man. I'm traveling with one of your people. Gaetan? Of the Chihinne?"

The old man said a few sentences to the others, and the stony expressions dissolved in amusement. One of them even laughed.

"You need to learn to lie better, woman. Did your man see us and run away and leave you?"

Katherine, who considered herself a skilled practitioner of the art of the necessary lie, was indignant at not being believed now. "I'm not lying. I'm telling you the truth. You're right that Gaetan wouldn't have anything to do with me usually, but his brother took me captive, and then he was killed by Rurales, and.... It's a long story."

"Gaetan would kill you before you spoke his name."

"You must know him."

He shook his head. "I know of him. No white would live in his presence."

"Not usually," Katherine said agreeably. "Why don't you get down. I'll make coffee, and if you're hungry, I'll cook. My story will entertain you, I think. My name is Katherine Grant."

"I am called Agocho," the old man said as he dismounted.

One of the others shoved the carcass of a small antelope off his horse near the fire. Katherine looked at it with distaste. Before cutting into it, she could tell the meat would be stringy. She started to slice bacon into the frying pan when Agocho stopped her with an angry exclamation.

"No pig meat! You prove yourself a liar when you try to cook pig meat for us."

Gaetan had crunched his way through several strips of bacon that very morning. Katherine put the bacon aside and said, "I cooked other things for Gaetan. No Apache eats meat from a pig?"

"No."

"Are there other forbidden things?"

"No pig. No bear. Nothing with scales."

"No fish?"

"No fish."

She wondered what the Apache unbeliever would say to a nice fat trout, but more than that she prayed for the sight of him. Three of these men were already pawing through the miners' packs and saddlebags in a very proprietary way. Agocho sat patiently, waiting, she supposed, for her to tell him a story he wouldn't believe. The fifth man watched her with undisguised lust.

After pouring coffee for the men—and keeping quiet when they added prodigious amounts of sugar to their cups—Katherine told Agocho an edited version of her adventures, surprised to realize how short a time it had been since she saw her first Apache. Agocho and his friends didn't need to know everything. They wouldn't believe most of it, and the details of what happened in Hierra's camp were none of their business.

Every time she paused, Agocho spoke at length in Apache, not just translating her words but, she suspected, commenting on them. Talking didn't stop the sick feeling in her stomach, but her heart slowed and her breathing steadied. Did Apaches kill and steal from other Apaches? If so, Gaetan would be a fool to show his face here now. And if he didn't, what was she going to do?

Gaetan lay concealed on a hill overlooking the campsite, studying the men below. They were Coyotero, not Chiricahua, and had the look of those who sought each other out after being cast out of their bands.

In his grandfather's time, or even his father's, no Apache would steal from another, but those days were gone. The horses and mules needed to graze in the valley, but he regretted not taking the time to cache the packs in the hills where he'd hidden the guns and ammunition.

He watched two of the men pulling the contents out of the packs, showing things to each other gleefully, and knew they would steal if they could. And they could. One of him. Five of them. Bad odds. Foolish odds, yet the thought of returning to the people with nothing, no better than Chishogi, galled him.

The woman cooked for them as she did for him. He glanced at the dead quail beside him and felt a flash of resentment. If nothing else, the woman was a good cook. She could make even the white man's flour taste good.

Since the Coyotero hadn't killed her immediately, they planned to take the woman too, which would free him from the promise. A promise not to kill her or hurt her brought no obligation to take risks for her.

The old man who led the small raiding party and the woman talked as if they were old friends. If the woman considered the men her enemies, she would, of course, smile at them until she found a way to shoot them in the heart or stab them in the belly.

Unless he could think of a way to keep the horses and mules, there was no use going down there. Standing by while others rode away with his spoils would be unnecessarily humiliating at best and dangerous at worst.

Still, the Coyotero couldn't know what the white woman was like. No man would ever believe what this woman was capable of unless he had seen her moving into firelight, shaking down her hair and holding out her hands to the Rurales as if asking for help.

Gaetan had half-expected to have to guard against her himself after using her to rob the miners. Even waking to see her own blood on his knife, she didn't show fear. The fact she held no grudge and had thanked him for going back for her surprised him.

He shook his head as if to throw the thought out of his mind and concentrated on the problem of the Coyotero. There had to be a way to use the woman to improve the odds.

The antelope was as tough and stringy as Katherine expected, and she hoped Agocho and his men wore themselves out chewing it. She piled each tin plate high with the roasted meat and added cornbread and a spoonful of beans. The amount of beans she had prepared for two didn't stretch any further.

The men ate with single-minded attention to the food, and she didn't try to eat with them. Part caution, but also lack of appetite. She toyed with her coffee cup but put it down when she noticed her hands shaking.

Agocho finished and belched in appreciation. "You cook good." He thrust his chin toward the younger man who had stayed at his side when the others rifled through the packs. "Kloshchu says he will forgive your lies. You deserve a better husband than the one who ran away. You can be his second wife."

Oh, no, not that again. Katherine gave a small smile at first Agocho and then Kloshchu. "Thank you. That would be an honor, but I can't marry anyone here. I'm going home to New York—my home is way to the east."

Agocho shrugged. "You'll come with us in the morning and be Kloshchu's wife."

"He only thinks he wants me for a wife. I don't want to live in this part of the country. I want to go home. I'd be a bad wife."

"Kloshchu will teach you to be a good wife, and after you learn, he won't hurt you. A woman doesn't say how it will be."

"Gaetan's brother said your people don't force women to marry."

"You're not Apache. You will do as I say."

Nasty old man. As she tried to think of another argument, a voice came from the gathering dusk around the fire. Dizzying relief swept through her at the sound of the incomprehensible words. Even though she hadn't heard Gaetan's voice for days, she knew it instantly. She closed her eyes and controlled the urge to run and hide behind him.

He took a place near the fire with the other men and threw a quail at her without looking her way. Katherine fixed him a cup of coffee, four heaping spoonfuls of sugar and all. She kept her head down and her posture submissive as she put it beside him.

The conversation sounded friendly. Maybe now that these other Apaches knew everything here really did belong to one of their own, they would just socialize a little and ride on.

When the quail was done, she heaped a plate with the best pieces, topped them with more cornbread and took it to Gaetan like the most humble of maidservants. Her appetite had returned. As she wondered whether she dared eat, Kloshchu walked over and stabbed a piece of the meat with his knife.

Squatting in front of Katherine, he bit into the succulent flesh, reached out and ran a dirty hand over the side of her face. She jerked away without thinking. He frowned, said something that sounded ugly and threw the meat in the fire.

The men ignored her after that, so she gathered the pots and pans and took them to the stream to scour with sand and elbow grease. Halfway back to the fire, she saw Gaetan rise, say a few more words to Agocho and head into the darkness. She dumped the pots and pans on the ground, grabbed a blanket from her seat by the saddle and hurried after him.

He stopped and turned so suddenly she almost ran into him. *Stay.* She pretended not to see the dog signal. "I'm not staying here with them. I'm coming with you."

Stay.

"No. I won't stay." In the light of the rising full moon, his eyes looked more empty and frightening than ever before. But Katherine felt more desperate than ever before. "The only way you can make me stay is to kill me. Do that if you have to, but don't try to make me stay with them."

He took a step forward. His hips moved in a way so sensually provocative her body flooded with the sensations that had overwhelmed her when she watched him bathe. The embarrassing intensity of her reaction stiffened her spine and enabled her to stay standing toe to toe with him.

"I don't believe you. A man who won't speak English because it soils his mouth wouldn't do that with a white woman." She forced herself to say the rest. "And if I'm wrong and that's your price, I'll pay it. I won't stay here with them."

She met the terrible eyes for long moments, determined not to beg. She wouldn't beg. She wouldn't. "Please, Gaetan. *Por favor.*"

He turned and walked away, one hand flipping off to the side in another dog signal she recognized. *Heel.*

Agocho and the others hooted and shouted. She didn't need to know Apache to understand them, and she didn't care what they said. She followed Gaetan, filled with a mixture of emotions, some of which she didn't want to admit and some of which she didn't want to identify.

He led the way across the little valley and into the hills beyond. Katherine stuck as close to him as she had the first night fleeing the Mexicans. He stopped on a small ledge on the side of one hill. Before her dread had time to build, he bounced her down on her rear as hard as he had once before, and then he was gone.

She leaned forward, hugged her knees and squeezed her eyelids shut in a futile effort to keep tears inside. When she finally got control of her heaving stomach and shaking limbs, she said loudly into the night, "Thank you, Gaetan, for keeping me safe. *Gracias, Gaetan, por guardarme.*"

The night was warm, but she wrapped up in the blanket anyway and lay staring at the sky for a long time before falling into troubled sleep.

Katherine woke before dawn but lay unmoving as strengthening light chased the stars. The thought of having to go near Agocho and any of his men repelled her. The thought of facing Gaetan didn't hold much appeal either.

A bird twittered nearby. The day was well and truly beginning, and if she didn't hop to soon, an Apache would probably drag her to the fire by her hair. She sat up and gasped at the sight of a coiled form near her feet under the blanket. A snake that large could spit venom from ten feet away and kill a big man.

The longer she looked, the more she realized the coiled shape wasn't exactly snake-like. She flipped the blanket aside and stared at a sight every bit as strange. The gun belt. With the Colt in the holster. She smiled the smile that wasn't a smile and pulled the gun out. Loaded, ready to go.

Feeling more like herself than she had since Agocho and his men showed up, Katherine buckled the belt around her waist, arranged the big shirt to cover it and folded the blanket over her arm to give additional cover.

As she climbed down toward the floor of the valley, Katherine pondered the meaning of the gun. Did he mean she had to fight off Kloshchu on her own? Considering what Kloshchu and the rest must believe after last night, that didn't make sense, did it? Maybe it made more sense.

She slowed almost to a halt and headed for the creek and the shelter of the trees. It wouldn't hurt to approach the campsite slowly from cover. Agocho and his friends wouldn't starve if they had to wait a little longer for breakfast. Maybe a quiet peek at what the Apaches were up to before walking out in plain sight would be a good idea.

As she got close to the fire, the scent in the air told Katherine no one had waited for her to make coffee. She moved through the trees as quietly as possible and stopped as soon as she could see the men clearly. Their positions struck her as strange. Slipping a little closer, she assessed them, trying to understand the tableau they presented.

Agocho faced Gaetan, leaning forward, talking intently. Kloshchu and one other sat on each side of Agocho, their rifles held casually across their chests. No one had kept hands on a rifle last night.

The other two men stood on each side of Gaetan, slightly behind and also holding rifles in a deceptively casual way. Gaetan had a pistol at his waist, but his rifle lay on the ground beside him. So Agocho did intend to steal the horses and packs. His men not only had Gaetan outnumbered but braced.

And this morning Gaetan had given her a gun. Katherine stepped out from the trees and called out cheerily, "Good morning. I'm sorry I'm late. I'll get breakfast started right away."

Agocho turned toward her. "No breakfast. We're leaving. Kloshchu no longer wants you for a wife, but you come with us."

Kloshchu started toward Katherine with a very unhusbandly look on his face. Katherine pulled the pistol and put a bullet between his feet. He jumped straight up with a yelp.

Gaetan's hand snaked for his rifle. He smashed the man on his left in the side of the head with the stock and knocked the man on his right sideways with the barrel.

When everyone stopped moving, one of the men who had been behind Gaetan was unconscious, the other stunned.

Katherine held the pistol in both hands, aimed at the middle of Kloshchu's chest, and Gaetan had his rifle pointed at Agocho. The last of Agocho's men looked uncertain for a moment and dropped his gun when Gaetan spoke.

Gaetan spoke again, and Agocho nodded. The disarmed men went to catch horses, and everyone waited. By the time they had all five horses caught up and saddled, the man who had been unconscious was sitting up, shaking his head.

Agocho got to his feet and looked at Katherine. "You'll be sorry. Gaetan will make you sorry."

Katherine shrugged. "Probably so. He just made you sorry."

When they were gone, she left it to Gaetan to watch and make sure they kept going while she checked the coffee the men had made. It wasn't bad. She poured a cup for herself and one for Gaetan. She put two teaspoonfuls of sugar in his and took it to him.

"I'll start breakfast."

He walked to the fire and kicked dirt on it. Katherine took the hint, doused the fire and started packing.

Even with both of them working, the morning was almost gone by the time they had the packs reassembled and on the mules. The loads were lighter because Gaetan threw aside all the mining equipment. He also ignored the extra saddles.

Katherine caught a sturdy black gelding for herself. She smoothed the saddle blanket over the gelding's back, hoisted the saddle into place, and was reaching under its belly for the cinch when she felt Gaetan's hands pushing her shirt up and unbuckling the gun belt. She twisted away, almost fell under the horse and lost the battle before it started.

"You, pig! You bacon-eating Apache! I need that gun, and when you need your black-hearted self saved again and I don't have it, you'll be sorry. Give that back!"

She didn't expect a reaction and didn't get one. Repositioning the saddle, she cinched it tight and tied off the latigo angrily.

Before they had gone a mile, Katherine could tell Gaetan's direction was south, a little southwest maybe. Thank goodness for the canteen and sack of supplies she had stashed along the creek back in the valley. All she had to do was go back, pick up those things and start north. The loss of the gun rankled, but she still had a knife, and the nearest American town couldn't be that far.

She pulled her horse beside Gaetan's. "I know you need to get these supplies south to your people, but I need to go north. Since you won't let me have the pistol, I guess I'll go without it. Thank you. I…. Thank you."

Before she could repeat her words, much less turn her horse, Gaetan pulled the reins out of her hand, leading her horse as if she were a child on a leadline.

"No! Wait a minute. You can't do that. That wasn't our deal."

She tried to yank the reins loose and take them back and had no more success than at keeping the pistol. They rode side by side like that, Katherine's mind whirling with indecision. She had no choice but to go with him, but she had a choice whether to fight him at every turn and use anything she could get her hands on as a weapon or go willingly.

A mile passed. Another. She thought about Agocho's prediction. *Gaetan will make you sorry.* She thought about her own words the night before. *Thank you, Gaetan, for keeping me safe.* She thought about Nilchi's assertion that Gaetan would never take a captive. He rode with his eyes straight ahead, never glancing toward her, and Katherine examined the clean, strong lines of his profile even though she knew she would find no hint as to his intentions.

She remembered the way she felt stretched beside him on the butte watching Hierra and his men turn back, remembered the same feeling of common purpose when she held the Colt aimed at Kloshchu's chest. She remembered huddling on her knees, sobbing, and the first tremors of hooves drumming on the earth, returning.

Most of all she remembered touching his cheek as he loomed over her, assuming the worst as his body blocked the sun and his weight pinned her to the ground. The knife had flashed and her blood had dripped, yet instead of never waking again she had awakened with the throbbing pain in her breast and raging fever in her blood gone.

Heaven help her, knowing what she did about his hate and anger, she trusted him and wasn't going to fight him. As if sensing he no longer needed them, Gaetan threw the reins back at her and kicked his horse on ahead. Katherine watched him go, hoping she wasn't ten kinds of a fool.

11

After five days of non-stop dawn to dark travel deeper and deeper into the mountains she knew were Mexico's Sierra Madres, Katherine was too tired to fear the killing drop alongside the wicked switch-backed trail that wound through heavily forested mountain slopes. As the trail widened enough that the sides of the packs on the mules no longer hung into empty space, she heard the sound of voices and lifted her chin off her chest.

An Apache boy spoke to Gaetan while staring wide-eyed at her. She smiled and waved, and he jerked his gaze away. The boy ran ahead, his shouts echoing through the trees as he called out the news.

Katherine felt a stab of disappointment as the Apache village came into sight. Less than two dozen brush-covered dwellings squatted at considerable distances from each other across a large valley—not a village, more of a sprawling camp.

A crowd gathered along the path Gaetan followed, perhaps as many as fifty people staring with expressionless faces. Only one person approached, a woman of singular beauty, slim and petite, with huge dark eyes that set off delicate features. Shining blue-black hair hung past her waist. She ran to Gaetan, walking beside his horse, and Katherine watched curiously. He didn't seem to be talking to the woman any more than he did to her. Well, one word was more, and he did speak a few words.

The woman slowed her pace, halted and stared at Katherine as she passed by. Hostility changed the beautiful face to something ugly.

"If he was yours, he's still yours, and welcome to him," Katherine muttered.

When Gaetan dismounted in front of one of the domed huts, Katherine did too. The boy who had heralded their arrival climbed on Gaetan's horse and herded all the horses away. Unsure what she should do, Katherine watched Gaetan pull the packs off the mules where they stood, and then the mules were gone too. *Heel.*

She resented the dog signal as much as ever, but with so many curious eyes fastened on her, she obeyed without a murmur and ducked into the hut behind him. He took the knife from her as easily as he had the pistol and left her fuming. *Stay.*

Katherine looked around in the gloom. The only light filtered down through a smoke hole at the top of the dwelling. A blackened fire pit sat cold in the center of the dirt floor. Two beds with blankets spread over grass mattresses were the only sign of human occupation.

Sitting cross-legged, Katherine watched the people outside through the space between the edge of the blanket in the doorway and the brush of the hut. One woman after another came forward with baskets, helped herself to staples and left. So far as Katherine could tell, no one oversaw the process. Each woman took what she wanted and could carry. As one pannier after another sagged empty, half-naked children played peek-a-boo in them and then followed their mothers away. Silence descended.

No longer able to catch sight of a single person, Katherine kept watch, aware of hours passing as the shadows of what little she could see lengthened. *Stay.* She fought a strong urge to ignore the command and go look for him. There had to be someone among these people who spoke English, or more likely Spanish, well enough to explain what Gaetan was up to.

A heavyset older woman appeared, carrying clothing of the kind the Apache women wore, a pair of moccasins swinging from one hand. Guessing the woman's destination, Katherine scooted over to the closest bed and waited.

The woman pushed her way inside and said a few garbled words. Because of the clothing she carried, if not her words, her meaning was clear. Katherine spoke to her in Spanish. "All right. I'll change. My name is Katherine."

The woman gave no acknowledgment, just shoved the clothes at Katherine. Getting into a shoving match with someone's rude mother would not be a good way to start meeting Apaches. Katherine squelched the desire to push back, pulled off the miner's shirt, and put on the simple calico blouse. Taking off her boots, she wriggled out of Hierra's trousers and reached for the skirt.

The woman tugged at Katherine's drawers. "Take off."

This time Katherine recognized the words as Spanish, almost incomprehensible Spanish, but Spanish. Katherine hoped the woman understood better than she spoke because the Apache clothing did not include undergarments of any kind, and Katherine Grant was not wearing a skirt with nothing underneath.

"No," Katherine said, her words slow and careful as if talking to a child. "You try to take those, and you'll have a fight on your hands." She half-expected the woman to give more orders or call for reinforcements, but nothing happened.

After a similar argument over the boots, Katherine followed the woman outside. A man waited there holding a burning branch. He touched it to the hut, and flames raced across the dry brush. Was her presence in that hut so offensive, they had to burn it?

"Why?" Katherine asked the old woman. "Why fire?"

"Brother dead. Burn his house."

Relieved she wasn't the reason for the destruction, Katherine followed the old woman across the camp to another one of the huts. An old man who could be a bookend with the woman sat by the door. He glanced at Katherine then quickly away.

A rotten smell rose around this hut, and bones lay scattered on the dirt around the entrance. Katherine balked when the old woman gestured toward the doorway.

"No. I want to see Gaetan. I want to go where he is."

"Gone."

Katherine's stomach clenched. "What do you mean gone? Gone where?"

The woman thrust her chin toward the north. "Gone. He fights."

The world tilted, a roaring sounded in her ears, and for the first time in her life Katherine fought to keep from fainting. How could she have been so stupid? Why, oh, why, when there had been a weapon in her hands hadn't she shot him right through his black heart? Praying she would live long enough to have another chance, she followed the old woman into darkness.

GAETAN STOOD ON the edge of a rock cliff high above the camp. From here he could see so far down the mountain that rocks and trees looked tiny. Sometimes a hawk or eagle circled below him, its feathers iridescent in the sun, and he imagined how it would be to fly over the earth, everything small and unimportant below, free on the wind. Looking down on the world from such high places usually calmed him. Today making the climb had been a waste.

Bringing the white woman here had been a mistake, and today he had paid dearly for it. At least nothing like this would ever happen again. He would ride north alone to hunt the enemy. Until they killed him, he would kill them. With Nilchi gone, there would never again be a reason to raid with others as foolish as Chishogi or to have anything to do with such a well deserved failure.

At the thought of Chishogi, Gaetan spit to one side. The man should be in such disgrace he would sit in silence in a council of warriors. Instead he spoke long and loud today, his eyes hot with spite. There would never be a reason to sit through that again either.

A saddle horse and spare mount waited below. He should go down and start north. Loose dirt rattled on the hill behind him as someone climbed with no attempt at concealment. Gaetan wished he had not lingered, hoping for peace he never found.

"I need to talk to you more before you leave."

The voice was that of Bácho, who had been accepted as leader of this small band even though years ago a crippling wound had left him with an atrophied, weak arm and he no longer rode with warriors.

Gaetan would never show disrespect to Bácho. The chief was gray-haired and showing his age in all ways now, but when Gaetan first escaped the school, Bácho had still been strong and handsome.

Most of the people had wanted to turn away a boy who knew only the names of his parents and who could barely make himself understood in Apache. "Let him go back to the whites," they said, but Bácho had taken him in and trained him as a warrior.

In spite of their good history, a bitter weariness washed over Gaetan. "We've said all the words, Grandfather. Now we will each do as we have agreed. There are no more words to say."

"I have no more to say about the white captive."

Gaetan took a last look at the scene far below and turned to Bácho. "She's not a captive."

Bácho's conciliatory tone turned peevish. "She's not Apache. She's not your mother, sister, or wife. She's a captive."

Gaetan didn't bother replying. Truly all the words had been said.

"The woman is nothing," Bácho continued. "I know you didn't mean the words you spoke in anger."

Gaetan had meant every word. He drew his knife, cut his palm and let blood drip to the ground. "My brother was my blood, and I meant what I said. Make sure everyone understands how it will be. If you don't believe me about this, tell me now."

Bácho looked out over the far mountains, stubborn reluctance on his face. In the end, he nodded. "I believe you."

They climbed down the mountain together but neither spoke again as Gaetan mounted his horse and rode away.

12

IN THE FIRST days of living with Tliish and her husband, Goshé, Katherine daydreamed nonstop about revenge and escape. She pictured the scene of the stage robbery except that in her mind the man who pursued her into the rocks was not one of the robbers at all, but Gaetan. She centered the sights of her Remington on his chest and squeezed the trigger. She watched him waver on his feet the way the robber had before dropping to the ground dead and rolling not just down the mountainside but straight into the flames of hell.

She dreamed of escaping, of sneaking through the Apache camp the way she had through the Rurales' camp. In the confusion of the dream, she saw Gaetan on the wheel again, but this time she walked up to one of the Rurales, politely asked to borrow his rifle, and ran the bayonet through that blackest of hearts before skipping off into the night by herself, light-hearted and free.

What she did not do was study the people and place around her, find their weaknesses and devise a plan. The remoteness of the mountain valley, the terrible, narrow trail to it and the lookout she had seen greet Gaetan combined to make escape seem impossible.

She fell into a melancholy so deep she floated through each day in a fog of indifference. Fighting for survival with all her strength and cunning had only brought her this misery. She had no fight left.

Languages had always come easily to Katherine. In one foreign port after another she effortlessly picked up enough of the local language to get by. Spanish and French just soaked in during her first years of travel. Now she closed her ears to what she heard around her, resented the few Apache words and phrases she could not help absorbing.

Tliish worked ceaselessly gathering firewood, preparing food and making new clothes for herself, her husband and her grown son. Yards of new cloth appeared as magically out of nowhere as did fresh meat and staples. The Apaches must have some kind of communal system that supported everyone because Goshé didn't hunt and rarely left his place beside the doorway. He sat looking off into the distance with vacant eyes.

Debechu, Tliish's son, visited every day. Maybe there was good reason for Tliish's pride in her son, but in Katherine's experience men who strutted around the way Debechu did were the ones who ran below decks and hid when a hurricane hit instead of helping batten the hatches.

He was handsome if you liked short men with darting, beady eyes, but he had no wife. Of course the way his mother fawned over him, he hardly needed a wife.

The suspicion Katherine had once harbored that Apache women ate when the menfolk were done proved true. Tliish's considerable bulk benefited from the amount of food left over when the men finished. The bits of gristle and bone left when Tliish finished disgusted Katherine, which didn't matter. She had no appetite.

She obeyed Tliish's orders to help gather firewood and do other work, but obeyed slowly, less from defiance than because her limbs felt so heavy, her head so full of cotton. Without Tliish's threats, shoves and pinches, Katherine would have slept away every hour of both night and day.

She knew her behavior provoked the old woman and wondered when Tliish would escalate to hitting. Katherine told herself she'd fight back then, that she would escape before then, and some days she even believed it.

The summer months drifted by. As pounds melted off her body, Katherine tied her ragged skirt tighter around her waist and learned to ignore the crawling sensation in her matted hair. Nothing aroused emotion—until she almost retched with revulsion the first time Debechu touched her.

That night Katherine didn't dive into the oblivion of sleep the moment she curled into a self-protective ball in her dirty blanket. She stayed awake, her mind churning. No man could be attracted to what she had become. That proprietary squeeze of the shoulder had to be just that. Probably he had plans to make his mother's slave sew him another fancy shirt. Once she convinced herself, she fell asleep.

The touching continued and progressed day by day, making it impossible to deny what Debechu had in mind. And day by day fear and fury tore away the mists of despair. The other Apaches no longer avoided her. In fact, some of them were beginning to give orders and do the same kind of pushing and shoving Tliish did. The mystery was why they had waited so long.

Sigesh, the beautiful woman who had behaved with jealousy over Gaetan the first time Katherine saw her, never came close, but her sly looks as she talked to the others told Katherine who instigated most of the shoving.

You'll get yours, you beauty. Men with no honor betray everyone before they're through.

Because she ate so little, her physical strength was gone, but the need to move, to do something, returned. For the first time she gathered enough firewood on her own to make a full bundle, then struggled to figure out how to carry it.

"Let me show you the way to do that," said a mellifluous voice in Spanish.

Katherine look up in surprise. "You speak Spanish!"

"My mother was Mexican. Tliish speaks Spanish to you also."

"Is that what you call it?" Katherine said sourly. She expected a reprimand for the criticism but got only a laugh as the other woman bent to show her how to tie the wood.

"Thank you. My name is Katherine."

"I know. I'm called Lupe."

As Katherine watched Lupe walk away, a wave of shame washed through her. The Apache woman was not an extraordinary beauty like Sigesh. Lupe's figure was sturdy, not lithe, and pockmarks marred the smooth brown skin of her round face. However, she walked with an erect pride and her hair shone in the sun. She was clean.

Studying the other women around her, Katherine realized every one of them except Tliish was at least as clean as you could expect after a day working in the sun. No more sulking and avoiding facing her own mistakes, Katherine vowed. Neither Tliish nor anyone else was going to keep her from bathing, taking care of herself and finding a way to escape. If escape meant going over or through Tliish, Goshé and Debechu so much the better.

The Apache women all bathed early in the morning in a secluded part of the stream, and from that day forward, Katherine joined them. No one bothered her at the stream, and as the women and girls chattered around her, more and more words and phrases of their speech began to make sense.

Still, washing, even stealing dry clothing from Tliish long enough to wash her own filthy rags, only solved part of Katherine's problem. Every day she sat on the stream bank and worked on the mat of her hair. Little by little she finger-combed most of the heavy mass, but she despaired of ever achieving more than many smaller mats.

"See if this will help."

The very sound of Lupe's soft voice and good Spanish lifted Katherine's spirits. She took the proffered steel comb, wondering if once upon a time it had come from a miner's saddlebag. Before long the pile of broken, torn out hair in her lap grew large enough to stuff a pillow, but she could draw the comb right through her hair.

"Thank you," she said to Lupe, returning the comb. "I don't know how I'm going to keep it this way, but thank you."

"You should use a brush every day."

"I'd love to, but I don't have one."

"You have a brush."

"No, Tliish has a brush, but even if she'd let me use it...." Katherine made a face and shuddered.

Lupe frowned at her. "You're very thin. You need to eat more."

"Yes, I do," Katherine said, knowing it was true and wondering if she could.

Embarrassed, she rose to her feet. "I'm sorry. Thank you again. I need to get back before the old—before Tliish comes looking for me."

Two days later, Katherine walked to the stream to bathe feeling strangely light-headed. As she stood on the bank, debating the wisdom of disrobing and walking into the water, her knees gave way, and she fell in a graceless heap.

The interior of the wickiup that greeted Katherine's eyes when she came to was unlike anything she had imagined. Baskets and leather bags hung from the pole supports in what looked like an orderly fashion. Hides covered the floor, and the bed she lay on was comfortable. Someone might actually regard this little dwelling as a home.

Lupe knelt by the fire. The rich scent of roasted meat filled the air. Katherine's stomach clamored.

"I fainted, didn't I?" she said with wonder. "I never did that before. How did I get here?"

"Other women helped me carry you. Eat this."

What Lupe offered was a bowl of stew. Chunks of meat, onions and beans floated in thick gravy. Katherine cleaned the bowl, mopped the last of the gravy with a piece of flat bread and settled it all down with a cup of heavily sugared coffee.

"Now you will tell me why you eat my food, but do not eat the food Tliish has for you."

"I—she—what's left for me isn't very.... My appetite has been poor."

Lupe looked at the empty bowl. "Today is different?"

"You're a better cook. Even what she gives her son isn't as good as that stew."

"Her son," Lupe said faintly, as if she didn't know that Tliish had a son.

"Yes, Debechu. She feeds him and makes him so many new clothes, the girls must all be very impressed, although he...."

Lupe waited, but Katherine didn't finish the sentence. If she told Lupe about the problem with Debechu, she would only hear how she must submit, and Katherine had no intention of submitting.

In fact as she left the wickiup, she felt a slight stab of regret. Lupe had not been as careful with her knife as Tliish was. A rifle leaned against the brush wall in plain sight near the door to the wickiup. Another time Katherine would like to be friends with Lupe, but as her father said, desperate times called for desperate measures. She walked back toward Tliish's wickiup working on a plan to take advantage of Lupe's carelessness.

Two days later, for the first time since she had been in the Apache camp, Katherine did wrap a hand around a weapon. Tliish handed her an awl, pointed at the moccasins she was making for Debechu and said, "You. Make holes."

An awl made of bone was not much of a weapon, but the feel of it in her hand and the sight of the point mesmerized Katherine.

"Work, lazy woman."

Katherine looked up and gave the smile that wasn't a smile. Tliish recognized the look for what it was and grabbed the awl back.

"My son wants you for wife. I tell him no, but he wants you. You work harder."

Katherine pressed her fist to her mouth, but it did no good. Giggles escaped around it. Back home she had tried so hard. Dress, grooming, hair style and manners had all been directed at finding a man who would marry her in spite of her limitations, and Henry Dumont had been the best she could do.

If only she'd known, she could have come West long ago and inspired a long line of suitors. Of course, the men who had proposed in the last months didn't know what she had disclosed to every man who looked vaguely interested back home.

She'd turned Nilchi down with a smile and Kloshchu with a bullet. The pure malice in Tliish's eyes told her both of those ways had been smarter than laughing. Katherine couldn't bring herself to apologize, but the truth might undo some of the damage.

"He doesn't want to marry me. I can't have children."

"I know. All know. When you come here, we think there is baby in you from white man, Gaetan and brother. Now know. No baby. Never bleed. Not real woman."

She was *not* going to react to the sound of *that* name in *that* context. "Then your son can't want to marry a woman who isn't *real*."

"He is man. He wants to stick cock in you. After, he will marry real woman. You will be whore for all."

"A cock has to stiffen to get inside a woman," Katherine said. "A weak boy's mother can't stiffen his spine or his cock for him."

The woman came at her with the awl. Katherine blocked the blow easily and walked outside. Maybe a visit to Lupe would get her some decent food and another look at the knife and rifle.

GAETAN UNLOADED ONE pannier after another from the line of mules in front of Itsá's wickiup with satisfaction. Women were already approaching, ready to take a share of the plunder as soon as Lupe finished choosing. Raiding along the routes of the white freighters all summer had paid off handsomely.

Itsá worked on the other side of the mule, lifting heavy sacks with an ease that belied his slender form and average stature.

"Will you stay here tonight this time?" Itsá asked as they finished.

Gaetan shook his head. All summer he had brought back provisions from the north, but he never stayed more than a few hours.

"Everyone is grateful to you. The women have made you a wickiup of your own. You should sleep there to show appreciation." He grinned. "You could bring Sigesh there instead of going to her."

Gaetan just looked at Itsá. The man had been Nilchi's friend. He was half a dozen years older, but like Nilchi in many ways. Gaetan knew he should respond to the teasing in kind, but no words came.

"If you won't stay, at least eat with me before you go."

Gaetan started to refuse the invitation, when Itsá continued. "I promised my wife I'd talk to you the next time you returned."

"A meal would be good," Gaetan said, tacitly acknowledging what they both knew—if Lupe wanted Itsá to talk, he would do it, even if it meant shouting the words at an unwilling listener.

They watched boys herd the mules away and ducked inside Itsá's wickiup. Gaetan sat beside his brother's friend and wondered idly if Itsá valued his wife so highly because she cooked as well as the white woman. Batting the thought away like a pesky fly, Gaetan wished he could kill it like a persistent insect and knew he couldn't. He forced his attention back to Itsá's somber face.

"I miss your brother," Itsá said.

"I miss him also. I should never have taken him from the school."

"What you did was good. He was happy when you came for him, glad to live free with us."

"At first maybe. He never hated them. He was content there." Gaetan clamped his mouth shut after that. Admitting such a thing brought the grief back as fresh as months ago.

"I don't hate them the way you do either, although I hate the ones who killed my son, and I won't let them make me live like them on the reservation."

Itsá's words were bitter. His infant son had been killed in his cradleboard by soldiers more than three years ago.

Lupe brought food and sat quietly on the far side of the wickiup while the men ate. She would bring more food or drink if they wished and stay quiet as a woman should instead of helping herself to the food and babbling at them while they ate.

Once more, Gaetan shoved the unwelcome memory from his mind. He set himself to speculating as to what Lupe could want her husband to talk to him about.

When they finished eating, Itsá said, "My wife has become friends with the white woman. She believes you need to...." He looked at his wife as if for help with the words. "Do something."

Gaetan didn't want to talk about the white woman. He didn't want to think about her, and of course as with everything about the woman, what he wanted made no difference. All too many times through the summer thoughts of her had arisen unbidden and unwanted, one more reason he never should have brought her here. If he'd taken her north first, she would be long gone, memories of her fading instead of riding with him.

His people believed in ghosts. Gaetan heartily wished his brother's ghost would appear to claim the memories of the white woman for himself and take them away.

Nilchi could have the memory of her voice in the night as she cut the thong the Rurales had tied so as to almost but not quite stop his breathing. Let Nilchi, who had wanted her, remember her waving her fists as she shrieked and danced on the rocks or the way she had put a bullet inches from Kloshchu's feet.

A ghost probably could not have the memory of a touch. Gaetan decided he would have to keep the memory of her touching his cheek as he sat across her hips, her blood dripping from his knife onto her bare breast.

Itsá waited patiently for some response.

"You agreed with Bácho and the others," Gaetan said. "I did as you asked. What would you have me do now?"

"Yes, I agreed, but you haven't looked at the woman since you brought her here. Everyone—some believe that you didn't mean the things you said in anger. Since they no longer believe, they begin to look at the woman differently and treat her differently. After all, she's a captive."

"She's not a captive," Gaetan said. Even to his own ears, his voice sounded harsher than he intended.

Itsá didn't pick up the argument. "I take fresh meat to Tliish as we agreed, and my wife takes the best things from the provisions you bring, but the woman told my wife that Tliish feeds her son well with the food and makes him many things to wear with the cloth."

"She's white. She'll lie if it suits her," Gaetan said. "Has she tried to escape?"

Itsá looked as if he didn't know what to say for a moment. "No, she hasn't tried to escape. I know you're angry that we didn't believe you about her, but consider that Bácho was right. Being alone with her changed the way you looked at her. My grandfather told of a captive who decided to die and made herself die in spite of all he did. The woman is like that. She has no spirit." He glanced at his wife. "A little better lately maybe."

Gaetan got to his feet and thanked Itsá for the food. He controlled the rising anger until he was well away from the others. So she had fooled Bácho and everyone else who had refused to believe him about her, and they were more convinced than ever that they were right.

He should be pleased because sooner or later, she'd make them all sorry. She would be dangerous to people who refused to believe and were careless, but the thought of her going after Chishogi or even Itsá or Bácho with a knife didn't particularly bother him. An Apache could handle any white woman, even this one.

He didn't want to see the woman again, didn't want to hear what she would say to him, not in any language, much less two. No matter how Tliish had explained to the woman why she had to remain here, the woman would blame him. What a white woman thought was of no importance. What ate at him was the fact he agreed with her.

Tomorrow, he decided. If Sigesh had no other visitors, he would spend a little time with her, sleep in the wickiup the women had built for him and deal with the white woman tomorrow.

Except the next day he spent alone in high places, and the morning after that he convinced himself Itsá was wrong. Bácho and the others insisted the woman had to stay. Let them handle whatever trouble she caused. No ghost would come to relieve him of the memories of the woman he already had. He didn't need new ones. Saddling his horse, he left the camp and made it to the foot of the trail before reluctantly turning back.

13

Katherine tried to visit Lupe every day. Not only did she need the decent meal she got there, for the first time since arriving at the Apache camp, she wanted to learn as much about the people around her as she could. Getting her hands on Itsá's rifle would be easy. If there was a way to get her hands on it without anyone missing it until after she was long gone, Katherine couldn't see it.

Chiding herself for fixating on one weapon in a place that held so many, she turned her attention to the other Apache men. Every one of them was heavily armed, and not all of them were careful.

Given time, there was no doubt in Katherine's mind she could steal what she needed and get away. She also knew she could avoid recapture—one way or another—but the mistake she had made by laughing and insulting Debechu loomed larger and larger.

Since that day, Tliish had all but ignored Katherine. Debechu no longer touched her back, shoulders, or face as often as he could, but he stared at her with an unsettling sly malice. She wanted to believe a weakling like that couldn't pose a danger, but in her heart she knew better.

Three days ago, Tliish had pulled and pushed Katherine up the mountain into a heavily forested area. The old woman's explanation they were going to look for herbs sounded warning bells. Tliish never explained anything; she gave orders. Still, Katherine felt confident she could handle whatever nasty tricks Tliish had in mind, and maybe from high up in the mountains, she could get a good overall view of the lay of the land.

Tliish started Katherine picking some plants that didn't look like herbs to her and disappeared. The instant she realized what the old woman had done, Katherine took off down the mountain at a run, skidding across steep rock slides, grabbing for trees to keep from plunging headfirst into rocks and other trees. Twice she glimpsed Debechu pursuing her but far behind.

Since then, Katherine had expected the two of them to try again, but something had happened. She heartily wished she had not closed her ears to the Apache language for so long. Mother and son were so sure she couldn't understand them, they talked freely in front of her. And they were right for the most part. She caught only a few words and phrases here and there. "Wait." "He will go." And the name that scraped right across her nerves, "Gaetan."

This morning, Tliish's concern had passed. She gave orders with something close to glee. "We go. Herbs."

Katherine shrugged off the old woman's hand. "All right. I'm coming, but I can outrun him, you know."

They had only gone half the distance as before when Debechu appeared through the trees. Tliish latched on to Katherine's arm and held on like a leech. Before Katherine could twist free, Debechu reached them and took her other arm.

"Run now," the old woman said as she walked away.

He has to be at least an inch shorter than I am, Katherine thought, *but I should have hit the old woman to make her let go*. Fighting panic, she took in the ugly mix of hate and lust in the handsome face. *After all the food his mother stuffs into him, he's starting to get the same kind of pot belly as Henry.* Even so, she couldn't break the bruising grip on her arm.

When he spoke, the only words she understood were "hurt you."

"No, you won't," Katherine said in English.

She kicked the toe of one boot into the bottom of his knee as if to pry off the kneecap. He screamed and almost went down, his grip loosening. She wrenched free and ran.

Her head start wasn't enough this time. He caught her before she could disappear in the trees, both of them falling on the steep slope and rolling. The free fall ended against a tree with a crash that drove the air out of Katherine's lungs. As she fought to drag in a breath, Debechu pulled himself on top of her, slapped her hard across the face and ripped her blouse open.

Katherine arched her fingers into claws and jabbed them at his eyes. He jerked his head to one side, saving one eye but not the other and howling as he slapped both hands to the wounded eye. She squirmed free. He grabbed an ankle and yanked her back. She battered his face and arm with her other boot until he let go.

He caught her again on rocky ground. She went down across a rock so hard she cried out. Her vision blurred; her leg went numb. Assault was no longer Debechu's intent, at least not his only intent. He knelt on her stomach and pulled his knife, his face a bloody mask of rage.

Scrabbling her hands across the rocks, she seized the first one she found loose, too small, but better than her fist. She smashed it into the side of his head with all her strength.

Stunned, he sagged to one side. She hit him again and pushed him off. The numbness in her leg had turned to fire. The leg refused to work. She dragged it along—hopping, sliding, rolling. Anything that took her away from Debechu and toward the camp.

The thought of what the Apaches would do to a captive who resisted one of their own so violently flashed through her mind. Too late. She should have hit him again, she thought wildly, found a bigger rock and made sure he was dead. It would have bought her some time. She should have run in the other direction, over the mountain, and kept going. Except going downhill at a snail's pace was all she could manage. Maybe there was some taboo against assaulting women in front of wives and children.

As the forest thinned, she caught glimpses of open land and wickiups through the trees. Labored breathing sounded behind her, growing louder. She tried to hobble faster and fell. Debechu staggered after her, a one-eyed monster glaring through a veil of blood.

If he got her down again, she would never get up, and she knew it. If anyone at all would help her, she needed to find out and find out now. She struggled to her feet and screamed, a feeble effort between frantic, gasping breaths. Sucking in more air, she tried again.

Debechu kept coming. Katherine screamed a third time, tried to run, fell, rolled and came up facing him and his knife. He lurched forward another few steps, then stopped as if he'd hit a wall, dropped the knife and backed away.

"No! Gaetan, no!" The rest of his words were a whining babble.

Katherine risked a glance over her shoulder. Gaetan. Raising his rifle toward Debechu, with a look on his face that could make a bullet unnecessary. Bácho pushed the rifle barrel to one side and down, talking fast. Several other men clustered around the two.

Bácho turned to Debechu without taking his hands off the rifle. "Go. Go now."

Debechu went, his gait an unsteady half-run. Katherine crawled toward his knife. She almost made it, her outstretched fingers mere inches away when Gaetan reached past her and grabbed it first. She glared up into eyes as angry as her own, wordlessly letting him know what she had intended to do with the knife, what she would do with any weapon she got her hands on.

"Cover yourself."

She'd forgotten how deep his voice was, how powerful his presence. Killing him was going to take some doing. She didn't look away, considered pretending she didn't understand the Apache words.

Her torn blouse hung over her back and around her arms. Even without the feel of cool fall air on her sweaty, heaving chest, she knew her breasts were exposed. She just didn't care, and if he did, they could stay bare.

She made no move to cover herself and wiped the back of one hand across her runny nose instead, surprised at the smear of blood that appeared.

"Cover yourself, or I will do it."

Oh, no, he wouldn't. She pulled the torn edges of her blouse around from in back and tied them in a knot in front. Maybe her breasts were small, but the knot pushed them up, and the torn cloth covered no more than her nipples. She knew full well the Apaches wouldn't consider the arrangement properly modest any more than Aunt Meg and her friends back in New York.

He pivoted toward the village, flipping one hand in a dog signal. *Heel.* Katherine lunged to her feet on a tidal wave of fury that would have lifted a battleship, forgetting all about her leg until pain shrieked through it and she almost toppled right back down. She caught herself, balanced on the good leg and assessed the men around her. They were all armed, she could....

Gaetan spoke a few more words without turning back. She didn't have to understand the language to know what he said. Each of the other men put a hand over the haft of his knife.

To kill him, she had to be able to see him. Katherine hobbled through the camp, her eyes fixed on the perfect place on his back for a blade or bullet.

By the time Gaetan stopped in front of a wickiup, Katherine had fallen far behind. Even hate-filled thoughts of vengeance couldn't keep her going as the pain increased. The bone had metamorphosed into a column of fire. The agony radiated up through her hip and down into her knee.

She gave up and stood in place, swaying on one leg, touching only the toes of the other to the ground. To her surprise, the wickiup Gaetan had gone to was Lupe's.

Lupe appeared in the doorway, tipped her head as she listened to Gaetan for a moment and hurried to Katherine. "Lean on me."

The smaller woman helped Katherine inside and eased her down on the bed. "How much are you hurt?"

"I'm not sure. Scrapes, cuts and bruises all over. I fell with my leg right across a big rock. I don't think it's broken, but the pain is—ugly. Debechu attacked me in the woods."

"I know. Gaetan said what happened."

Katherine didn't want to hear that name, much less know anything he said. She stretched her legs out straight in front of her and lifted her skirt. Her left thigh had already swollen to half again its normal size. Deep reddish purple bruising spread down to her knee. She didn't try to see how high it went.

Lupe wiped Katherine's face with a damp cloth. "Echo will be here soon. Her medicine is good. She'll know what to do."

Concern and a gentle touch after all the fear and fury brought tears to Katherine's eyes. "I was afraid," she admitted. "My brothers taught me how to fight long ago, but I was afraid I couldn't hold him off, afraid when I got here no one would stop him."

Lupe sounded indignant. "Of course we would stop him. Apache men don't do such things."

Katherine gave her the look that deserved, and Lupe looked away. "He'll be gone before the sun sets."

"Will he take his mother and father with him?" Katherine fought a wave of panic. "I won't go with them. You can kill me, and I won't go with them!"

"Sssh. His mother and father will go with him, but you will stay."

What did that mean? Stay where? Stay how? Before she could ask, Lupe said, "What he tried to do? Did he succeed?"

Why did that matter to anyone? Did they think she was a virgin? If Debechu had his way, did that make her less valuable? No matter, she didn't have to decide between the truth and a lie.

She flipped her skirt up again, showing her intact drawers. "No. I don't think he was even trying at the end. After I jabbed him in the eye he was so mad, all he wanted was to kill me."

Katherine gave brief consideration to admitting her part in provoking the attack and rejected the thought. Bad enough she'd let her pride and temper get away from her, she wasn't telling anyone unless she had to.

Lupe was already giving her a suspicious look. "Stay here. I'll be back," Lupe said.

Voices sounded from outside, Lupe's higher and male voices lower. Katherine recognized Gaetan's and grimaced. Why was he here? Why did he care what happened? Was he going to have to give Tliish a refund?

Lupe returned with Echo. The Apaches here depended on the frail, white-haired woman for treatment of their illnesses and injuries. Echo examined Katherine with gentle hands and then conversed with Lupe.

"She says she thinks you will be well, but she needs the light of the sun to see these days and wants to see your leg outside. She wants to see if you can use it."

"Good," Katherine said. "Will she look at my leg by the stream? I really, really want to wash his blood off. Please?"

The other women consulted then helped Katherine to her feet. Echo didn't feel as fragile as she looked. No men were in sight. Walking with support on each side still hurt but was much easier.

After helping Lupe ease Katherine into the water of the stream, Echo said a few words and left. "She's bringing medicine that will ease the pain," Lupe said. "I have this for you." She held out a cake of amole.

Katherine's eyes widened at the sight. "Soap! Oh, yes. Washing with soap is medicine in itself." She scrubbed from the top of her head to her toes with enthusiasm, rinsed and did it again.

When Katherine finished, she dried off with a piece of blanket and put on a clean blouse and skirt way too short that Lupe gave her. "Are these your things? Thank you."

"When you feel better I'll help you make clothes of your own. These we tear up for rags." Lupe picked up the clothes Katherine had shed.

When she felt better. The words, with their implication of a future, made her feel better all by themselves. "Not the drawers," Katherine said. "I want to keep those."

"They're for a man."

"Yes, I stole them from the commandant of the Rurales. I need—I'm used to feeling covered."

Lupe pulled up her skirt and showed Katherine an abbreviated breechclout. "We'll make you new clothes."

Katherine laughed out loud. Maybe Lupe was fooling her and only cleaning her up for the gallows so to speak, but it felt good. Katherine's spirit lifted. She wanted to believe.

"Thank you. Thank you for everything, but especially for the amole."

"Gaetan asked me to give that to you. He said you would like soap."

Katherine had placed the wet cake of yucca root soap on a dry stone with care. Now she snatched it up and threw it. It skidded across the grass, picking up dirt and twigs as it went.

"If he had anything to do with it, I need to wash again without it."

"Don't say such a thing. Gaetan protects you."

"Protects me! I saved his worthless life from the Mexicans, and he sold me to the filthiest, most disgusting, useless people he could find. He used me, and he betrayed me! I'm going to kill him. If I have to tear his rotten, black heart out with my fingernails, I'm going to kill him!"

Shaking and panting with the intensity of her emotion, no longer caring the consequences, Katherine glared at Lupe, waiting for her to call for help. Nothing happened.

After a moment, Lupe said softly, "Gaetan did not sell you."

"Traded? Gave? Loaned? Rented?"

"I don't know this last word, but you are still Gaetan's. At least everyone except Gaetan says you are his."

Katherine stared in disbelief.

"Gaetan says you aren't a captive. He wouldn't take a captive. Bácho says you aren't Apache, so you must be a captive. What did Tliish tell you about why you're here?"

"Nothing. I know why I'm here," Katherine said furiously. "He brought me here. I wanted to go north, and he forced me to come here. I trusted him. I trusted that whatever he was doing, it would be for the best, and he—he did this!" Her last words were a hoarse shout as she waved her hand at the camp and everything beyond.

Lupe took Katherine's hand in hers. Katherine stiffened, but didn't pull away.

"When Gaetan brought you here, he wanted to take you north to your people the next day. Bácho said no. He said Gaetan couldn't do that because you would tell the Americans where we are, and they would tell the Mexicans, and the soldiers would come. Gaetan said you wouldn't tell. He said white, Mexican, Apache, you see any who hurt you as an enemy and fight beside those who help you. He argued with Bácho, and in the end, all the warriors met in council. My husband told me how it was. There were many angry words."

As Katherine heard about the promise Nilchi had extracted from his brother, she remembered those last minutes, the terrible, bloody struggle to talk, and her anger turned to sorrow. She stopped resisting and folded her hand around Lupe's.

Lupe said, "The warriors believed you helped Gaetan escape from the Mexicans, but they didn't believe everything he said. He was alone with you for many days."

Lupe hesitated, and Katherine said, "Tliish told me what they thought—of him and of me."

"Bácho said such a promise should have no power. He said only a man bewitched by a woman would believe the things Gaetan said about you. No white woman could escape Mexican soldiers by killing with a knife." She gave Katherine a questioning look.

"It was a sword."

"Ah, that makes a difference," Lupe said with a slight smile. "Bácho and Chishogi said they would kill you before they would let Gaetan take you away. Gaetan said he would give you a rifle and die fighting his own people beside a white woman before he would break the promise."

Lupe stopped and seemed to consider before adding, "Gaetan was so angry he said he didn't think he would die in such a fight. He would win because you are a better warrior than Chishogi. Gaetan and Chishogi...."

"Don't like each other much?" Katherine said.

Lupe nodded. "My husband and others made Bácho and Gaetan agree that you would live here among us. We need to move to another place soon. The grass here is wearing out. We've been here two years, and it's not good to stay in one place so long. When we move, Gaetan will take you back to your people."

Katherine felt the words in her stomach like a blow. She pulled her hand free, crawled to where the amole had come to rest, picked it up and returned to sit next to Lupe. Keeping her eyes down as she picked the bits of stick and dirt from the soap, she said, "Then why did he give me to Tliish? Why the most worthless people among you?"

Lupe sighed. "My husband says it's a sad thing that Gaetan knows more about his white captive than about his own people. Goshé was once a great warrior. He and Bácho rode together when they were young, but a bullet hit him in the head and now he's like a child. So Bácho said you should stay with Goshé and Tliish. He said Tliish could speak Spanish and would tell you enough so you'd understand why you have to stay. Gaetan would provide for you with a little extra for Tliish and Goshé, and this would be a good thing. I don't believe Bácho thought Tliish would use the things Gaetan provided for you for her son."

"Gaetan really didn't know?"

Lupe shook her head. "As my husband says, he doesn't know us. He wants only to kill your people. He agreed to what Bácho said, and he left. Before he left he said we must keep the promise he made to his brother, no one could hurt you. At first everyone believed and was careful, but through the summer, he returned, he brought provisions and he left without asking about you or looking at you. People began to say Gaetan's grief for his brother and bad feelings for Chishogi made him speak the way he did and that he didn't really care what happened to you. Now we see he still means to keep the promise. He would have killed Debechu today. Bácho and the other men stopped him."

Katherine had finished picking the detritus out of the soap. She put the cake back on the rock with care, and she started to cry—cry great, big, gulping sobs. Lupe pulled her into her arms.

"Sssh. You're all right now. Your leg will heal."

Her leg was no longer the worst pain. "I wanted to kill him. I would have killed him if I had a weapon. I thought he betrayed me."

Lupe pushed Katherine away and touched her face. "You must not feel like this about Gaetan."

"Feel?" The thought slowed the wracking sobs. "It's not a feeling. There was a bond. I can't tell you—I can't describe it, but I saved his life, and he saved mine, and we helped each other, and even though I knew he'd rather kill me, I trusted him. I can't explain it, but there was a bond, and I thought he broke it."

Lupe was still shaking her head when Echo returned with medicine. The two women helped Katherine to her feet, but not before Katherine picked up the soap and tucked it into the waistband of her skirt for safekeeping.

14

A SLIGHT BREEZE brought the scent of pine resin. The fall air cooled his skin but not the heat of the killing rage in his blood. An eagle dove from above down into the canyon, its white head gleaming in the sun, but the sight gave no pleasure, brought no ease.

Gaetan considered going back down the mountain rather than staying until Bácho and perhaps others came to this place and talked at him but decided listening with respect and dealing with them would be difficult no matter where. Let them make the climb and be short of breath when they started talking.

When Bácho and Chishogi had threatened to kill the woman before allowing her to leave the camp, they had also insisted that Goshé and Tliish would be ideal caretakers for her during the time she had to stay with the people. Gaetan had never liked or trusted Chishogi, but he wanted to believe Bácho had spoken in good faith. Wanted to but couldn't.

This summer Gaetan had abandoned his one-man war against the U.S. Army and raided along the freight routes and more than kept his part of the compromise over the woman. He had provided for her and provided well, with more than enough extra for Tliish and Goshé.

Thinking about Debechu consuming, wearing and gambling away things intended for the woman knotted Gaetan's stomach. Knowing Lupe and Itsá were the only ones of his own people willing to tell him what was happening brought a fresh wave of fury.

If Chishogi brought a white woman to the camp and wanted to take her back to her people right away would anyone stop him? Worse than that disloyal thought was the certainty that if Chishogi had brought the woman to the camp and wanted her cared for, Bácho would have made sure his friends actually cared for her.

At last he let himself think of the woman. Itsá's description of her behavior since she'd been in the camp didn't match what Gaetan knew of her in any way. She must have been really sick, not pretending. And today—thin, bloody and wild-eyed, she didn't resemble the woman he remembered until he took the knife before she could reach it. Then he saw the woman he knew in the hate-filled blue eyes.

No matter that no one believed him, she still was as she had been, fierce to the core. If she had reached the knife first, she would have tried to use it. For some reason, the thought calmed him.

He heard a man climbing the slope behind him. Only one. Good.

Bácho's voice. "We must talk."

"Yes."

"Echo says Debechu is hurt far worse than the white woman. She says his eye will heal but he may never see from it again."

"Good. Is he gone?"

"Not yet. I gave them horses, panniers. They're packing. He says the woman flaunted herself before him and tempted him. His mother says this is true."

"She did this so she could get him alone, beat him to death and come back here?"

"Who knows why she did it? You of all men know the evil of the whites."

"I was alone with the woman for many days. I know she wouldn't behave like that."

"You said she tempted the Mexicans so you could kill them."

"She called to them and made them turn to her. She didn't use her body to tempt them. I saw her with my brother and the Coyoteros. I traveled with her on foot and on horseback. She has a bad temper and too much pride for a woman. She has no manners. But she's modest."

"She sat on the ground with her breasts exposed in front of us all today."

Gaetan fought the feeling the woman's actions had evoked before answering.

"That had nothing to do with modesty. She wanted to defy me. You know Debechu lies and his mother protects him."

Bácho sighed and gave up the effort to make an argument he had to know was baseless.

"I'll see for myself," he said. "I'll take charge of her for you now."

However much respect he had for Bácho in every other way, Gaetan had no intention of ever trusting the old chief in any matter concerning Kath... concerning the white woman again. In fact Bácho was about to find out turning a blind eye to what Tliish had done carried a price.

"No," Gaetan said, staring Bácho in the eye in a way that bordered on disrespect among the Chiricahua. "You say she's my captive. She can live in my wickiup."

"You're never here. Who will watch her?"

"Lupe is her friend. She can teach her."

"You can't let her live alone!"

"You say she's mine. I'll do as I please with her."

Bácho's face reflected his frustration. "You help the people here in many ways, but since your brother's death, you lose your way."

"Banish me then."

Bácho broke the tension with a laugh. "I wouldn't be so foolish. Not only would we lose what you bring from the north, but you'd be entitled to take what's yours with you—like the woman. She can live as you say until she causes trouble."

"Don't think because I let you stop me from killing Debechu today I won't do as I said before, Grandfather. If he had forced himself on her or if Echo didn't tell me the woman will be fine soon, I'd kill him. The woman already killed him in all the ways that matter, but if I see him, I'll kill what's left. Make sure everyone knows what will happen if they hurt her."

Bácho made an annoyed sound, but he agreed in the end. When he left, Gaetan stayed on the mountain until the eagle rose high toward the sun. This time he took pleasure from the sight, let the bird's harsh cry pierce through him.

He watched as the eagle rose on the wind and headed north, shrinking first to a dark speck and then becoming part of the sky.

AFTER DRINKING THE foul black concoction Echo prescribed, Katherine obediently rubbed greasy ointment over her swollen and bruised leg. She basked in Lupe's concern and slept dreamlessly across the fire from Lupe and her husband.

The next morning, she dressed in the borrowed clothes and searched in vain for her boots, ignoring a pair of worn moccasins placed near where she had slept.

"The boots are gone, Katherine. Burned."

Katherine looked at her supposed friend indignantly. "If I'd been wearing moccasins, Debechu would have won, you know. That's why the boots are gone, isn't it? Because they were a weapon. Did *he* tell you to take them?"

Lupe's face closed into the impassive expression Katherine knew too well. Lupe wasn't going to give her any more information. Since the boots were already gone, Katherine yanked the moccasins on angrily and said no more.

Leaning heavily on a stout stick from Lupe's firewood instead of depending on the other woman, Katherine followed Lupe to a wickiup on the outskirts of the camp.

"You will stay here," Lupe said.

"Who lives here?" Katherine asked warily.

"You. The wickiup Gaetan shared with his brother had to be burned. We made this for Gaetan, but he only slept here a few times. He says you will live here."

Katherine peered inside to see nothing but a dirt floor without even a sign that a fire had once burned inside. A single burden basket sat near the doorway. "I can see he made a real home of it," she said.

Lupe's face opened again, and her look said she didn't approve of sarcasm. Katherine considered shocking her with stories of the Apache unbeliever crunching his way through strips of bacon and wearing his dead brother's clothes and moccasins but decided to save that for another day.

"You need these things," Lupe said, pulling out the burden basket and removing blankets, a fire starter, a gourd cup and bowl and an iron kettle.

"Oh, thank you," Katherine said, abandoning her grudge over the boots. "That's like...." Her words tapered off as a group of women walked straight to the wickiup. One left a bundle of firewood beside the door. Each of the others left an item necessary to an Apache household. Each smiled and left without speaking.

Katherine knew her version of the Apache expression of gratitude had no more finesse than Tliish's Spanish, but she gave it her best anyway.

"It's like a house warming," she said to Lupe when the others were gone.

"The house isn't warm. You have to build your own fire."

"No, back home we call it a house warming when people give gifts to someone moving into a new home."

"The gifts are to thank Gaetan. Everything here comes from him—except the firewood. This is from him also. He says you should have it. You'll need it to cut meat."

With those words Lupe pulled a belt from the basket, a belt that had a scabbard hanging from it, a scabbard that had a knife in it. Katherine took the belt with something approaching reverence, loving the solid feel, the weight.

"I'm sorry I was cranky about the boots. This is better."

"The knife is to cut meat. There's no other reason for you to have it. Don't give Bácho or Chishogi reason to...." Lupe paused, obviously searching for the best way to finish the statement. "Don't give them a reason to make Gaetan unhappy."

Katherine buckled the belt around her waist. Even her leg felt better. "Of course not. Gaetan's happiness is of primary concern to me."

"Hunh." With that disapproving sound, Lupe left Katherine to set up her household.

As KATHERINE WORKED on her own in the wickiup, she vacillated about what to do. Waiting to travel north with Gaetan would be safer than escaping. Why flee alone with the entire Mexican army on the alert for her if she could have a guide who ran that gauntlet successfully every few weeks? Still, thoughts of the grief her father and brothers must be suffering preyed on her mind.

In the end she decided it would be better to get home in one piece later than end up dead or in a Mexican prison sooner. The thought of traveling with Gaetan again had nothing to do with the decision. Nothing. What had happened to her, what *was* happening to her was a great adventure—better than any big game hunt. She spent her days working side by side with Lupe, trying not to be too much of a pest as she soaked up as much knowledge as possible.

What the small group of Apache fugitives around her all had in common was a determination to stay free and live as they had always lived, but the more Katherine talked with Lupe, the more she realized their lives had already changed beyond recognition. A traditional Apache group consisted of families belonging to only one band. The people around her were from all the Chiricahua bands—Chihinne like Gaetan, Nilchi and Bácho; Nednhi like Lupe and Itsá; and also Chokonen and Bedonkohe.

The Chiricahua had always been nomads who ranged all over parts of Arizona, New Mexico and Mexico, following their food supply. Even when the men raided and made war, the woman and children had followed and stayed hidden nearby. Now, for two years the women and children had lived in one place and the raiders had traveled far to the north in an effort to keep either Mexicans or Americans from locating them.

Lupe's description of Apache family life didn't match what Katherine saw around her either.

"If a man moves in with his wife's family when he marries, why aren't you living in a Mexican town? Was your mother a captive?"

"No. In the time my mother was young, we traded with the Mexicans and visited their towns. My father and mother saw each other one time and neither one could look away. Her family is large. He brought them four horses, and they let her marry him."

"But he didn't move in with her family."

"That was different. She's not Apache, and her family didn't want him."

"Do they live on the reservation?"

Lupe shook her head. "Soldiers killed my father when I was twelve years old. My mother took me, my sister and brother back to her family. She married a Mexican, and she still lives there. My sister and brother still live there. When I was seventeen, Apache raiders came to our village, I called out to them and told them I am Nednhi and asked them to take me back to the people, and they did."

Katherine's hands stopped scraping deerskin as she looked at the other woman in surprise. "Just like that? You left your family like that?"

"My mother knew I would go if I could."

"You've never seen her or your brother and sister again?"

"The Mexicans only kill us now. We don't trade or talk. I am Nednhi. They are Mexican."

Lupe's circumstances might be unique, but Katherine didn't see large family groups around her. Bácho and one other older man headed a family group of unmarried children, married daughter and husband, but the rest of the people here consisted of married couples who had no extended families or whose families were on the reservation, a few single men and Sigesh, who was divorced and lived alone.

Hunting was circumscribed by the need for the group to remain undetected. Only bow and arrows could be used. Firing a gun within a day's ride of the camp would be a grievous sin. Lupe beamed with pride as she described Itsá as the best hunter in the camp. He didn't raid, she said. He provided with his bow.

As Lupe described the foods on which the people had always relied, Katherine realized how much the determination to stay hidden limited what could be gathered. Mescal was so important the women risked traveling to where the agave plant grew to harvest the plants in the spring, but the band did without other foods. Many berries and seeds could be found in these mountains, but some plants could not.

All the restrictions left the people dependent on plunder. Chishogi had led several successful raids throughout the summer. The livestock he brought back meant plenty of meat, but the herd had grown too large for the limited pasture in their mountain valley.

The band needed to move and move soon. Katherine listened to the debates over pasturage with a mixture of satisfaction and sadness. The sooner the men decided to move, the sooner she could start home.

As she came to understand the problems of people cut off from their traditional food supplies who couldn't buy or trade for provisions, she also understood why the people appreciated Gaetan. Although his stated single-minded purpose was to kill enemies, he had never passed up an opportunity like the one Cal and his miner friends had presented.

Charged with providing for her, he brought more supplies more regularly. Gaetan didn't bring herds of horses and cattle home. He brought the kind of supplies the miners' mules had carried—beans, flour, salt, sugar and coffee—also weapons, ammunition and sometimes utensils and yard goods. Canvas that had once covered packs fluttered throughout the camp. Gaetan provided the kind of staples the people couldn't get otherwise, and the women loved him for it.

Sigesh loved him a little too much, Katherine thought sourly. Even married couples among the Chiricahua showed great reserve with each other. Sigesh was not openly promiscuous, but Katherine saw several of the unmarried men slip into her wickiup at one time or another. Her instinct was to dislike the woman, but she started to wonder if she should pity her instead. Finally she worked up her nerve and questioned Lupe.

"Does Sigesh have to allow men to visit her?"

"Her husband divorced her."

"I know, but does that mean she has to have many men?"

"No. She chooses."

"Why would any woman choose that?"

"She has no man of her own. This way she has men to help her and bring her gifts." Lupe slid a quick glance at Katherine. "Gaetan visits her sometimes. She tries to make him want to be her husband, I think."

Katherine refused to let the small stab of annoyance—or something—show. "I knew that from the first day I came here. She came to meet him and made her feelings clear. Why would he marry a divorced woman who chooses to do that when there are unmarried girls he could have?"

"Young girls listen to their mother and father, and no mother or father would want Gaetan for a son-in-law."

"Why not?" Katherine said, surprised. "He'd be the best provider, wouldn't he?"

"Yes, but families have expectations of a son-in-law, and Gaetan goes his own way. He was in the white school too long. He wouldn't be a good son-in-law or a good husband."

Nilchi had hinted at this attitude toward him and his brother among their own people. How sad that boys who had already suffered so much were subject to such suspicion. Katherine got hold of herself. Nilchi had not been, and Gaetan most definitely was not, a boy.

She said, "But Sigesh would marry Gaetan."

A slight smile crossed Lupe's face. "She wants him for the reasons others do not, I think. She'd like a husband who would give her many good things, but who wouldn't be here often."

Katherine said no more. It was none of her business. Except she couldn't stop thinking that arrogant, black-hearted devil that he was, Gaetan deserved better. Unbidden, the memory of what she'd seen watching him bathe floated through her mind. Any woman he married who didn't want him as often as possible had more wrong with her than she did.

15

KATHERINE LEARNED MANY things from Lupe and the other Apache women but began to accept in the time she had left with them, she would never master basket weaving and she would never speak decent Apache. The first didn't matter. No one she knew in New York would ever expect her to weave a usable basket. No one in New York would ever expect her to speak fluent Apache either, but her failure in that regard stung her pride.

Her comprehension grew by leaps and bounds, but her ability to speak languished at the level of Tliish's Spanish. She needed teachers willing to criticize subtle mispronunciations. Lupe and the other women smiled and nodded encouragement at any effort, even when she could tell they had no idea what she'd said.

One morning as Katherine walked to Lupe's, fretting about her lack of progress, a young boy raced by, touching her hand. She laughed at him as she always did when it happened, knowing the boys dared each other to touch her.

The bigger boys had tired of the game sometime ago, but today's hero looked no more than seven. As he slowed and looked back, ready to run to his watching friends, Katherine had an idea. She called out to him.

"You're very brave. Are you brave enough to help me learn to speak better?"

He ran, and they all took off, laughing, leaving her to wonder if any of them had understood a word she said, which was the problem, of course.

The same thing happened with a different boy the next day and the next. On the fourth day one of the older boys faced her. "We are brave. How could we help you learn to speak?"

"I need to practice. I need to practice with helpers who will make me say the words until they're right. The women are too gentle. I need boys strong enough to tell me when I'm wrong."

"Hunh." He turned and walked away, a little Gaetan in the making.

Katherine sighed. It had been worth a try. She'd just have to work harder with the women.

The next day three of the boys approached her. "We'll help you."

Safety in numbers, she thought, smiling at them. At least the early winter day was warm, for she knew they wouldn't go inside with her. Not yet.

As the days passed, more and more of the few children in the camp came to Katherine's wickiup in the afternoon. Winter was a time of storytelling for the Apache, and her plan fit right in. Telling the stories of her own childhood stretched Katherine's vocabulary. And if these children gained a little knowledge of what American children were like, maybe it would help them down the road.

Katherine scoured her memory of Aesop's fables. Tortoises and hares. Grasshoppers and ants. She told Lupe each story first, wanting to at least have the necessary vocabulary. She knew enough to avoid or change any story that mentioned a witch. The Apache belief in witches made talk of them dangerous, particularly for a stranger. She also learned which animals could not feature in her stories because they harbored evil spirits.

To thank the children for their help, she experimented with cookie-like doughs that she could fry in a pan. The results varied but were always edible. A few of the mothers visited in the first days, but for the most part the children remained her sole audience and teachers.

On a cold, gray day with hard pellets of snow adding to the sting of the wind, Katherine pulled her latest fried dough experiment from the fire as the first children arrived. Aware of an adult with the children, she looked up, expecting to see one of the children's mother, and dropped the pan back into the fire. Gaetan.

Seeing him surrounded by children disconcerted her. They showed no sign of fear or awe. In fact Ya-kos, the youngest of them all, sat close and smiled at him shyly. She should have known. If there was an Apache who didn't love children, treat them kindly and give them guidance, that one wasn't in this camp.

She yanked the pan back out of the fire and set it aside to cool. For a moment every single Apache word deserted her. Finally she managed to say, "Today I will tell you the story of the rabbit and the dog."

As she told the short stories, Katherine always watched faces and listened for giggles. The children were no more inclined to correct her as she spoke than Lupe, but if she identified her mistakes from their behavior and asked afterwards, they would vie with each other to help her.

Today the older boys corrected her with more vigor and fussed at her longer over perfect pronunciation. They wanted to impress Gaetan the way she had once wanted to impress her brothers, and like her brothers, he gave no sign of being impressed.

The children ate their treats and hurried toward their own homes, eager to be safely inside before dark. Gaetan stayed. Katherine's pulse quickened. Memories of him didn't match the reality of his presence. He was bigger than the memories, his eyes darker and more hypnotic, the lines of his face stronger.

"Are you here to make sure I'm not poisoning young minds with my stories?"

Without realizing it she expected him to ignore her as he always had. The deep voice, actually answering her, gave her a start.

"Yes. Bácho worries. It's his responsibility to be sure the children are safe."

"He could come listen himself instead of waiting until you're back to do it, but that would be beneath him, wouldn't it?"

"Yes."

"But it's not beneath you."

"All the people are his responsibility. You are my responsibility."

"Aah, so what will you tell him?"

"You won't hurt the children. But you can't help them either. You think you can help them, and you can't. The Mexicans will kill them soon, or your people will."

"You're wrong. If the Mexican army came tomorrow, some would escape. You know that. And people who go north of the border can be safe on the reservation. Maybe you'll fight to the death, but some of these children will live and so will their children. Knowing a little bit about how other people think might help them."

He got up and for a moment she thought he'd walk out without saying more, but then his voice came, deep and low.

"Do you know what we called ourselves on the reservation?" He didn't wait for her to guess or admit she didn't know but gave the answer. "*Indeh.*"

When he was gone, Katherine hugged her knees, almost unable to believe she had just had a conversation with him, however short and intense.

The next day she asked Lupe the meaning of the new word. *Indeh.* The dead.

KATHERINE DIDN'T EXPECT to so much as see Gaetan again unless Bácho found another reason to worry she was sabotaging his people and wanted someone to spy on her. She was wrong.

The next time he returned from the north, Gaetan joined the children again. He took a place across the fire, sitting motionless until little Ya-kos tried to climb in his lap and fell into the empty space between his crossed legs.

Katherine heard the rumble of his deep voice but couldn't make out the words as he pulled the little girl to a seat on one thigh. The fact that thigh was under heavy leggings didn't keep Katherine from remembering it and the lean belly above it bare. Or all of the rest of him.

Fortunately by the time Gaetan finished talking to Ya-kos and they both looked up expectantly, Katherine had forced her eyes up from his stomach, across the broad chest to his face. She was having less luck forcing her imagination to behave, but surely the gleam in his dark eyes was a reflection from the fire, not awareness of her guilty thoughts.

This time he listened as the children told her stories, and she repeated each part back to them. When they left, he stayed as he had before.

"You speak well now," he said. "You don't need their help."

"I'll never speak as if born to it, and I enjoy them."

She waited for him to forbid her to continue with the children, but what he said surprised her. "What is a rifle with a 'scope?"

She decided not to point out he had spoken an English word. "Have you seen a telescope, a spyglass?"

"A long tube. Faraway things look close."

"Yes. Some of them are very large, but some are smaller, and a smaller one can be fastened to a rifle in place of the sights. That's a telescopic sight, and it's aligned so that when you look through it, you see a faraway target so clearly you can chose where the bullet will go. There are hairs set in the glass, like this." She held her forefingers up crossed. "You center those cross hairs on the target. That's a rifle with a 'scope ."

"You've used such a thing."

"Yes. My father has one, and he let me use it a few times. Did your brother tell you about my family?"

"Yes. The ships."

Earlier in the day Katherine had roasted and ground a portion of her share of the coffee he had brought. Now she added all of it to a pot of water and pushed it close enough to the fire to boil. As she did it, he asked another question.

"Why did you decide the Mexicans were your enemies? They cooperate with the Americans."

She told him the things the Rurales had said in her presence and then asked a question of her own. "What did they mean when they talked about a bounty for the scalps?"

"The Mexicans pay for Apache scalps. Sometimes they pay for other scalps because they can't tell the difference, I think, but when they find their own people dead and scalped, they pretend we did the killing so they have more reason to hunt us."

A year ago, back in the civilized world, she wouldn't have believed a word of it. Now she felt only sorrow—because she did believe it.

"Why didn't you let me die? You wanted to kill me, so why not let me die from the wound?"

He was silent so long she thought he had gone back to ignoring her, but finally he said, "When I pulled you off the horse I saw the wetness on you from the wound. Until then I thought you were sick."

She didn't see what difference that made but waited. After a while he went on. "I left you there and thought you would die and that would be good, but when I unloaded the mules, a can rolled out of one of the packs. A can of honey."

"That's what you used? Honey?"

He nodded, looking into the fire, not at her.

Admitting he'd made any effort to save her life probably embarrassed him. Another thought came to her, and the words popped out before she thought. "Did you think your brother's ghost pushed that can out of the pack to give you a hint?"

"No, I thought it would be easy to put honey on the wound and you would live or die as Ussen decided, but when I looked at the wound...." He shrugged and changed the subject. "You were afraid when you cut me free."

"I was. I thought you might go crazy and kill me and everyone else you could until they stopped you, but I also thought if you did that it would be my revenge on them." She felt the corners of her mouth pulling back and pressed her lips together to stop it.

"You're very fierce. I thought you would escape after I left you here."

She looked down, ashamed. "I was sick for a while. Everything seemed—too much."

"I never should have brought you here."

Recognizing the closest thing to an apology she would ever get, Katherine accepted. "I understand how it was."

"The people won't move from here until next fall, I think. Will you wait, or will you try to escape before then?"

Katherine laughed out loud. "Do you think I'd tell you?" After considering it a moment, she said, "Maybe I would. You'd probably keep the secret and hope I succeed so you don't have to bother with me again, but no, I'll wait and go with you. I like living here." She gestured around the wickiup, which was beginning to have the same comfortable look as Lupe's.

"You want to go back where there are things like rifles with 'scopes."

"That's not what I miss, although a pistol tucked in a purse is always nice to have. What I miss most is the big bathtub we have at home. Especially in cold weather like this, to be able to sink into a hot bath is wonderful. That's what I miss most, hot baths and clean sheets that smell like sunshine. I know you hated the school, but wasn't there anything there you liked? Did they have a bathtub?"

"They had a big tub, and on the day before their church day they filled it with hot water and made us wash so we'd be clean for their church. They put the little children in first and washed them. Even the first year I was there, when I got to the tub, the water was cold and dirty and gray with scum. I don't miss it."

"You mean they didn't change the water, or—or add more hot or anything?"

He just shook his head.

"Sheets?" Katherine said, expecting him to tell her there weren't any.

"I think they washed the sheets in the tub after all of us. They didn't smell of sunshine."

Was that some vestigial sign of a sense of humor? *Dear God, don't let it be. Don't let him have a sense of humor. It's hard enough as it is.* Realizing she was praying and what she was praying about, Katherine made herself stop.

The rich scent of coffee reminded her of the boiling pot. Pulling it back from the fire, she sprinkled a little cold water across the surface to settle the grounds and filled two cups. Moving around the fire to hand him one, her heart accelerated and stomach dropped. She hesitated there, studying him as he stirred two spoonfuls of sugar into the cup. This close to him she could see how tired he looked, gaunt and worn down.

Without thinking, she said, "Are you hungry? Would you like to eat with me?" What she was saying struck her as the words came out. "I'm sorry. That's silly. It's your wickiup and your food. You don't need an invitation from me."

"The food is yours. Share it as you choose. Yes, I'm hungry. If I eat here, will you talk at me the whole time?"

Katherine opened her mouth to give that the answer it deserved, then closed it again. She cooked without saying another word. When they finished eating, he was the one who spoke.

"You didn't eat at the same time as Agocho and his men."

"As my brother George says, wisdom is the better part of valor, and it didn't seem wise. Of course, I didn't really want any of that stringy antelope, especially after he told me using some bacon fat to make it taste better would bring the wrath of Apache gods down on my head."

He ignored the jibe. "Ussen is our only god. He's the same as the white god, I think. You mislead enemies so they think you're a meek woman. You did that with my brother."

"Did I?" Katherine thought back. "He knew I shot the stage robber. You all knew that. Did you think I was meek?"

"I thought you were dangerous. He laughed. He didn't believe any woman would be dangerous to him."

That made her smile. "He was right. I remember looking at him and thinking that given enough time he could charm me into marrying him or doing anything else he wanted. But there wasn't any time, was there? I wish—I wish something different happened."

"You felt that way because you saw inside him and saw his heart was weak and white. He wanted you because you're white. He told you about the school. They did that to him there."

"I don't believe there was anything weak about him. He defied you when he took me. Would any of the others have dared do that?"

He didn't answer.

"I worried about it, though. I could see how he was baiting you on purpose, and I thought if he took me only to anger you, he'd tire of it and I'd be in a bad way. He did tell me about the school. He told me how you escaped and came back for him, and that it was hard for him because he didn't even speak Apache any more. I wondered if he was angry at you over that."

"He was."

He no longer looked tired, but intense, the firelight glittering from his eyes, his mouth a hard, straight line. Wisdom would be to agree with him, but Katherine didn't like that weak heart statement, and whatever Gaetan provoked in her, it never seemed to be wisdom.

"No. I asked him and that's not what he said. He said he was glad you came and got him from the school. He said if he stayed there until he graduated, he would have ended up as a drunken beggar. He was glad you took him from the school, but he was tired of you treating him like a boy when he was a man."

Gaetan didn't move and didn't look any more inclined to violence—or any less. She felt compelled to admit. "I didn't tell him, but I understood how you felt. Even after he told me how old he was, I kept thinking of him as much younger. But he thought you were bossy and overprotective, and it annoyed him, and he wanted to annoy you back. I don't think he realized that you only annoyed him, but he enraged you."

He got to his feet and stalked out so suddenly Katherine flinched. When he was gone, she tied the door covering closed against the night. The absence of him made the little dwelling seem very empty.

GAETAN WALKED A short way from the wickiup and stopped, staring up at stars hanging like ice chips in the night sky. The woman had no idea the gift she had given him. For years he had lived with the burden of believing Nilchi would have stayed at the white school if he had the choice. Gaetan had given him no choice.

He would never have asked his brother such a thing outright. No Chihinne would. The woman, so fierce she'd make plans to murder them all in their blankets if she got a wrong answer, wanted to know, so she asked. He felt a terrible weight lifting from his shoulders.

Grief washed through him the way it always would at the thought of Nilchi, but living with the memory of a younger brother who had been annoyed at an overprotective older brother was easier than believing Nilchi had never forgiven him for the school.

Gaetan wore no coat, carried no blanket to throw around his shoulders. The sharp wind cutting through his wool shirt started him moving. He crossed through the center of the camp, his steps slowing as he approached Sigesh's wickiup.

Going to see what the white woman was up to had been a spur of the moment decision when he saw the children headed that way. He knew now he needed to check on her each time he returned to the camp. Checking on her didn't require spending time with her, but the thought of listening to her practicing Apache with the children held a strange appeal. Watching her narrow the strange blue-gray eyes as she worked on a difficult sound and then laugh when she mastered it pleased him. And after all there were things he had wanted to know, and now he did.

His intention had been to go to Sigesh tonight. Sigesh never talked about anything except her own wants and needs, but she would accommodate him, and he could spend the night by her fire.

Only he didn't want to be accommodated. The change in the white woman's expression when she saw him today reminded him of the way her face lit up when she saw him the night she sat with Agocho. She had feared for herself that night. That was all. *Thank you, Gaetan, for keeping me safe.*

He had blankets and supplies cached across the valley in a cleft in the mountain that provided protection from the wind. Resigned to a night no warmer than on the trail, he turned his steps in that direction.

16

KATHERINE HELD UP the first basket she had ever judged worth finishing and twisted it one way then the other, admiring her handiwork. The smooth feel of the tight weave she had finally achieved pleased her even more. "I can't believe it. It looks like a real basket. It *feels* like a real basket."

"I'll show you how to heat piñon pitch and make it waterproof tomorrow," Lupe said.

"Maybe that should wait until I do a second one. I don't want to take a chance setting my very first basket on fire trying to spread hot pitch in it."

Lupe's only answer was an understanding smile. Instead of choosing more sumac and starting that second basket, Katherine watched her friend as she wove with practiced skill. *If I don't ask the question, I'll never get an answer.*

"When you spent so many years with your mother's people, you must have learned far more about their ways than I've learned about the Apache in these last months. Do you ever think the Mexican customs are better, or the Catholic beliefs? Maybe just for some small thing?"

Lupe's hands stopped and for a moment, Katherine thought her face would close in that way the Apache had when they wanted to shut someone out, but in the end she answered. "When I chose to return to the people, I chose to be Nednhi in all ways. The Mexicans have their ways. We have ours."

"So it never makes it harder for you."

Lupe hesitated and looked down at her basket. When she spoke again her voice was so soft Katherine could barely hear. "Sometimes, but I chose when I returned, and I chose when I married. My husband is Nednhi, and so am I."

"N–, I mean Gaetan's brother told me things that made me believe it was hard for him."

"He was a little boy when the whites took him. I was twelve when my mother went back to her family."

"Gaetan was nine."

Lupe frowned. "You will only hurt yourself if you think too much about Gaetan."

"I don't...." Katherine gave up the pretense with a sigh. "You don't have to worry about me. I'm used to wanting what I can't have. It's not as if I'm going to do anything foolish about an attraction."

"When you return to your home, you'll find a good husband, and you will be happy."

"No, I won't. American men don't want women who can't have children any more than Apache men do. Once I'm home, I'll find a way to make a life as an unmarried woman. Someone has to be the maiden aunt."

To Katherine's surprise a look of anguish crossed Lupe's face and her fingers fumbled on the basket. "I'm sorry. I didn't.... You had a child. I never thought. I'm sorry."

The effort Lupe made to smile tugged at Katherine's heart.

"You couldn't know," the little woman said. "There are shamans who have curing ceremonies. My husband will take me to the reservation when he thinks we can be safe. We'll have to be careful, but I *will* have the ceremony. You should do that too."

"I wish it were that simple," Katherine said wistfully. "When we realized there was a problem, my aunt took me to doctors. They all agree. There's something wrong inside me, and there won't be children. One of them even agreed with Tliish—he said I wasn't entirely female. My aunt certainly seized on that as an explanation for why I'm—I'm...."

Her voice choked with tears, and Katherine stopped before she could embarrass herself further.

"You're strong. Strong is a good thing. Didn't you ever bleed, even when you first came of age?"

Twirling her finished basket again, avoiding the sympathy in Lupe's eyes, Katherine sniffled before saying, "I did. That's how we knew there was a problem. It happened once and then not again for a year, and it's been that way ever since, once or twice a year, and my aunt says.... She says it's not even right when it happens. It's only for a day or two and not really a—a flow. So after that I knew, and if you tell a suitor there won't be children, he becomes an ex-suitor instantly."

"But you had a husband where you came from. You divorced him before you came here."

"No, I didn't. There was a man I was going to marry. He was older and already had children, but I—I changed my mind."

"Because he hit you."

Katherine stared at the other woman in amazement. "The Apache grapevine is a wonderful and amazing thing."

"Grapevine?"

"The way everyone learns all there is to know about everyone else."

"Gaetan had to tell Bácho and the other men everything he knew about you when they argued over what to do with you."

"Well, he got it wrong, or maybe his brother got it wrong and told him that. I never married Henry. We were engaged, and yes, I broke the engagement because he hit me."

"Why did he hit you?"

"He wanted me to do something I thought was wrong, and I wouldn't. He tried to force me to do it."

"What did you do to him?" Lupe said, her eyes alive with curiosity.

"I broke a lamp over his head and ran."

The two of them were still laughing as Lupe helped Katherine start another basket.

KATHERINE HURRIED HOME thinking she really should have made herself a coat months ago. Maybe winter temperatures in the Sierra Madres didn't usually get as frigid as New York, but a trip across the Atlantic in January would be better than the last few days. Cold rain alternated with icy, stinging snowflakes and sleet, all driven by winds that swirled through the mountains in vicious gusts.

Still, spring couldn't hold off forever. She wouldn't be spending another winter here, and she had plenty of coats at home.

After the short trip through what had turned to freezing drizzle, her wickiup seemed especially cozy. She prepared for bed, thankful for the flannel nightdress she had made herself, much to Lupe's amusement.

"Why not just sleep in your clothes on cold nights?" Lupe asked.

"Because," Katherine replied.

Tonight she lay listening to the wind howling outside and hoped her family was somewhere safe and warm, not in a storm like this on some faraway sea. Careful not to examine her own motives, she admitted she wanted *him* to be safe too. Feeling that way was probably one more sin blotting her celestial record, but she didn't care. She wanted him safe because she needed him to keep her safe, and she wanted him safe—because.

Hours later, an unfamiliar sound woke Katherine from a fitful sleep. Her heart leapt to her mouth at the sight of the hulking figure in the shadows. Bear!

She groped for the knife beside the bed, wondering if she could get away while the animal searched for easier food than a woman who would fight. As her hand closed on the knife, she saw the figure was human, a man wrapped in a blanket. Easier to deal with than a bear, but still....

The man stirred the coals of the fire to life awkwardly with his left hand, and a single flame leapt up, highlighting his profile. Letting go of the knife, Katherine rose from the bed and went to him. "What are you doing here in the middle of the...."

Her words died in her throat when he turned. Gaetan's eyes were neither cold and hard nor burning and intense but sunk deep in gray hollows and dull. His hair hung in wet strands, ice crystals beginning to melt and drip onto the blanket around his shoulders.

Her mind churned frantically. Why had he ridden through the storm instead of holing up somewhere. Why was he here? She got hold of herself. He was here and he needed help. She heaped more wood on the fire. Once the flames blazed, she pushed a pot of water close to the heat and tackled the man.

"Sit."

He did, his movements so slow and clumsy he had to be chilled to the bone.

She toweled his hair dry with a piece of flour sack. Even dry, the skin of his face and neck felt cold and clammy, and he was shaking. Reality never did match imagination. The few times she had allowed herself to imagine touching him....

His clothes were soaked. "The wet clothes have to come off."

He nodded slightly but didn't move. She pulled the blanket off his shoulders. Half frozen, the wool held its shape. Pushing the blanket aside, she reached down, ready to peel his shirt off if she had to. "Oh."

The gross distortion of his swollen right forearm showed even through the heavy, wet shirt. Blood glued the fabric to his shoulder and down his chest. Katherine swallowed hard and without thinking reacted in the way of a woman of people hiding from enemies. "Did anyone follow you?"

"No."

"How long ago did it happen?"

"Three days." The hoarse voice didn't sound like Gaetan's, but at least he could speak.

"You need Echo. I'll go get her."

"Tomorrow."

Katherine thought about defying him. He couldn't make it to his feet in time to stop her if she took off into the night and got help. *He came here for help.*

She pulled his knife out of its sheath. "I'm going to cut the shirt off."

If he gave any sign of permission, she didn't detect it. Without asking again or waiting, she cut his sleeve at the shoulder and pulled it off his arm, holding her breath until she was sure no bones protruded through the bulging, discolored skin. She eased the cloth of the shirt away from his shoulder as gently as possible. In spite of her care, fresh blood welled in bullet wound.

"The bullet's still in there, isn't it?"

"Yes."

Rubbing his torso briskly had no warming effect. His skin stayed cold and didn't feel dry in spite of her efforts. Giving up, she tore the skirt she had washed on the last warm day into strips and bandaged the shoulder with a thick pad over the wound.

"Echo could set that arm by feel."

"Tomorrow."

"I'm going to splint it then, just to keep the bones from moving any more. If that bone comes through the skin, it will kill you."

She started toward the firewood she had brought in when the weather turned ugly, saw the pot of water steaming and filled a cup. Rummaging through a parfleche, she found the small pouch of medicine Echo had given her for the pain in her leg months ago. After two doses, Katherine had hidden the concoction out of sight. The stuff was so foul it probably still had some potency. She poured half of what was left into the hot water and stirred it.

"Drink this," she said, putting it in Gaetan's left hand. "Echo gave it to me for the pain in my leg. It tastes terrible, but it will help."

His hand shook so badly as he raised the cup to his mouth, liquid spilled over the side. Better he get half of it down than she offend male pride holding it for him. Turning back to the woodpile, she chose the straightest sticks she could find, broke them to the right length and padded them with pieces of blanket. When she returned to Gaetan, he had put the cup aside, still almost full. She picked it up and held it out.

"You drink that or so help me, I'll hold your nose and pour it down your throat."

For a second a familiar spark gleamed in his eyes, but before she could take comfort from the sight, it disappeared. He drank the medicine. Most of it.

"How long since you had anything to eat or drink?"

"Three days."

"Why didn't the lookout on the trail help you?"

"He did. He took the horses."

Katherine stifled an urge to yell at him, rinsed out the cup and filled it with plain water. "Here. You can chase away the taste with this. If I cook something, can you eat?"

He shook his head. Katherine stopped questioning him and bound a protective splint around the arm as gently as she could. His fingers were icicles. She envisioned them turning black and rotting away and wanted to cry.

Pulling off his moccasins, she found his feet in worse shape than his hands. They were blocks of ice right past his ankles. In spite of his dark skin and the poor light, she felt sure she could see a bluish tint.

"Stand up."

He didn't move. Throwing fears about male pride to the wind, she crouched beside him, levered him up and stripped off the rest of his clothes. His lower body was no better than the rest of him. She dried him as fast as possible, keeping her hands away from male places more successfully than her eyes.

"Get in bed."

She glimpsed that same reassuring spark, longer this time, and almost smiled.

"Please get in bed."

He lowered himself to her bed like an old man. She made sure he was covered, then wondered what else to do. Hanging his wet clothes on her rawhide line, she argued with herself. Maybe she should get Echo in spite of what he wanted. But what could the old woman do in the middle of the night? Daylight wasn't that many hours away. Of course if the storm didn't break, Echo would have to work by firelight anyway.

Picking up his moccasins and setting them by the fire, she had an idea, used them as potholders and lifted one of the hot fireplace stones. After bundling the stone in every scrap of cloth left in the wickiup, she slid her improvised foot warmer near Gaetan's feet and tucked the blankets back in. He looked asleep already, or maybe passed out, or maybe.... Touching his shoulder reassured her, except how reassuring was violent shivering?

Back home she could fill that bathtub they once talked about with hot water and warm him up properly, but what else could she do tonight? He really was asleep. The disgusting medicine had made her sleepy too, and she hadn't been hurt like this.

She tiptoed to the bed as if he could hear her and slid in next to him. Her body heat could at least warm his good side. As she touched him, he rolled, pulling her against him, her back to his chest. His good arm fit under her in the curve of her waist, the splinted forearm hung over her ribs.

A protest slipped from her throat as she started to fight, but he gave her nothing to fight against—he didn't try to hold her. Because she was free to leave, she stayed, sinking back down and relaxing against him. He was cold, so cold. Diving into a snowbank back home had to be warmer than this, and snowbanks didn't shiver.

After a time she straightened her legs, letting her thighs touch his, his knees fit behind hers. Holding her breath, she forced herself to press her feet against his, managing not to whimper at the feel. She shouldn't have bothered with the hot stone. It couldn't be doing a particle of good.

Why had he come to her instead of Echo, Sigesh, Bácho, or Lupe and Itsá? Because of the bond. Probably he would deny such a thing existed, but it did. Getting away from Hierra had forged some strange bond that wove its way around the hate, fear and distrust, and everything that happened after only strengthened that bond. He knew she would help him if she could, just as she knew he would keep her safe if he could.

She touched the icy fingers of his splinted arm. What if she had bound it too tight and cut off his circulation? She pressed his cold fingers flat between both of her hands. At least she could feel that he was still breathing.

In fact she could feel everything she had seen so many months ago by the stream, and in spite of the fact he now shivered behind her under skin so cold touching it took courage, her foolish body was reacting. Her breasts felt heavier, her nipples taut.

She shifted slightly. Just in case he was half-awake, she had better make sure he couldn't detect the wetness flooding female places. He would put her quickened breath down to fear or nerves, wouldn't he?

The shivering stopped. That had to be good. The hand in hers felt more like flesh. What about the wound? Had he bled through her clumsy bandage? She reached back and felt the cloth. Still dry, at least on the outside. Instead of pressing just his one hand between both of hers, she cupped the fingers of each hand over his, startled when his fingers tightened, curling back around hers.

He didn't move again. His breathing stayed slow and regular. Keeping her feet against his no longer demanded a martyr's dedication. If her feet were better, his had to be too, didn't they? Maybe the stone had been worth bothering over after all. She moved a foot slightly, feeling the extra length of his. Not just his foot, she realized. Her body lay curved inside the larger curve of his. He was taller, every limb longer, his shoulders wider.

For the first time in memory, Katherine felt not just female, but feminine. This was what other women had and she never would. If she had been able to marry a man she wanted instead of one who would have her, it would be like this every night. She would lie in a husband's arms and feel like this. She swallowed the lump in her throat and blinked away tears. Every one of her brothers could give her a stern lecture on the soul-sapping effects of self-pity.

Tonight she wasn't giving way to regret or self-pity. Tonight she was staying awake and glorying in every minute of this one chance to know how it felt. He was warm now and sleeping peacefully. In the morning, Echo would set the arm and doctor the wound, and he would be fine. He would. And for this one night Katherine Grant was going to pretend the man holding her was hers and would still be hers tomorrow.

In spite of her every effort, Katherine fell asleep shortly before dawn. When she woke, he was gone.

17

GAETAN WALKED THROUGH the camp toward his cache on the mountain. The pain in his right shoulder and arm made it hard to think, yet he knew he hurt less now than he would once Echo was through with him, and he wanted dry clothes. The cold bit into his flesh under the damp things he'd dragged back on, and exhaustion slowed his movements, but he no longer felt as if his next breath might be a death rattle.

What he had done last night had no meaning. After all, Bácho insisted the woman was a captive, and a man was entitled to order his captive to help him. Of course he hadn't exactly ordered her to help. *Sit. Drink this. Stand up. Get in bed.* He ought to be grateful she hadn't taken the opportunity to get even by waving her hands at him in what she called dog signals.

He admitted to himself he had gone there last night knowing she would help. There were others he could have asked for help, but with the white woman he didn't have to ask. She helped as her part of whatever bargain they had sealed last spring. He didn't understand it, didn't like it, but no longer tried to deny it.

He hadn't expected her to help quite so thoroughly, though. A woman so fierce shouldn't feel so good to hold. A woman who danced on rocks shrieking with temper shouldn't curl warm fingers around icy ones so gently or press warm feet against cold ones so willingly. A man shouldn't wake from sleeping with a woman of a hated enemy people in his arms feeling more at peace than he could ever remember.

As soon as Echo set the arm and dug the bullet out, he would go north again. The less time he spent here until he could take the woman to her people the better. The first day they saw her, fighting for survival on her own, he had warned Nilchi she was dangerous. She was more dangerous in more ways than he had ever imagined.

By the time he reached Echo's, bright sun reflected off the thin ice sheathing every stick and blade of grass. In another hour or two, the last traces of the storm would be gone. He called out, waiting for the old woman to invite him inside, but she came out to him instead.

"How bad are you hurt?"

"My arm is broken, and I have a bullet in my shoulder. Did you dream I'd come to you with wounds?"

"I heard it in your voice. Let me see."

He wondered how much the clouded eyes really saw, even in the sunlight, but knew it didn't matter. She probably could have set the arm by feel in the night, and maybe she could have dug the bullet out that way too.

She patted his cheek. "How did this happen?"

"Mexicans ambushed me three days north. They shot my horse first, and when the horse went down...."

"Can they follow you here?"

The anger that had allowed him to ignore pain and go after enemies flared. "They'll never follow anyone again."

"You didn't put this splint on yourself," she said as she cut through the bindings and removed the padded sticks.

"The white woman did it last night."

"Hunh. She's very smart. And kind too. She wrapped the sticks so they can't rub your tender skin."

He ignored her teasing and concentrated on giving no sign of the effect of her exploration of his injuries. The throbbing ache in his forearm spread until it merged with the fiery pain in his shoulder, each gaining power from the other.

She patted his cheek again. "We need help for the arm and maybe for the bullet. I'll get Itsá."

"I'll get him."

"No. You sit here and don't move your arm."

He stared at his arm. Had it looked that bad last night? He remembered the white woman's hands, her voice and her scent, but he couldn't remember seeing his own arm. Closing his eyes, he sat as commanded. The cold seeped back into his bones but so did the strange, unfamiliar calm.

By the time Echo set the arm and turned the bullet hole in his shoulder into a crater in her search for the bullet, sweat soaked him from head to toe, and he shook almost as hard as the night before. Itsá helped him inside Echo's wickiup, gave him a sympathetic look and left.

Echo bustled around her fire, and Gaetan sat and watched her, knowing he couldn't make it to his feet on his own yet. When she brought him a cup of something thick and black, he regarded it with suspicion.

"The white woman gave me medicine last night. She said you gave it to her for the pain in her leg. I don't want more of it."

"She was supposed to drink that medicine herself!"

"No one would drink it willingly."

"You will drink it. Now."

Or I'll hold your nose and pour it down your throat. The worst part about needing help was putting up with women giving orders. He drank and decided he could not only stand but walk.

"Thank you for your help, Grandmother," he said, placing a pouch of tobacco near the fire. "I feel better and will go now."

"Not yet." The old woman sat down next to him, her face serious. "I know how you are. You think you're fixed. You hurt, and you're tired, but you think you can ride away tomorrow, maybe the next day."

"I...."

"No, you listen. Your arm is broken in two places and the bones were all over. I got it back together the way it should be, and I was afraid maybe I couldn't do that. If you treat that arm as if it's made of wet clay until the bones heal, it will be good. If you're foolish, you'll have an arm that will never be strong. You'll be a cripple like Bácho. Are you hearing my words?"

"How long?"

"The moon is new now. Two more times, and you come let me take the splint off and look at your arm before you use it. If it gets dirt underneath and you itch, if it gets wet, you come back and let me fix it. You hear my words?"

"I hear you, Grandmother." He wasn't sure he was going to do what she said, but he heard her.

He left Echo and started across the camp toward his cache. He could get a fire going there, sleep, eat some dried meat—or he could go where a fire already burned, a bed waited, and someone else would cook better food. Much better.

The wickiup was empty. What looked at first glance like two loaves of bread sat close enough to the fire to stay warm. On closer inspection the loaves turned into tortillas, plump with a filling inside. He checked the filling by biting into one. Spicy meat, onions, beans and corn. He ate both of them, wished she had left a third, drank enough water to quench his thirst for the first time in days and collapsed in the woman's bed.

KATHERINE'S BREATH PLUMED in the frosty early morning air as she stared at the provisions heaped near Lupe's wickiup.

"You need to take your share so that others can take what they need," Lupe said.

Gaetan had laid down the law months ago. Lupe chose first. Katherine chose second. Then everyone else. The longer Katherine looked at the pile on the ground, the more trouble she had believing her eyes. Half-dead from cold and injuries, he had led a string of pack animals up the tortuous trail of switchbacks in the storm last night.

Lupe touched Katherine's sleeve, reminding her she should get busy.

"Do you know when we were hiding from the Mexicans, one of them stuck a bayonet right through Gaetan's arm, and he never moved?"

Lupe sighed. "Do you want me to help you get your baskets?"

Katherine got her own baskets, filled them and took them home. She didn't believe she'd see Gaetan again soon. Certainly not to talk to. Echo would set the arm and remove the bullet, and he'd be off again, back to whatever murderous pursuits he planned.

Still, cooking a little extra food this morning and leaving it out hadn't hurt anything. It would still be there when she got back from replenishing her woodpile, and she could have it herself later.

By the time Katherine returned home with the firewood, the sun beamed down from as high in the sky as it ever climbed this time of year. After stacking the wood beside the door, she ducked inside, then backed right out again, smiling. The smile faded to a frown as she stood there.

He ate. That had to be good. But sound asleep in her bed in the middle of the day? She glared up at the sun as if it were to blame. Maybe Echo would enjoy a visit.

In spite of the cold, the old woman sat outside her home, a cheerful bundle of blankets and furs. "You need to wrap up better," she said, patting Katherine's covering of a single blanket.

"I should. I always think I'm only going to be away from the fire for a little while."

As Katherine worked on how to ask the question, Echo gave the answer. "He's going to be fine unless he's foolish. I don't think Gaetan is foolish."

Unless? "I had a bullet wound last spring," Katherine said hesitantly, demonstrating the path by moving her hand across her chest. "It was so shallow I thought it was nothing, but it suppurated and almost killed me."

Echo made a face. "That can happen, but I think he'll have a fever from the wound for a few days and that's all. It bled clean, and he's young and healthy. The arm is the problem. He needs to be very careful with the arm until the moon is new two more times. You tell him. I think he listened to me, but you tell him too."

"Me?" The word came out as a squeak. Katherine cleared her throat and tried again. "I probably won't get a chance to talk to him. He doesn't have much to do with me, and he certainly won't listen to me. I can't tell him anything."

"He was hurt and he came to you. He'll listen."

Echo didn't understand. The bond didn't include listening.

Katherine headed off the children with excuses as to why she couldn't tell stories. She worked beside Lupe, debating the whole time whether to tell her about Gaetan. In the end she decided against it. Lupe's position on Gaetan was clear, and Katherine didn't want to hear it.

Twice during the day she slipped into the wickiup and built up the fire. The second time she fought the urge to touch him, make sure he was breathing.

Dark came early in the mountains, and the temperature plummeted under the clear sky. Hurrying home from Lupe's, Katherine decided she was going to shake him awake if she had to. Hurt or not, no one should sleep for so long without at least turning over.

He was gone. Gone without a sign except that the fire burned so high he had added more wood recently. Katherine looked around, feeling strangely bereft. What had she expected, a thank you note pinned to the pillow she didn't have?

She looked at her pots and utensils and decided they could stay where they were. Food held no appeal. She should think about replacing the skirt she had torn for bandages. She should....

He came in slowly, hunched and favoring his right side, a draft of cold air swirling around him. Unable to control her face, Katherine bent over the fire, hoping to hide her expression. Memory of the intimacy of the night before hung between them like a third living being in the wickiup.

"Thank you, Katherine."

They were not words she ever expected to hear from him, even spoken in such a low voice. She dared look up. Dark circles still shadowed eyes that held no trace of the usual glowering intensity.

"I have more of Echo's medicine."

"No. Tonight you're not strong enough to force me to swallow it."

"She says your arm is very bad."

"You talked to her about me?"

"When I saw you asleep in the day, I was...," *worried*, "curious."

"She exaggerates."

He was hurt and he came to you. He'll listen. "I don't think she'd do that. She told me she was afraid she couldn't get the bones straight this time. Please be careful."

"You don't have to worry. I'll be able to take you north when the time comes."

"I have every confidence you can take me north, even with one arm, especially if you let me have a gun so I can save you if you get into trouble."

"You're fierce enough without a gun."

"You can't think I'd shoot you."

"There were many times you would have shot me, and there will be more, I think."

She glared at him, wanting to deny it, and couldn't. As she started preparing the food her stomach now grumbled over, she wondered how to convince him to sleep in the bed again. She could sleep across the fire on the floor wrapped in a blanket.

If he argued, she planned to win.

18

Echo's prediction proved true. Fever plagued Gaetan for the next several days. Katherine made a second bed on the far side of the fire, expecting the effort to be wasted, that he would disappear as soon as he felt well enough. He didn't disappear. He continued to sleep in her original bed. He showed up in the evenings to eat with her as he had on the trail, and to Katherine's surprise, he answered her questions about the ambush and then about other things.

He was, in fact, a much better source of information about his people, their beliefs and customs than Lupe, who often acted as if she were an insider guarding secrets from an outsider. Katherine wondered if the difference in attitude was because Lupe was determined to believe and Gaetan was not. So she asked him.

"Your brother told me once, 'Gaetan believes what he wants to.' Do you believe as your people do, or did some of the things they taught at the school take root?"

About the time she wondered if not answering was his way of telling her to mind her own business, he said, "My brother was wrong. If I could choose, I would choose the Chihinne way. The things I learned in the school make that impossible, so I believe what I can, not what I want to."

"Do you believe some of the things they taught at the school?"

"No, the whites there were like all the rest of you. They lied and they said things they didn't believe themselves or they wouldn't have acted the way they did. The most important things I learned at the school they didn't teach, but I saw."

All the rest of you. The words hurt, but she wasn't going to let him see that. When he didn't continue, she prompted, "Such as?"

"I learned that we can't win against you. You are too many, and we are too few. We fight better, but we can't make guns or bullets. We have to steal those things from you, and we'll never have rifles with 'scopes. In the end, you will win."

The dark menace of his eyes was so strong in the firelight, Katherine knew she should drop the subject, but a perverse compulsion drove her on. "If you know that, why keep fighting? Even if the reservation is less why not make what you can of life there?"

"You said you freed me in the Mexican camp because even if I killed you, I would also kill them, and you'd have revenge. You can understand how it is, I think. Your people will kill us all, but before then we'll soak the earth with so much of their blood their grandchildren's grandchildren will remember the price they paid to take our lives and our land."

He got up and walked out into the night then and didn't return until long after Katherine was in bed.

Over the next days, she did her best to ignore him. He was, after all, merely one more man who found her lacking, even if his reasons were different. She refused to worry about what he did during the day just because every occupation of the Apache male was dangerous.

He wouldn't be foolish enough to ignore his arm and play some hoop and pole game so violent that women weren't even allowed to watch. If he did, she'd volunteer to amputate his arm with a dull knife.

Gentle probing of Lupe yielded a little information. "He helps my husband hunt sometimes."

"Hunt? He can't hunt with that arm. Pulling back a bowstring could pull his bones apart!"

"He helps. He helps track and holds while my husband skins. Holds with his good arm."

"Oh."

"You must not...."

"Don't tell me," Katherine said sadly. "It's too late."

"Gaetan will never...."

"I know!"

"You want to return to your people."

"Yes, I do, and I'm going to. It's still too late."

That night Katherine lost her resolve to ignore him. They had barely finished eating when she said, "I never lied to you."

The look he gave her made her wish she'd kept quiet. "You lied to my brother."

"Because I was meek when I was in the middle of a dozen men who wanted to kill me? Do you consider it a lie to be careful in a situation like that?"

"Would you have told him there could be no children?"

Her heart seemed to stop beating. Of course the women told him, and why should it matter if he knew? It shouldn't. It didn't. It did.

"I don't know. I thought about telling him just to make him stop wanting to marry me, but I was afraid he'd slit my useless throat—or let you do it."

"To take you back to your people isn't so hard when I know you won't have sons who will be enemies as fierce as you are.

When I first made the promise, I thought that was the worst part of it."

The fire had died down. She hoped he couldn't see the humiliating tears that welled and slipped one by one down her cheeks.

"Lucky for you, I'm not female enough to have sons—or daughters."

"You feel female to hold."

Heat flooded her face and dried the tears. Those words shouldn't feel like a compliment, but they did. She couldn't remember ever hearing words that made her feel quite like this.

"I thought you were asleep."

"I know."

"If his spirit came to you tonight and released you from the promise, would you kill me?"

"No."

The moon was almost full, and the time when his arm would be healed was close. If she could keep from bringing up any more contentious subjects, maybe she could hold on to this feeling that long. Maybe even longer.

KATHERINE FOUND AN open place high in the pines that framed a magnificent view of miles of the surrounding mountain range. Spring sun warmed her shoulders, and a fresh breeze played across her face. She sat listening to the birds in the trees, daydreaming about the past and the future, when Gaetan startled her by dropping down beside her.

Why would he track her here? "Are you hungry? Do you need something?" Glancing at him with the words, she noticed his arm, covered by nothing but his shirt sleeve, and his face, as relaxed as she'd ever seen it. He looked younger, his true age.

"She took the splint off."

"Yes. The arm is weak like a boy's now. She says it will strengthen soon."

"My brother Lewis broke an arm once and that happened. It only took a couple of weeks—fourteen days maybe—for it to strengthen."

"Then my arm will be better tomorrow."

"I'm sure your arm is superior, but maybe you should give it three or four days."

She didn't expect him to respond, and he didn't, but she did expect him to give a reason for coming here. Believing he had sought her out only to share his pleasure at having the splint off would be one more step along a road that led to misery.

Not that it mattered. Already every part of her was reacting to his presence so close beside her. Once again she felt both female and feminine, and she allowed herself to enjoy it.

"I like to watch from high places also," he said. "There are better places than this."

"I suppose so, but I happened on this one. We call the way I feel today spring fever." She pointed higher up the mountainside. "I also found a beautiful pool up there, but there are no paths to it and no sign people ever go there. Is it something to do with not eating fish? Apaches don't swim?"

"We like to swim, but a boy drowned in the pool the first summer we came here. There was talk of moving to another place, but Bácho did ghost medicine instead. Since then no one goes near there."

"So I can't swim there." Katherine heard the disappointment in her own voice and added, "I don't mean to sound like that. The stream is fine."

"Swim if you want to. If anyone finds out, tell them I said you're not Apache, and it doesn't matter."

"You don't believe in ghosts, do you? You're still wearing N–, your brother's moccasins. You just resole them."

"Do you believe in angels?"

"No."

They sat in companionable silence for a while, Katherine wishing she could feel the way she did right then forever. "I should get back to gathering wood," she said finally, more to say something than because she meant it.

"You'll be happy to go back where you don't have to work."

"How do you know I don't work back home?"

"Your hands were soft."

Katherine turned her hands palm up and fingered her calluses. "I suppose they were, but that wasn't a source of happiness. The happiest time in my life was when I traveled the world with my father and brothers. All of us had callused hands from swinging all over the ships. And when we were on land, my father took us on his hunting trips. I cooked and took care of the camp in ways not that different from here. And I was free, free to laugh too loud, free to argue with my brothers and run, free to ride a horse astride and to listen to the stories the sailors told, to talk to people I met and learn their languages."

Hearing the passion in her own voice, Katherine gazed off into the distance for a moment until she could go on in a normal tone.

"Part of what I was sitting here thinking about is what I'm going to do when I get back to New York. There's no way around having to wear layers of clothes and ride sidesaddle if I ever get on a horse again, but I'm not going to spend my days visiting my aunt's friends or worrying about whether servants did *their* work properly. Maybe I can teach. I like being with the children."

The mountains darkened as clouds floated past the sun. A hawk circled in the distance, and the clouds drifted on, letting the sun paint the scene in pink and gold. Katherine relaxed, an easy contentment sweeping through her. Gaetan destroyed that with his next words.

"Will you marry another white man?"

He didn't look at her, and Katherine's temper stirred. He had a talent for squelching any good feelings developing between them. "I think your brother and Lupe both told you everything I ever confided to them, and that means you know I wasn't married to Henry. We were engaged, and I refused to marry him in the end."

He said nothing, but it felt as if he'd called her a liar again, and that made her madder. "You call him my husband because you think I lay with him. You think because I crawled in your bed when you were cold, I must have crawled in his sometime, and if it makes you happy to know I'm as bad as you think, go ahead. Yes. He said with my problems he wanted to make sure I'd be suitable. I never would have listened except I wanted to know myself. I didn't love him, and I wanted to make sure I could bear it. Happy? Unlike your beautiful, chaste Apache women, I'm a mess."

"I thought in the beginning you wouldn't give the pistol to my brother if you were a virgin. He didn't care."

"He was a nicer man than you are."

"Yes."

He'd found out what he wanted to know. If he wasn't going to leave, she ought to get up and leave herself. Except she'd been here first, enjoying the day he'd just spoiled. She decided to stay put until her bottom wore out.

"If you felt like that, why would you marry him?"

She sighed. "Because the life of a married woman is easier than the life of an old maid, and he was willing to have me. His wife died and left him with seven children. He didn't want more. He did want someone to take care of the ones he had. He was perfect for me, except he was as old as my father and—and like your arm."

"A white man is like my arm?"

"Superior."

"So you were meek around him because you wanted him to marry you, and that made him brave, and he hit you, and then you hit him."

She hated conceding the point, but he was right. "Yes, but he got even. He told my father and brothers what I did, what I let him do, and he told everyone else, and I couldn't deny it. My family was so angry they all but disowned me, and my reputation was so ruined no one would have anything to do with me."

"Why did he hit you?"

"He wanted me to do something I didn't want to do."

Once again his silence made her speak when a question might not have. "He wanted me to do something—unnatural."

"You should have killed him."

Was that sympathy? "I thought what I did do was bad enough at the time. I broke a lamp over his head. The last time I saw him he had broken glass in his hair and lamp oil dripping off his nose." She felt the smile that wasn't a smile tugging the corners of her mouth and changed it to a real smile.

"Hunh."

Oddly enough disapproval wasn't radiating from him the way it had from every other person who knew about Henry. They all assumed her bad temper had caused the quarrel, and no force on earth could induce her to tell her father or brothers what Henry had tried to make her do. Everyone, including Henry, thought she should have begged forgiveness and married him anyway. She liked Gaetan's attitude much better. *You should have killed him.*

"Did my brother tell you how I escaped from the school?"

Happy at the change of subject, she thought back. "He said one of the teachers took you outside the walls."

He nodded. "Every year that teacher chose a favorite from the older boys. That year she chose me."

"A favorite she took places and did things with?"

"She only did one thing with her favorite."

Katherine gaped at him. "You mean...?"

"Yes. She taught me many things."

Anger swept over Katherine. "That's dreadful. For a teacher to do that to children...."

"I was sixteen, not a child. She knew she could do as she liked with us, I think. We could give her pleasure, but what we thought or felt didn't matter. I heard sometimes she chose a boy who couldn't do what she wanted, but even then she just chose another. We were always hungry at the school. The food was bad and there was never enough. To be her favorite meant many good things. My brother and I both ate better that year."

"If she did it every year to someone different, why didn't someone tell? Why didn't you?"

His look was more cynical than anything Nilchi had ever managed and made her realize how foolish her question was.

"No one would believe you."

"And I didn't want to tell. The school was easier that year, and before long I knew she was going to help me get away."

"She fell in love and helped you?"

He shook his head. "She wanted me to do something—something I wouldn't do."

"Oh." She met his eyes, understanding what he was telling her.

"I told her if we went away from the school where my brother wasn't close and others could never know, I'd do what she wanted."

"So she took you outside."

"She had a horse and a wagon and a basket of food. She called it a...."

Unsure whether he wouldn't say the English word or didn't remember it, Katherine filled in for him. "Picnic."

"Yes. She drove the horse far from the school."

"Did you kill her?"

"I was young and had no weapons. I took the horse and the food and left her there. I thought she'd tell the people at the school I forced her to take me away and they'd believe her, but my brother said she never came back to the school."

"They'd pretend to believe her, but they wouldn't. She wouldn't be a teacher who could pick on favorites after that."

"Maybe she moved far to the east. Maybe she'll meet Henry someday."

Katherine laughed. His expression never changed, but his eyes gleamed with something very different from anger.

"My wife is roasting fresh venison. Come eat with me."

Refusing an invitation to eat with Bácho would be rude, but Gaetan came close anyway. He had a strong suspicion the food would be accompanied by advice he didn't want and that it wouldn't taste as good as what awaited in his own wickiup.

After eating enough to be polite, he leaned against a willow backrest, considering how to hint to Katherine that she should practice her basket weaving on such a thing without asking. Seeing Bácho studying him as if he could read the thought, Gaetan concentrated on the old man and what he was up to.

"Echo says your arm is healed and the bones are as they should be."

"Yes. She's a good healer."

"You'll go north again soon then."

"In fourteen days, I think."

Bácho frowned. "She said that?"

"No, she said it would take time for the strength to come back."

"It's good that while you were hurt you could make the white woman serve you."

Making Katherine do anything would be dangerous. On the other hand, as with the backrest, thinking of ways to make her *want* to do things had been an entertaining diversion for a man stuck in camp with a broken arm. He said nothing and waited for the rest of Bácho's unwelcome advice.

"Now that you understand how pleasant life can be with a woman to cook and make a home, you should marry. Sigesh would make you a good wife, and she'd welcome you as a husband."

She'd probably welcome half the other men in the camp every time he was gone too, but Gaetan didn't say so. "We don't suit, Grandfather. I use her sometimes and she uses me, but she makes the darkness in me darker. I wouldn't take her as a wife."

"I could speak to Klosen for you. Maybe he'd accept a few extra horses for his daughter."

"Maybe he would, but the daughter wouldn't agree. She has eyes for that young Nednhi warrior. I don't need a wife. Soon I'll be gone all the time again."

"In fourteen days."

"Yes."

"No Chihinne would marry a white woman, even if she weren't barren."

It wasn't a question. Gaetan said nothing.

After a moment, Bácho continued with his concern over Katherine. "We may leave here before fall. The grass is down to the roots in some places. If we go when you're not here, we'll leave the woman. You can find her and take her north before you join us."

Gaetan nodded, not liking it. Katherine would never sit here alone and wait for him. She'd start out on her own.

"Have you decided where to go?" he asked.

An evasive look crossed Bácho's face. "No, not yet."

As Gaetan walked back to his own wickiup, he mulled over the things Bácho had said. The chief had a daughter of marriageable age he never mentioned as a candidate for Gaetan to marry—because she wasn't. His years in the white school meant traditional Chiricahua families would never consider him suitable for a desirable daughter. Gaetan had never wanted to marry Bácho's daughter or anyone else, yet in the past the insult would have provoked a rush of the black rage. Today it only made him thoughtful.

It occurred to him he should have been more sympathetic with Nilchi's determination to keep Katherine, except Nilchi had never seemed eager to marry either. And, of course, if Nilchi had set his sights on Bácho's daughter or any other girl, he would have charmed both the girl and her parents into forgetting all about the school and accepting him in no time at all.

Gaetan had no illusions about his own ability to charm. Most of the time staying polite was the best he could manage. Katherine was the only one who had ever shown any sign of finding him charming, and as Bácho said, no Chihinne would consider marrying a white woman.

Better to marry a promiscuous woman or one who didn't want him than a woman whose face lit with inner fire at the sight of him.

Bácho's evasiveness about where the band would move was part of the same problem, less true distrust than lack of confidence that a man who had spent so much time under the thumb of whites could resist telling Katherine anything she wanted to know.

Gaetan envisioned piling the bodies of every white he had ever killed in one place and showing them to Bácho. Would it make a difference in his attitude? No, it wouldn't.

Only one thing Bácho had said bothered him. That one thing didn't provoke anger but a concern he could do something about. Fourteen days after the splint came off his arm, Gaetan rode north. Early that morning, he hid a pistol, a rifle and ammunition under Katherine's bed.

19

THE GIFT OF the guns pleased Katherine enormously but also puzzled her. Did it simply mean Gaetan trusted her with them or that he expected her to need them? One way or the other, no one else needed to know.

She hid the rifle and ammunition out of sight in the wickiup, and she made a rawhide pouch the perfect size for the pistol and hung it at her waist. Several of the Apache women carried such pouches, although they made them of soft buckskin. They had no need to conceal three pounds of steel.

The guns and what had passed between them also gave her hope that when Gaetan returned he would stay for a day. Or two. Or three. He did. As spring turned to summer, his times away grew shorter, and his time at home stretched from overnight to two days, then three.

Katherine tried to ignore the disapproval emanating from the Apaches. The children had stopped sharing stories as the days lengthened. Now they avoided her. Lupe still worked beside her and taught her, but there was a reserve in her manner. Only Echo remained cheerful.

"We each must walk our own path, and you'll find your way soon," she said, giving Katherine a reassuring pat on the cheek.

Little did Echo know. Katherine had lost her way a year ago in a little valley where she had watched a man bathe, followed him away from danger into the night and taken his side against his own people with a gun. Now here she was, storing up memories to take back to New York with her because she was being stupid again.

Other women managed their lives sensibly. Why couldn't she? They didn't yearn for the impossible but settled for the possible.

She had looked on the one night in his arms as a good thing, a chance to know something otherwise denied her. She had been wrong. The memory haunted her, stoked desires that could never be satisfied, made the nights he was gone lonelier and the nights he slept across the fire from her an aching torment.

If only she had never learned a word of Apache, never been able to talk to him and see him other than as a hate-filled devil who wanted to kill her. Katherine had no illusions about her own veneer of civilization. If she had been born Apache, lived as Gaetan had, she would be as he was, fighting for vengeance and survival with a single-minded fury. Getting to know him had been her undoing as much as what she had seen by the stream and felt in his arms.

She jerked her thoughts back to the moccasins she was making, then threw them down and headed up the mountain to the ghost pool. Now that the weather had turned hot, she swam every afternoon. She thought the Apaches knew and that was part of their disapproval, but she didn't care. In a few months she'd be gone, and they could tell stories around their fires in winters to come about the lazy, disrespectful white woman who had lived with them for a little while.

GAETAN PULLED THE panniers off the last pack horse in the string he'd brought this trip, pretending total concentration on the task while keeping one eye on the women beginning to gather round. He wanted to catch the look on Katherine's face when she first saw him.

"She's not here," Itsá said.

"She escaped?" A stone formed in his stomach at the thought.

"No, she goes to the pool up on the mountain every afternoon. The women will soon tell you about it and that you should punish her and make her stop."

Even as Itsá spoke, Gaetan could see Sigesh angling her way through the other women toward him. He didn't believe Sigesh had ever felt any more affection for him than he felt for her, and he hadn't been to her bed since he broke his arm. Her reasons for bringing him tales about everything Katherine did eluded him, and he was in no mood to hear more.

"It would be good if your wife set aside Katherine's share for her so that others can choose," he said to Itsá, already moving away with the words.

He spoke respectfully to several of the older women as he walked by them. Sigesh would never make a spectacle of herself running after him, and she wouldn't catch him without running. In moments he was away from them all, striding across the valley, into the trees, up the mountain.

He climbed high then worked his way down to a place that overlooked the pool and sat down, studying the scene below. Watching a woman not his wife bathing or swimming could get a Chiricahua man killed, but Katherine wasn't Apache, and none of the people would come here. Gaetan would kill any other man who watched her like this, but he wasn't spying. He was deciding.

Either she hadn't been at the pool long or had changed her mind about swimming. Her moccasins were off and her hair hung loose down her back, but she was fully clothed. Close to the edge of the pool, she sat much as he was sitting, arms folded on bent knees, chin resting on arms. Unlike his gaze, intent on her, hers seemed dreamy and unfocused.

He wanted to know what she was thinking, wanted to see the look on her face if he showed himself. He wanted her, and he was sure she wouldn't resist but would give herself, give something he was sure he'd never had.

Without rising, she undid her belt and pulled her blouse over her head. When she did get up, she dropped her skirt, then stood for a moment in a ridiculous short breechclout made of bright yellow calico. The strange feeling she'd evoked for the first time when she'd danced on the rocks and shrieked at him returned. The yellow cloth fluttered to the ground, and his blood raced faster, buzzing in his ears.

He had been wrong to think she could not be beautiful. He liked everything about her body, including the height that meant he could look her in the eye by merely tilting his head even when she stood toe to toe with him. Eyes that once seemed strange for their lightness were now familiar—and fascinating. Sometimes more blue, other times more gray, when her eyes met his, he knew she saw inside him, and she never turned away.

Her skin was not white or even pale, but golden brown, different from the bronze hue of his people, but warm. He hadn't been too cold to notice the softness of her hair against his naked chest the night he held her. The mass of it hung down her back now, the ends curling in very un-Apache waves. In his mind he saw the way the sun would pick out red glints in the dark brown.

She eased into the water, her slim body disappearing little by little, and began to swim. The thick heat in his groin hardened to an ache. The feeling had come often in the night sleeping in the wickiup so close to her, and he had willed it away, as he could again. If he decided to.

Deciding was why he was here. Maybe he should be doing it somewhere else, but far to the north, thoughts of Katherine had haunted him until he worried he would become careless among enemies. And he had never decided.

From the day he had found Bácho's band after escaping the school he had followed every custom of the people with care. He never allowed anyone to see disbelief or disrespect, yet they saw inside him and knew. They had always regarded him with varying amounts of suspicion and always would. The years in the school had made him different, and the people knew it.

The one rebellion he had made was a refusal to keep his eyebrows and eyelashes plucked. He'd done it when he first became a warrior, but it made no difference to the people and he considered it a vain waste of time. From Lupe he knew that Katherine had refused all suggestions she pluck brows or lashes, citing him as her excuse.

From Sigesh he knew that the hairy white woman had not only plucked body hair but rubbed stones over her arms and legs until they were as smooth as any Apache woman's. He wasn't close enough to see if that was true, but the idea of it increased the desire he'd thought already beyond increase.

Protecting Katherine and staying in the wickiup with her when he was home had already widened the gap between him and his own people, but when she was gone, things would return to the way they had been. If he took what he wanted from her, nothing could ever be the same.

If that's your price, I'll pay it.

He got to his feet and started down the hill.

AT LEAST SWIMMING with a ghost guaranteed privacy. Katherine slipped into the cool water with a gasp. Swimming to the rocks on the far side, she wondered as she always did how anyone had drowned here. A dozen crawling strokes took her from one side to the other. She could stand anywhere in the pool and keep her nose above water.

Maybe the boy was small. Maybe he tried to dive and hit his head. Maybe that's all a ghost ever was, a memory that haunted.

Shaking off the sad thoughts, she turned and swam to the rocks a second time, pushed off and started back. Color and motion brought her head out of the water, her feet scrabbled for the gravelly bottom. Red headband. Gaetan taking it off and throwing it on the grass.

After the first swift rush of joy at the sight of him, caution prevailed. She bent her knees until the water reached her chin.

"When did you get back?" Silly question. He wasn't there when she left the camp, and he was here now.

"What are you doing?" Sillier question. He was taking off his clothes, and he was going to be in this small pool with her in no time at all.

Shirt. Moccasins. Belt and everything else. She watched as mesmerized as the first time a year ago. So much smooth bronze skin. Such long limbs cloaked in curving muscle. And male. What she had seen before had stayed in her mind, but what she'd seen before hadn't been a fully aroused male standing on the bank while she was down in the water.

The exertion of swimming had quickened her breathing. Now, as she stood still, it grew ragged and deeper. Her stomach muscles contracted and rippled. Her breasts no longer felt small, but heavy, aching with their own weight. Nipples already peaked in the cool water tightened more—to something close to pain. The silk of the water on her skin made her more aware of the swelling heat between her legs and the thicker moisture there.

He didn't ease into the water but took two steps and came toward her in a long shallow dive. Her nerve shattered. She turned and swam for the rocks, arms and legs flailing.

Gaetan surfaced beside her and swam easily just behind her shoulder. When he rolled beside her in the water, she understood he wasn't trying to catch her. She reached the rocks, pushed off and started back. He stayed beside her, pacing her. She risked a glance at him, and he rolled again. She laughed and began to enjoy the chase.

This time as she turned, she felt his hand at the base of her neck, rough, warm strength sliding along her spine as she moved through the water. His hand curved over her bottom and fell away as she straightened and kicked forward. A small sound escaped her throat.

Across the pool, she turned again and his hand slid from her hip along her leg, cupped her foot and let go. Another lap and his hand seared its path across her shoulder and down her arm. No longer traversing the pool, Katherine circled him, wanting his hands on her breasts, her belly, all of her.

He rolled again and swam away. If he thought he was going to tease her like that and leave! She churned after him at her best speed, caught him when he turned, slippery arm muscle sliding away under her hand. She gave chase, touching him as he had touched her until they circled each other, hands touching, stroking.

He stood first, his hands sliding to her back, pulling her toward him. She flattened her hands on his chest, not to push away but to feel him. His nipples were as taut as hers, pebbles in the center of the smooth skin and firm muscle under her palms. And warm, such a contrast with the water around them.

He tightened his hold, and she slid her hands to his shoulders, then her arms around his neck. The water buoyed her as she climbed him and wrapped her legs around his waist.

She could feel his arousal, tried to maneuver herself onto him, but he cupped his hands under her bottom and pulled her up. "Gaetan!"

He carried her through the water and up the bank without apparent effort, lowering her onto the pile of their clothing. Unwilling to let go for a second, Katherine stayed wrapped around him and tried to pull him to her.

"No more teasing. Now!"

He entered her in a single hard thrust, opening her, stretching her and forcing a moan of surprise from her. She was ready, so ready, and yet totally unprepared. She'd been wrong. She was still virgin to this, to his strength and her need, to the pleasure and the pain and the sheer triumph of having him. He drove into her and she rose to him, clutched him tighter, harder. Her nails raked and dug into his back, her teeth into his neck.

Her world narrowed down to Gaetan. Wet strands of his hair clung to her breasts, shoulder and cheek. Skin slippery with a sheen of water dried to smooth satin over surging hard muscle as the heat of their bodies intensified scent and taste.

Feeling him inside her, *knowing* he was inside added a possessive ecstasy to the pleasure assaulting her, as each thrust echoed through every part of her. Reveling in the sensations, almost unable to bear them, she cried out as her back arched and body spasmed around his, drawing him deeper, holding him tighter. The aftermath of the internal storm left her passive prey for another half dozen strokes until he stiffened, filling her.

Katherine's heart and lungs had only started to slow when Gaetan shifted his weight from her. She made a small sound of protest, wanting to hold him longer, but he pulled away and sat up. Pushing herself up also, she looked at the wounds she'd left on his back and wanted to kiss them. Some strange, belated shyness held her back.

"Are you sorry?" she said.

"No."

He got up and walked back into the water. She followed. Some signs of what they had done could be washed away. The ones that mattered the most were indelible.

THE NEXT MORNING Katherine got up, pulled on her clothes and kicked the bed. Gaetan had managed to sneak away before she woke, of course, just as he'd waited until she was long abed before joining her. Worse, instead of giving his renewed silence the treatment it royally deserved, she'd curled in his arms, delighted to have him there and unable to hide it.

Whatever taboos he'd broken and prejudices he'd ignored, he could just *deal* with them. Didn't she have to deal with the fact she'd been colossally stupid? Again.

Being stupid over never-wanted-him-anyway Henry had cost her everything back home. Being stupid over wanted-him-so-much-she-ached Gaetan had already meant walking back here yesterday afternoon beside him in wet clothes, sporting the mark of a passion bite on her neck that her hair only covered if she kept her head bent in an awkward position. At least she'd bitten him down by the shoulder! All those expressionless Apache faces had watched them, and she'd half-expected them to start throwing stones.

And what did it mean? If anyone thought what happened meant she was like Sigesh, they had another think coming. She'd shoot them all, starting with Gaetan, except she didn't want to shoot him, at least not for a hundred years or so until she'd had enough of him.

Going outside meant braving all those faces again. She had to go out. Ducking through the door she stared at the baskets sitting to one side. Her own baskets. Full. Slowly it dawned on her. He'd come back yesterday and brought whatever he'd stolen north of the border with him. And no one except Lupe could take what she needed until after Katherine. And Katherine had been busy being stupid at the ghost pool.

She carried the baskets inside and took off up the mountain at a run. If he was hungry he could feed himself. She needed some time alone.

Katherine watched the last of the sunrise from the tree-framed mountain overlook she'd discovered months ago. As the delicate pinks faded with the coming of full daylight, she admitted to herself she had no right to be upset.

She'd wanted him, thought he could never set his hate and prejudice aside, and she'd been wrong. Wanting more was greedy. Wanting to hear her name or soft words—or any words—was unreasonable. She was going to calm down, make sure whatever she'd done didn't affect his protection and enjoy what she had, whatever that was.

"Katherine."

She whirled. "You're going to talk to me today?"

"Yes."

He sat beside her, and she remembered the last time they'd sat here, the time they'd shared about Henry and the school. She stretched her neck, trying to work out the lump in her throat without crying.

"Did you ask if I'm sorry because you are? If you changed your mind, you can divorce me."

It was as if she had never learned a word of Apache. She stared at him with no understanding.

"Or we can be married for a little while. I'll still take you back to your people when we leave this place."

Katherine's mind finally wrapped around a word. "Married?"

His brows furrowed as he looked at her. "What did you think we did yesterday?"

"I thought we…. I thought I…. Married?"

"Yes."

"When Datilye married Jágé, there were.... The families.... They didn't just.... There was a celebration."

"You're not a maiden and you have no family. I have no family. Would you have me give myself horses? Would you give yourself a wedding feast? No one would come. No one will celebrate our marriage. Bácho mourns already."

How anyone else felt was of absolutely no concern to Katherine.

"I do have family even if they couldn't attend. Lupe would come. Echo would come."

"Maybe."

"We're really married?"

"Yes."

"How do I divorce you?"

"You put everything of mine outside and don't let me in again."

"That's too easy. Things like that should be hard. Marrying should be hard. My people definitely do it better."

"How do they do it?"

"You go to church and take vows in front of family and friends. Even with no family, you'd go to the church and the preacher administers vows."

"What kind of vows?"

Unhappy and uncertain about marrying Henry Dumont, Katherine had read and reread the wedding vows until she could recite them, so she did.

"Those are hard promises."

"Yes, they are."

"Our way is better, I think."

"We're married because of what we did yesterday?"

"And because I moved in with you last night, and you let me."

"You've been living with me for months."

"Not in the same way."

Definitely not in the same way, but she still had trouble believing him. "How can you say we're married but you'll still take me north?"

He shrugged. "We can have a little time. You want to go back, and no matter how we try to hide, sooner or later they'll find us, and the soldiers will come."

Katherine pushed around on her bottom so she faced him. "Married is married. If we're married I'm not going anywhere."

"You want to go home."

"Not if we're married. If we're married, home is where you are."

He studied her as if he hadn't seen her before, his expression making him seem younger again. "The soldiers will come, and you'll go with them."

"If Mexican soldiers come, I'm going to have to run faster and hide better than anyone else. Maybe they won't do what Hierra was going to do, but they'll either throw me in prison forever or put me in front of a firing squad."

"There are many different soldiers. The ones who come won't be the same as the others."

"They don't have to be. By now every soldier in Mexico knows about a woman named Katherine Grant who looks like me, killed a Rurale and escaped with an Apache. If we're married, we're married. No soldiers."

"You said you want to go back to your family. You said it many times."

Married meant she could touch him didn't it? She touched his face tentatively. He didn't pull away. Maybe he leaned into her palm a little. Even as she pulled her hand back, something inside her gave a small, happy skip.

"I said it because I didn't think there could ever be anything here for me. The way you feel about whites is so strong. I didn't think...?"

Her last words weren't supposed to be a question, but they came out that way. She didn't expect an answer, but he surprised her.

"Your skin is white, but I think the white god made a mistake, or maybe he did it on purpose to play a joke. He gave you an Apache heart."

Whatever else it was, her heart was female enough to race at those words. If married meant she could touch, could she ask to be touched? "Hold me?"

He pulled her into his arms, and she rested her head on his shoulder, reveling in his strength, breathing deeply of his scent. A shadow of yesterday's feelings returned.

"What about children? I'm not going to let you take a second wife, you know."

"Even if you stay now, our time will be short. It will be better if there are no children. I won't stop fighting."

With her head against him, she could feel his words as well as hear them. Wanting to deny their meaning and knowing she couldn't, she said nothing. He would fight to the death, and she would never have the power to change that.

As if he knew the direction of her thoughts, he said, "You told me once that laying with me would be a price you'd pay."

Loving him would carry a terrible price, but that was in the future. Remembering when she had said those words brought a smile today. "Even then I hoped to get the chance, although you couldn't have made me admit it with a gun to my head. The thought of it made my knees shake. The first time I had enough strength to crawl to the creek and bathe, I saw you there. I started wanting you then."

"I watched you yesterday. Before I came to the pool."

"You did? Then we're even, and I don't have to feel guilty any more. I was napping in the shade and woke up and saw you and didn't dare move. Of course I didn't want to move either. I think I started loving you before then, when you came back for me. From the miners. I knew you didn't mean to, and I didn't care. It only mattered that you did come back."

He didn't say anything for long enough she knew he wouldn't speak of love. When he did speak he changed the subject.

"When we traveled together, I told you to stay so I could fill the canteen at the place only the people know. You were so angry you danced on the rocks, and I went to the spring and sat for a long time before I filled the canteen."

"I remember. I didn't think you were coming back."

"I stayed there because I fought a strange feeling. It happened again when you almost shot Kloshchu and told Agocho I made him sorry and again when you tied the knot in your shirt when I told you to cover yourself." He looked down at her, and for the first time she saw amusement in his eyes.

"You made me want to laugh."

"But you didn't laugh."

"No."

"I'll have to work harder at it."

"I can't give you what you want, Katherine. I think the anger has burned into places inside me that should hold other feelings. I'll be as good a husband as I can for as long as you want, and when you want to go back to your people, I'll take you."

She raised her head so she could look straight at him. "You've already given me what I want. I want you. You should know that I won't leave your people so long as you live. If you ever return and find me gone, know that they took me against my will. I will not leave you."

"That's a hard promise too."

"It's my promise." She toyed with the top button of his shirt. "Do Apaches kiss?"

"The people believe the mouth is only for eating."

"Oh." She didn't try to hide her disappointment.

He shifted her against him a little and cupped her breast with one hand, his thumb rubbing across the nipple. "They also believe a woman's breast is only for nursing a child."

Lowering his mouth over hers, he ran his tongue between her lips, exploring her tongue, making her shiver with a stroke along the roof of her mouth.

When he raised his head at last, she whispered, "I'm glad you're an unbeliever."

"I can do this more gently than yesterday. Yesterday I hurt you."

"Did you? I don't remember that part. How does your back feel?"

He didn't answer but the corners of his mouth curled up slightly as if against his will.

"Are you saying we don't have to come together like crazed grizzly bears every time?" she said.

"Not every time."

"You'll have to show me." She gave him a sharp nip on the shoulder, jumped up and took off running.

He made sure not to catch her until they were inside the wickiup.

20

Katherine made her way to Lupe's with her head down and shoulders slumped. Nodding a subdued greeting, she knelt by her metate, ready to help grind mesquite beans and find out what could be done with the flour.

Lupe diagnosed the cause of Katherine's blue mood at a glance. "He hasn't been gone that long this time, and you know he'll return soon."

"It's not just that he's gone. It's knowing how dangerous it is and worrying about him. Don't you worry about your husband when he goes hunting by himself?"

"Yes, but there's always danger. There always has been. I pray and ask Ussen to watch over him, and I think good thoughts."

Good thoughts. Not thoughts of Rurales and wagon wheels or Cal and his friends or Agocho and his. Katherine vowed to at least try to hold to good thoughts.

Lupe poured her ground flour into a basket and started again with more beans. "Since he became a warrior, Gaetan has never stayed with the people as much as he has since your marriage, even though the time of your hunting trip shouldn't be counted."

The memory of the "hunting trip" changed Katherine's expression to a smile. A most successful wedding gift, the trip had lasted twelve days and taken them far from home, far enough that Gaetan had let her practice with the rifle and hunt with him. Not much practice—ammunition was too precious—but enough to reassure her she could still hit the side of a barn.

"My people would call that hunting trip a honeymoon," Katherine said. "Although he did get a deer."

So did Katherine, but her success stayed a secret. The Apache regarded hunting as man's work, and she wasn't going to give anyone another thing to bedevil her husband over. His people gave him enough grief over taking a white wife.

"Of course, he gave away most of the meat," Katherine added.

"My husband does the same. A good man is generous."

"I suppose so, but no one needs the meat. We already have too much livestock here for the grass, and if Chishogi's raid is successful, he'll bring more."

"Then we'll move sooner."

They worked in silence for a while. "Can we really make bread from this? Katherine asked, looking at the growing pile of flour dubiously.

"Yes. It isn't like your white flour or like corn either, but it's good."

"I actually heard that Bedonkohe woman talking this morning about being out of coffee and sugar as if it's a hardship. As if Gaetan let everyone down by spending too much time lazing around here with his wife."

Lupe smiled mischievously. "I thought he was working very hard."

Katherine let go of the last of her bleak mood with a laugh. "He better not tell anyone that's work."

"Everyone did get used to having the things he brings. No one expected him to marry. If this is what you want, I'm happy for you. I thought you were like a young girl who wants foolish things just because she can't have them, and I didn't think he would ever...."

"I know. I didn't think he would ever either, and I thought I was being foolish, but I couldn't stop myself. You told me once when your mother and father first saw each other they never looked away. It didn't happen that fast for me, but when it did it was like that, and I thought it was stupid and hopeless, so I pretended it wasn't true."

"What about your family? You wanted so much to go back to your family."

"I wanted to go back because I thought there was nothing for me here. Now, I don't know. Part of me wants to find a way to get a letter to them and let them know I'm safe and happy. Part of me wonders if it's better not to. They must think I'm dead, and they're probably over the worst of the mourning. Maybe it's better to leave it that way."

"In the spring, my husband will take me to the reservation for the curing ceremony. If you tell me what to do, maybe I could send a letter for you if that's what you want."

"Would you? If someone gave it to the agent and asked him to send it, that would be enough. I think I can find a way to write on canvas or deerskin if I have to."

Shouting sounded from the direction of the trail up the mountain.

"Chishogi is back! Chishogi is back!"

"Maybe we'll have coffee tonight after all," Lupe said, getting to her feet.

"Not unless you find a way to brew a cow," Katherine said cynically, but she abandoned the grinding readily enough and went along to watch Chishogi strut and find out what he had brought.

Katherine hung at the edge of the crowd of celebrating women and proud raiders. When Gaetan returned with plunder, she had first choice. When Chishogi returned, she had last choice, which usually meant nothing.

Before long she noticed worried frowns on first a few faces then more and more. Chishogi still strode from one group to another like a conquering hero, but something was wrong. As she watched, the men disappeared in the direction of Bácho's wickiup.

Katherine worked her way to Lupe's side. "What's wrong? What's going on?"

"I don't know. There must have been trouble on the raid, but everyone's back. No one was hurt. My husband will find out, and he'll tell me soon."

In her most fair-minded moments, Katherine admitted that the grudge she held against Chishogi was unjustified. He hadn't killed Nilchi. If Nilchi hadn't been intent on giving Gaetan a hard time, he would have listened, and the three of them would have traveled one of the less direct routes and escaped the Rurales' attack.

Even so, she disliked the boastful man and agreed with Gaetan's low opinion. A sudden strong premonition came over her. Chishogi had done something careless and dangerous again.

The last of the beans were flour by the time Itsá returned home and relayed the news, which was every bit as bad as Katherine had feared. Half a day's ride from home, Chishogi's scouts had seen a small party of soldiers only a few miles away, and Chishogi attacked, killing several of the soldiers before the others got away. The Apaches had split up then, each man driving only a few head of cattle until they reformed the herd close to home.

"How could he have been so reckless?" Katherine asked. "Even I could track a man and several cows. How soon will the soldiers be here?"

Itsá didn't look as concerned as she thought he should. "Two or three days, maybe more. If we're ready for them, they can't reach us here. We'll drive them off and have time to move to the new place in ways they can't follow."

"Gaetan says if they're determined they'll come over the mountain behind us."

Itsá shook his head. "If they try to come that way, it will be a year. Finding a way through the pass and over the mountain is too hard. They'll try the trail and fail."

"They could leave enough men at the foot of trail to keep us trapped here until they find the back way, couldn't they?"

"They have no patience. They chase and they kill, but they never surround and hold. Your people are the ones who do that."

His expression and tone were neutral, but Katherine took her share of the flour and left as soon as she could. Finding out what to do with mesquite flour could wait until tomorrow. Alone and out of sight in her own wickiup, she cleaned the rifle and pistol, checked her ammunition and tried not to think about Gaetan making his way home not knowing that Chishogi had ensured the Mexican army was on the same path.

Days passed, and the people began to relax. They talked more about the upcoming move to a site days to the west than an attack by the Mexican army. Katherine didn't feel so sanguine. When Gaetan returned, leading fewer pack animals than usual and looking worn out, she all but forgot prudish Chiricahua attitudes about such things and threw herself at him.

As he unloaded the provisions, Katherine took her share and listened to several people telling him what Chishogi had done and how the attack had been a victory over the Mexicans that they would never be able to avenge.

The minute they were alone, Katherine asked Gaetan what he really thought. "They're foolish to believe because the army's slow to react, they won't come, aren't they?"

"Yes. The longer it takes, the more will come and the more likely they'll come over the mountain."

"That's what I thought. What are you going to do?"

"Tonight I'm going to enjoy my wife like a man who has been away for almost a month. They aren't coming over the mountain in the dark." His bandolier hit the ground with a thump, and his belt followed.

Katherine walked into his arms and abandoned her own worries. Come first light, she'd ask again.

In the predawn darkness the next morning, she found out what Gaetan planned—a solitary watch on the back way to the camp. As he prepared for a day on the heights, so did Katherine. Gaetan didn't pay much attention as she gathered a water jug, food and blankets against the cold of the fall morning. When she slung her rifle over one shoulder, he noticed.

"I don't need help to keep watch," he said.

"What are you going to do if you see them?"

"Kill them."

"How will that warn anyone? The way sound echoes around the valley, people will think any gunfire they hear comes from the trail because that's what they're expecting. I can run back down and warn everyone while you're shooting."

"That's why you have the rifle? For running?"

"Just in case."

"And the food? Is that for a picnic?"

Katherine wiggled her eyebrows at him. "Maybe we could figure a way to keep watch and have a picnic too."

He hesitated and Katherine prepared for an argument, but all he said was, "Come on then. Let's go make them sorry."

By the third day, Katherine struggled against her own doubts, although she kept them to herself. After all, keeping watch with her husband was pure pleasure. Early in the afternoon, gunfire sounded in the distance, and Gaetan changed from husband to the warrior she had first seen in an instant.

"You stay here," he ordered. "If you see them first, wait until they're close enough to hit, shoot one and run to warn the women and children. If you hear me fire, don't wait, run."

Katherine had expected to go toward where the other warriors had already engaged the army. "You still think they're coming this way?"

"Maybe not, but Bácho doesn't need us by the trail. If more soldiers come this way, I'll slow them down. You run and warn."

"I don't want to run. I want to stay with you."

He gripped her shoulders so hard it hurt. "You will run and warn everyone. I'll come behind you soon enough. Say it."

Arguing was useless, and he knew what he was doing. "All right. Yes, I promise."

He melted away into the trees. She knew he would work his way to another vantage point but didn't like it. It didn't matter anyway, she told herself, the soldiers had attacked along the trail as everyone had known they would. Being up here was only an extra precaution, useless now. Soon they'd both walk down the hill together.

She had herself as good as convinced when a flash of blue and movement in the distance caught her eye. More blue appeared between the trees as the first of the Mexican cavalrymen urged their horses down the slope. She lined up her sights on a gap in the trees, waiting for a uniform to appear, but Gaetan's rifle barked before she fired. Katherine lowered her rifle, jumped up and ran.

Women and children milled around in the camp, excited and certain their men could keep the soldiers from coming up the trail. They didn't want to believe Katherine, but the source of the sporadic shots high on the mountain became more evident by the minute. She saw one of the boys who had helped her learn Apache and stopped him.

"Go tell the warriors. Tell them more soldiers are coming down the mountain. Many more, and Gaetan is there alone. Go!"

The boy stared at her unmoving, until she seized him by the shoulders and shook. Even if he didn't believe, there was no doubt as he took off that he would tell Bácho, Chishogi and the others what she had said and done.

The women no longer doubted. They gathered their children and scattered into the trees like quail. For a person on foot, there were ways out of the valley other than down the trail or over the mountain, every one difficult and dangerous. Katherine sent a silent prayer with the women as she raced back up the mountain.

The gunfire stopped and so did Katherine's heart. The first of the Apache warriors overtook her and moved into position around her. They would fight and delay the soldiers as long as they could, giving the women and children time to escape, then fade away after their families.

Katherine wasn't going anywhere except back to Gaetan. Once she got to him she'd worry about getting away, and if that meant dragging him with her, wounded or able-bodied, she'd find a way.

Halfway down the mountain already, the soldiers advanced steadily, infantry on the heels of the cavalry. Katherine imitated the warriors, firing from the cover of trees, brush and rocks, then darting to different cover. Searching for her next target, she saw movement on the flank of the foot soldiers, ducked down, then popped up for another quick look.

Gaetan moved parallel to the soldiers, hitting them with enfilade fire from one position after another. The relief that flooded her at the sight changed to something else as she saw one of the soldiers pointing toward Gaetan. Aware of the danger on their flank now, several of them redirected fire toward Gaetan, who broke from an inadequate brush cover, zigzagging his way toward the Apache line. One of the cavalrymen yanked his horse around and charged after Gaetan, saber drawn.

Katherine heard Peter, the best marksman in her family, the one who had taught her to shoot. *Don't hurry. If you hurry and miss you've wasted more time than being deliberate in the first place. Take your time. Be sure.*

She shut out everything around her, narrowing the world down to nothing but a blue target, and squeezed the trigger. The soldier sagged and slumped, his horse lost direction, wavered and slowed. Gaetan kept coming, and Katherine focused on another of the soldiers targeting him. She missed and didn't care as Gaetan landed beside her.

"The stream," he said, yanking her to her feet.

Katherine took off for the stream, Gaetan at her side. As she ran, a blow smashed into the back of her thigh, numbing the whole leg as it crumpled and took her to the ground. Even before pain started shrieking along her nerves, Katherine knew she'd been shot. Gaetan skidded to a halt no more than three steps beyond, turned back and threw her over his shoulder. He barely slowed, but she could feel his muscles straining.

"You can't...."

"Can you shoot?"

She had dropped her rifle. Hanging onto Gaetan's shirt with one hand, she squirmed and reached the pistol with the other. An eager face bringing a rifle to bear appeared through the trees behind them. She snapped off the kind of hurried shot Peter would have deplored and followed it with two more. Maybe she couldn't aim or hit, but she could make them cautious, and cautious would be slower.

Gaetan jumped into the stream without slowing down, splashing water up onto both banks before whirling around and doubling back on his own trail. He eased Katherine down in the first brush they came to, pushed her skirt up and tied his headband over the ugly red holes in her thigh. At least it was the other leg from the one smashed in the summer.

Katherine's urge to giggle dissolved as she took in the amount of blood that puddled under the leg in the few seconds before the headband slowed the flow. The bullet had hit her in the back of the leg and exited the front, tearing a good chunk of flesh out on the way. The bleeding wasn't an arterial spurt, but it was a frightening flow. Gaetan pulled his shirt off and wrapped that around her leg too, tying the sleeves.

A trail of red drops glistened wherever afternoon sunlight dappled the ground between the trees. The Mexicans might think their prey tried to use the stream to hide the blood trail, but only if what they saw looked like a single trail to the water.

Gaetan picked her up again and left their original trail. He moved up the mountain, slowly and carefully now, listening for sounds of pursuit and keeping to the trees. Katherine hung like a long sack of flour over his shoulder, determined not to let pain wring a sound from her and trying not to bleed.

She had forgotten all about the things she left on the mountain when she ran to give warning. Gaetan had not. The blankets, food and water still sat in her abandoned lookout position. He set her down on her feet. "Can you stand?"

She tried. Her head swam with the pain, but the leg felt able. "If Echo could force some of her black medicine down me, I could stand, probably even walk."

Gaetan unwrapped his shirt and headband. Blood no longer flowed but oozed.

"With your shoulder, Echo said it 'bled clean,' Maybe it's good that it's bleeding."

"It's clean enough," he said, tearing a section of his shirt that wasn't yet blood soaked and wrapping it tight around the leg. "At least the bullet went right through."

Finished with the bandage, he wrapped her in the blankets, picked her up again and started climbing higher, angling around the side of the mountain. "Wait. What about the water and food?"

"I'll come back for them."

"Do you think they'll still come after us? Track us down tomorrow?" The setting sun already cast long shadows in the forest.

"I think tomorrow we'll find out."

They settled for the night in a rocky nest surrounded by the fresh scent of pine. When Katherine unwrapped the blankets around her, Gaetan objected.

"You can't stay up here tonight without even a shirt," she said.

"I can."

"Well, you're not going to."

In the end she stayed cocooned in one blanket. He draped the other around his back, tucked Katherine in the fork of his legs and closed the second blanket around them both. Wrapped in blankets and husband, Katherine refused to worry about what the next day would bring. She turned and kissed the side of his face.

"I'm sorry."

"You're not supposed to be sorry. You're supposed to make them sorry."

"I think I did a little. I'm sure you did."

"I'm sure you did too. Next time don't drop your rifle."

Next time. That sounded good. "It's like the beginning all over again, isn't it? Just the two of us hiding from Mexican soldiers." She kissed him again. "I love you."

"Go to sleep, Katherine."

So she did.

21

Being alone with the pistol in her lap held no horrors for Katherine. Worrying about Gaetan did. She fretted and fumed the whole time he was gone the next morning, sure the sun climbed across the sky more slowly than usual and hours were passing. Frost still covered the grass when he returned.

"They're gone."

"What did you find?"

"Four bodies. Everything burned."

"Lupe?" Katherine whispered. "Echo?" The old woman could hardly see and would be slow, so slow.

He shook his head, telling her of two dead women without naming names. Neither of the women had been willing to have much to do with a white woman in their midst, but sorrow slid through Katherine at lives ended in such a senseless way, so did dread, dread of what Gaetan had not yet told. She waited.

"The third woman was the one who was divorced."

Sigesh. Katherine could hardly accept that the beautiful woman was dead. "I'm sorry."

He merely nodded. "The fourth body is the one who led the raid when my brother died. From the way things look, he didn't retreat with the other men, he stayed and fought until the soldiers killed him, fought bravely."

Shame washed through her at the way she felt. Better Chishogi than any of the children. "Would he do that rather than face the disgrace of what he brought down on us this time?"

"Yes."

"Dying is easier than living sometimes, I suppose," Katherine said. "I didn't like him, and I still don't."

Gaetan frowned at her, and she waited for an Apache version of not speaking ill of the dead, but all he said was, "Can you walk if I help you?"

"Let's find out." Leaning, hopping and limping, she managed most of the trip down the mountain on her feet, but he carried her over some of the roughest places, this time in his arms. "A woman could get used to traveling like this," she said, hugging him around the neck.

He gave her a narrow-eyed glare, and she responded by kissing a corner of his mouth.

"If you don't stop that, I'll fall. We'll hit our heads and both freeze to death right here tonight."

"I don't think I'll ever freeze if you're close enough to touch."

"Does that leg feel good enough you're ready to sit down hard on your backside?"

She kissed his bare shoulder this time, but she stopped teasing. "Tomorrow maybe."

Down the mountain and across the valley—exhaustion dogged Katherine by the time they made it to the blackened sticks that had been their home. The smoky scent of burned wood, fabric and hide still hung in the air, and anger rose raw inside her. The little dwelling had been full of things she'd made, things that made life easier—and memories. Looking around at the other burned out wickiups, her anger turned to sorrow.

"What are we going to do?" she whispered.

"I'm going to bury the dead, and then I'm going to make a new house while you see what hasn't burned that we can use."

For the first time Katherine realized they weren't going to follow those who had fled, catch up with them and join them. The soldiers had taken all the livestock. Without a horse, she wasn't going anywhere until her leg healed.

"Will you bury them the way you did your brother?"

"No, there are caves on the south side of the mountain. I'll bury them there. Did you ever help when the women stored food in the caves?"

"No. They never let me go out of the valley. Well, except as far as the ghost pool to gather wood. I helped roast mescal when they brought it back here, but they didn't let me go to get it, and they didn't let me go to help fill the cache caves either. Are you thinking you could use one of those caves for burial?"

He shook his head. "I know where there are caves I can use for burying. After I do that, I'll look for a cache cave. If I find one, our winter will be good."

"Winter? My leg will be healed soon. We can follow the others before winter sets in."

"Most of them will spend the winter on the reservation now. The ones who stay out are going to have a hungry time. Joining them would be foolish."

"But if what they need is here...." As she spoke, the truth hit her. "They'll never come back, will they?"

"No. Even if they would, the Mexicans will hunt them until they're north of the border."

Looking around the valley with the burned out remains of the wickiups, she shivered at the thought of staying alone in the winter.

As if he could read her thoughts, Gaetan said, "The two of us will stay together."

She hardly dared believe his words. "But you never stay. You went back and forth all last winter."

His somber look lightened for a moment. "This winter I'll stay, and you'll work very hard to keep me content here."

Katherine's sorrow retreated and her sense of adventure advanced. "That's not work. I'll work hard at other things."

She began by fashioning a rake from twigs and sifting through the ashes.

Metal pots and utensils were all that survived the fires intact. Almost all. Raking through the ruins of Lupe and Itsá's home, Katherine found a metal comb. Holding it in her hand, she prayed Lupe was safe wherever she was. Maybe the comb never had been inside a miner's saddlebag, but help with her hair had been the first gift Lupe had given. Setting the comb aside with the pots, she went back to the search.

The speed at which Gaetan put their lives back together astonished Katherine and made her once more aware of why the government had so much trouble conquering the Apaches. Before she finished raking through the ruins, he built another wickiup out of sight among the trees and stocked it with food and goods from the cache he found.

Teasing words about how much woman's work he was doing danced at the edges of her mind, but for once she decided to listen to that advice about wisdom and valor and kept quiet.

By the time the first real storm of winter hit, Katherine's leg had healed, although it still had little strength. She and Gaetan played checkers on a board scratched out on the dirt floor, using stones and bits of wood for the checkers, and they shared stories.

He told Apache legends. She told of sailing around the world on her father's ships.

He told of hunting, raiding and making war throughout the Southwest. She told of hunts in Africa, Russia and India.

"I saw pictures of elephants and giraffes at the school," he said. "I didn't believe they were real."

"People who live there wouldn't believe about grizzly bears or moose either."

"I'm not sure I believe you about moose."

He had never seen a moose so his disbelief was reasonable. "Probably there are people who think they only dreamed about the moose the day after they see one."

He told of returning to the people at sixteen, knowing only the names of his mother and father.

"At that age, a Chihinne boy is well on the way to becoming a warrior. I had to learn quickly to get away from boys so young training with them was embarrassing."

"But you knew more about other things. You can speak three languages. You know about Americans and how we think."

"Those things didn't matter. Being able to run miles without breathing through the mouth did, and I couldn't do that for a long time."

"But now you can."

"Now I can."

"When I first followed you from the Rurales' camp, I was grateful they'd damaged you a little so you couldn't run that night. I had enough trouble keeping up as it was."

A slight smile played around his mouth. "I wanted to leave you behind very much. The promise and the other things were very aggravating."

"Did you always keep quiet about the things you don't believe," she asked, "or did you learn you had to do that after you came back?"

"There aren't so many things I don't believe. Our ways are good, and they make strong people. I had to pretend to believe many more stupid things when I was in the white school, but those who think the school made me different are right. I'm not what I would have been."

No, he wasn't, and Katherine would never stop being grateful. "You're more than you would have been."

"Less."

She knew better than to start an argument she couldn't win and changed the subject to how her family had put her ashore permanently at seventeen and ordered her to change into something she didn't want to be.

"It was different for me. You wanted to escape the school and start a different life. I wanted everything to stay the same. I did what they told me to do and tried to accept it, and maybe that was my mistake. Maybe I should have tried harder to make my father understand how much I hated it. That's why I was going to marry Henry, because a married woman has more freedom. I thought what he wanted was mostly someone to take care of his children, and I didn't think he wanted me that much."

"But he did want you."

"He wanted a woman desperate enough to put up with him. Unfortunately, I wasn't quite that desperate."

Gaetan laughed. Katherine stared open mouthed for a moment, then crowed. "I did it! I made you laugh!"

His face closed into expressionless Apache, his eyes still dancing. "No, you dreamed it, like the moose."

Katherine laughed with him as he dragged her through their checkerboard, scattering his pieces of stone and hers of wood as he rolled with her to the bed.

Sometime later, she rested on his chest and harkened back to their conversation. "Maybe we fit together so well because we're the same in some ways. Neither one of us fit in very well with our own people."

"We fit together well because I'm a man, and you're a woman. Ussen designed us that way."

"You know what I mean."

"I'm Chihinne. I'm Apache and always will be."

"I know that, but you fit better with me. There are places where people like us can be together and not have to worry about soldiers coming, you know."

"Faraway places across the ocean?"

She didn't want to admit it but had to. "Yes."

"This is my land. I was born here, and I'll die here. But not today. Today I'm hungry, and a good wife would get up and cook."

Katherine got up and started their meal. No words could change his mind, and arguing would only spoil some of whatever time Fate or Ussen would grant.

BREAKING ICE IN order to jump into frigid water for a quick bath horrified Katherine. By mid-winter she'd gotten over her conviction that Gaetan was going to die of pneumonia from doing it, but she absolutely refused to have any part of the process except for the pleasant task of warming him up afterward.

She still had regular dreams about tubs of hot water covered with soap bubbles and fragrant with the scent of lilac or roses, but she settled for heating water in every pot and kettle she had found in the burned wickiups, standing on a small square of canvas only slightly scorched around the edges, and scrubbing with a piece of cloth. She used only the tiniest bits of amole each time, hoarding the soap as a miser would gold.

In the beginning, every time she bathed, she feared Gaetan would pick her up, carry her to the stream and throw her in. He teased her unmercifully about how her method of bathing indicated a regrettable delicacy. As time passed and he always found something to occupy him outside when she started preparing to bathe, her fear of an icy drenching faded.

So when Gaetan ducked into the wickiup on a cloudy day in what she calculated had to be February, Katherine shivered at the cold air that followed him inside, but kept right on running her wash rag down her leg.

"I'll be done in a minute."

He didn't answer, dropped a rabbit by the fire and turned his back to her as he stripped off his wool poncho, then his moccasins. He must have gotten his feet wet while hunting, she thought, not paying much attention. When his shirt dropped onto the floor, she started to protest, then watched silently, her nipples tightening and goosebumps breaking out on her wet skin, as his headband, leggings and breechclout followed.

"Are you finally ready to try bathing inside with warm water?" Her voice sounded high and nervous, even to her own ears. He couldn't mean to throw her in the stream. He couldn't.

He didn't.

"No. I'm going to help you. There are places you missed, I think."

Taking her now cold cloth from her hand, he dipped it back in the hot water, turned her and touched the cloth to the nape of her neck, gently rubbing across her shoulders, down her spine and into the small of her back. The cloth lost its warmth quickly. His hand did not.

She tried to say something, managed only a small moan. "Aah."

"Turn around."

Facing him, she saw what she didn't need to see to know. Even if most wives experienced being washed by a fully aroused, naked husband, they would never know this—a man no words had been invented to describe, beyond handsome, beyond beautiful. His skin glowed copper in the light from the fire, shadows emphasizing the curves of muscle and planes of bone. His erection was hers, for her. She reached to wrap a hand around the hot thickness, and he stopped her.

"No. I'm washing you."

He followed the cloth down her neck and across her collarbones with his mouth. Warm cloth, water droplets running chilly trails down her body, lips and tongue that scalded their way across her skin—the sensations contrasted and blended until her head spun and her knees threatened to give way. He bent his head to her breasts, abandoned the pretense of washing and dropped the cloth back into the kettle with a splash.

Holding his shoulders for support, Katherine arched back as the pleasure of each separate touch stabbed through her. He kissed each nipple, sucked one after the other, then bit down gently on one as his tongue swirled around the tip. Her knees buckled; his hands curved around her ribs and under her bottom and held her on her feet.

Down her belly, across skin so sensitive it quivered at his touch. Sinking to his knees, he kissed down the outside of one leg, up the inside. Her body tried to crumple again as his breath feathered across skin left hot and moist by his tongue. His mouth blazed the sweet trail behind her knee, his cheek rubbing against her other leg, his hair tickling as he moved. Up the inside of her thigh, up—until his tongue stroked once slowly into the apex of her thighs. She jerked with shock and white hot pleasure, sagging against his hands as he moved down the other leg, up again.

This time the shock was less, the pleasure greater when his tongue slid into the cleft at the juncture of her legs, sucking and teasing the throbbing bit of flesh there as he had her nipples. The pleasure—for a moment the world blurred and she floated, then spasms shot through her, her fingers dug into his back, and even the strength of his hands couldn't keep her upright. She collapsed in his arms, still purring with pleasure as he carried her to the bed.

He laid her on her stomach, pushed her hair to one side and began kissing her again. Behind the ear, along her hairline. Her languor was so deep she registered the pleasure of his touch as if through a haze at first, but gradually her body began to recover and clamor for more. More as in Gaetan moving inside her, the familiar feel of skin, muscle and weight.

As she started to turn over, he slid an arm under her hips, pulled her to her knees. A small sound of protest rose in her throat but died there as she felt the hard heat of him pressing against her, stretching her open and sliding into her willing, ready depths. The sensations she needed all assaulted her, yet each was different, his cheek against her shoulder, the heat of his skin and his weight over her back.

"Gaetan." She gasped more than spoke, his thrusts rocking her, his arms holding her. The pleasure blended with the memory of what had gone on before, spiraling from their joining through her belly, across her breasts.

The image of him bathing in the stream so long ago arose behind her closed eyelids. Even more than their grizzly bear couplings, this mating seemed as he had then, a man who wouldn't speak to her but who would press the blade of his knife across her lips or materialize out of the night on a racing horse to save her from the danger he had himself thrown her into.

She opened her eyes so as to turn and see him as she knew him now, and saw instead between her own breasts, along her own belly to where each stroke invaded her. The feeling and the knowing and the seeing combined until her body jerked so violently she would have thrown a weaker man off, even as her contracting muscles tightened around him. Aftershocks still rocked her with every thrust until he made the deep sound of his own pleasure and poured himself into her.

She expected him to straighten and pull away. Instead he dropped to his side, still holding her with her back to his chest, rump in his loin. She straightened her legs as she had the first time they lay together, wanting every possible inch of skin against skin.

Close as they were to the fire, cool air on her damp body brought a slight shiver. He pulled the blanket over them both, and Katherine concentrated on the feel of him behind her, the way her breath slowed in time with his.

She wanted to say something but had no words. If she spoke of love, he'd claim to be hungry or get up, dress and leave. After a while, she wriggled around to face him, searching his expressionless face and dark eyes almost lost in the shadows.

She still found no words and settled for kissing him hard on the mouth before nestling back down against his side, one hand spread as wide as possible over the center of his chest.

When his breathing stayed deep and regular, Katherine peeked again. His eyes were closed, his face relaxed. She slipped from the bed, returned to her pots of hot water and finished her bath.

Dressed and bundled against the cold, she picked up the rabbit and took it outside to cut up. A long nap now, fresh meat for dinner—tonight he might be in a mood to let her experiment with what she had never yet been bold enough to try.

She would never ask him if what he had given her today was what he had refused to let a predatory teacher coerce him into doing. He would never ask if she gave him what she had violently refused to do for Henry. Some mysteries needed to remain between a husband and wife.

22

Gaetan concentrated on putting a razor's edge on both his knife and Katherine's. Mostly. Every time he lifted a blade to test, he glanced at his wife where she too worked in the pale spring sunshine. Her task was to assemble everything they would carry with them when they started north in the morning. She moved back and forth with grace, her hands quick and sure.

"How about this?" she asked, holding up her favorite frying pan.

"Put out everything you want, and when it's too heavy we'll decide what to leave."

That answer made her happy for now, but he could tell from the size of the two piles she had made she wouldn't be happy with the final results. Water, food and weapons took priority. After that, any item had to be worth its weight. Alone, he would carry no more than the rifle and knife, some dried meat and extra moccasin soles.

He wasn't alone. He had expected the months of this past winter to be a hardship, to feel constricted and burdened.

Instead, she truly had made him content. The fierceness of her was what calmed him, he had decided. When he was with her, the anger in him could subside because she saw the world as he did, and his enemies were hers.

The stories of her past life fascinated and entertained. When she broke down and confessed how she had turned Debechu from suitor to attacker with a few words, she didn't just make him laugh but roar. He smiled again thinking of it.

"Don't you laugh at me," Katherine said, looking up at him. "I *like* this spoon."

"We'll see. Maybe you like it more than the comb."

"Not that much, but they're both *very* small things."

The piles were high with small things, but he said nothing.

He wanted to believe her when she said she preferred her life with him to her white life, but she would never have to choose between a comb and a spoon on her father's ships or at her aunt's house. Someday she would go back to that life and have many good things again. The compulsion to fight enemies who would kill him or break his spirit and imprison him had not died this winter and never would. Their time together could not last.

She no longer spoke of love and that was a good thing. Love was a woman's soft emotion, not something for a man and certainly nothing for a Chiricahua. The feelings he had for Katherine were strong and proper for a husband—desire, pride, possessiveness.

Still, she was a good wife in all ways, and he wished he could show his appreciation with suitable gifts. Tubs of hot water and sheets that smelled of sunshine were not things he could give her, but he had thought of something she wanted that was in his power to give. And the more he thought of it, the more he realized he wanted that thing as much as she did.

Both knives had razor edges now. He shoved his in its sheath and rose to take Katherine hers and help her decide what could come with them tomorrow.

KATHERINE MISSED LUPE, Echo and some of the other Chiricahua women, but not enough to trade a minute of the winter alone with Gaetan. Since she couldn't hold back the inevitable coming of spring and end of their idyll, she tried to look forward to rejoining the others.

"How will we find them?" she asked.

"We'll ask people on the reservation."

"Just like that? We can just walk onto the reservation and ask?"

"No. You'll have to wait in the hills. The police there are Apache. If they see you, they'll tell the agent. If they see me, they'll look the other way."

Before starting down the switch-backed trail, Katherine stopped and took a long last look at the valley. She had known despair here, and she had known joy. Straightening under her pack, she hurried after Gaetan. What mattered was not where they lived but that Gaetan lived and lived with her.

In the middle of the third night of their trek, they detoured to the corrals of a large rancheria. Katherine marveled at her own attitude. Not long ago, no power on earth could have induced her to steal anything, much less a horse.

Sometime in the last two years she had adopted the Apache attitude. A prosperous ranch owner ought to expect to donate some livestock every so often to the people whose land he was using. He could count himself lucky that tonight, in the interests of avoiding raising an alarm or pursuit, they were only taking two horses.

She slipped into the corral, crooning soft Spanish words to convince horses that might regard an Apache with suspicion that she was trustworthy. In minutes, the most curious of the animals accepted the noose of a reata over his head in exchange for an ear rub. Gaetan opened the gate just enough for her to squeeze that one and then a second out, leaving the rest undisturbed to confound the vaqueros in the morning.

After riding bareback through the remainder of the night, Katherine's stiffness reached heights previously unknown. When Gaetan stopped and dismounted easily, she glared at him without making any effort to get off her horse. It couldn't be a man-woman thing. Her brothers used to complain loudly about soreness when they'd been on a horse too long.

Gaetan's eyes danced with knowledge. "I'm going to walk a while. You'd rather stay on your horse?"

"I'm quite sure Lupe told me that one of the duties of a Chihinne husband is to pry his wife off a horse when necessary," Katherine said through gritted teeth. "I also think really good husbands only steal horses with saddles."

He laughed at her, and the pleasure of eliciting his laughter washed away her temper and gave her the courage to half-fall off the horse on her own. Alternating walking and riding for the rest of the day did alleviate some of the soreness and stiffness as they worked their way through the mountains, staying to the tree-covered slopes and avoiding open areas.

By the next day Katherine had revived sufficiently to notice they no longer traveled northwest but straight west. Confident Gaetan had good reasons, she didn't question the direction but enjoyed the muffled sound of the horse's hooves on the pine-needle-covered earth and drank in mild spring air that held just a hint of the tang of horse and resin. Small birds fell silent as they passed, but the cry of a hawk sounded occasionally, and squirrels scolded overhead.

When dusk fell, Gaetan showed no sign of stopping to make camp. Katherine resigned herself to another night weaving through the forested hills with only shadowy light from a half moon to guide them, but to her surprise Gaetan led the way down the slope. Before long they rode on flat land. Splotches of moonlight showed that they rode parallel to and some distance from a rutted road. Edgy with concern, she peered into the night all around, searching for any sign of movement.

Unwilling to speak even in a whisper for fear the sound would carry to the enemies who used that road, Katherine kept all her questions locked inside, but she wanted to urge her horse forward, catch up with Gaetan and give him a hard pinch. What on earth were they doing here, and why hadn't he warned her?

Pinpoints of lamplight came into sight ahead. A town! He wouldn't risk entering a town for saddles, would he? No. She rejected the idea but couldn't find a better one.

They left the horses concealed in a dry wash before approaching the town on foot. Katherine couldn't stand it any longer. "Where are we going?" she whispered.

"To see the priest. We need to be ghosts in this place. No more talking."

Frustrated, Katherine kept quiet and followed as he skirted the town, keeping to the shadows of the adobe buildings. Less than a dozen buildings comprised the entire town. Only one showed signs of life—happy voices, whoops and guitar music—a cantina. Light glowed from a few other windows. Gaetan circled wide around the cantina and didn't stop until he reached a building distinguished from those around it by a cross on the roof.

Katherine almost jumped out of her skin when he left the shadows, walked to the door of the house next to the church and knocked. A short, heavyset Mexican woman opened the door after a second knock, showing no surprise at the sight of an Apache on the doorstep. When the woman stepped back, Gaetan pulled Katherine inside and closed the door behind them.

Heart racing, Katherine looked around the small room they had entered. A crucifix hung on one whitewashed wall, a plain wood chair stood behind a scarred desk.

"*Espera aquí,*" the woman said, putting the lamp she carried down on the desk and shuffling off toward the back of the house.

"What is this? What are we doing here?" Katherine said, keeping her voice as low as she could.

"The priest here is sympathetic to our people and will help us. I brought you here...." He broke off as a stooped, white-haired priest appeared.

"I'm Father Miguel Carillo, but I guess you know that. How can I help you two?" he said in Spanish. "I don't see any babies, so I guess you don't need a baptism. Marriage?"

Shock had Katherine staring at her husband wide-eyed as he answered in rusty, but easily understood Spanish, "My wife and I would marry in the way of your church."

The old priest all but rubbed his hands together. "Ah, that's a good thing. Now are either of you Catholic? Or even Christian?"

"I spent many years in St. Tilden's Indian Mission School, and they baptized me there."

Katherine's mind started working again. Gaetan hadn't exactly answered the question, but the priest didn't seem to notice the evasion.

"I was raised Presbyterian," she said, avoiding the unanswerable question of what religion she claimed now just as Gaetan had.

Father Miguel turned to her, amazement flooding his face. "You're American!"

"Yes," she admitted. "I suppose I still am."

The priest stepped closer, his tall frame stooping over further to stare at her features. "Holy Mother," he said. "You're her. You're the one everyone's looking for."

He rushed to his desk, yanked open a drawer and pulled out a stack of papers. Leafing through them, he pulled out first one stiff paper then another. "Here!" he said as if someone had argued with him and he now had proof he was right. "Katherine Grant. You're Katherine Grant."

She picked up the posters, one in each hand and held them in the lamplight so that Gaetan could see over her shoulder. Each one featured a reproduction of a photograph of her. "Can you still read as well as you speak Spanish?" she asked tartly.

He answered in Apache. Evidently now that the despised Spanish had served its purpose, he was through with it. "No. What do they say and how do they have a picture of you there?"

She waved one a little and set it down on the desk. "That one is a wanted poster put out by the Mexican government. It seems I'm wanted for questioning concerning the deaths of several Rurales in Sonora two years ago. I escaped in the company of a tall Apache. There's a reward of a hundred pesos, which strikes me as rather paltry."

As she read the second poster, Katherine's heart lifted. "'One Thousand Dollar Reward for information concerning Katherine Grant.' It describes me, hair and eye color, age and height. It says how I disappeared after the stage robbery and may have been taken by Apaches. And the person who put out this one is my brother. My brother Tom."

She didn't elaborate. Gaetan knew Tom was her youngest brother, the one she had been closest to growing up and who was in many ways her favorite.

"The address for contacting him isn't back in New York either. It's in Colorado. It reads as if he lives in Colorado. Tom didn't love the sea like Mark and Father. I wonder if he's really out here or if he has someone taking mail for him at this address."

Switching to Spanish, she asked the priest, "Was it my brother who gave you this?"

"No. The young man who gave it to me was Mexican. He led a donkey weighted down with these posters, and he said he had been paid to spread them in every town for miles around. He left one with me, one with the alcalde and one in the cantina. He said others were doing the same in other places."

"That sounds like Tom," Katherine said. "If he set out to do something, he'd do it thoroughly."

Gaetan touched her image on the poster. "How can they make a picture of you there?"

The photograph had been taken on the occasion of her betrothal to Henry Dumont, and Katherine had no intention of mentioning that event.

"I don't understand the process either, but I sat for that photograph back home about a year before I left. My family would be able to do whatever it takes to get these made." She tapped the wanted poster. "I don't know how they did that either, but I'm sure they used Tom's poster to make this one somehow. No one in the family would give them my photograph."

Turning to the priest, Katherine apologized. "I'm sorry, Father. It's rude of us to speak in Apache like this in your home."

Father Miguel had recovered from his initial surprise at her identity. "I can't believe that I'm the one who found you, but now that I have, we'll have to decide how to get you back to your family."

"No, I'm afraid not, Father. I'm married now and not going back to my family, but before we leave here, if you would be so kind as to let me have paper and pen, I'd like to write to my brother, and I know he'll pay you or your church the reward when he receives the letter. Other than that, all we need is marrying."

As she said the last words, Katherine leaned back just enough to touch Gaetan's arm and smiled over her shoulder at him.

"I can't do that. You know I can't marry you to a...."

His voice dwindled as he stopped himself from saying anything insulting, but the meaning hung in the air, not needing words.

A flash of temper stronger than she'd felt for over a year surged through Katherine. "Because I'm Presbyterian?" she said, not hiding the anger.

The priest opened his mouth as if to answer, then said nothing.

Katherine said to Gaetan in Apache. "The priest isn't really sympathetic, and he has no courage. He's no better than the Rurales. It's a beautiful gift you would give me, and maybe one day we'll come across a real man of God. Let's go."

Gaetan nodded, but the look on his face made Katherine start calculating how to get him out of the room with the priest still alive.

"Miss Grant."

She tore her eyes from Gaetan long enough to glance at the priest.

"I understand enough Apache to know how you shame me. Stay. If you truly want to marry, let me get Elena and her husband as witnesses, and I'll marry you."

Was his motivation shame or the thought of losing a thousand dollar reward? And would he try to collect the insulting, small reward of the Mexican government too?

Gaetan proved his mind worked along the same path when without a word he shifted his rifle to cover the priest.

"I'll get Elena and her husband," Katherine said. "You stay here and get to know my husband."

By the time she returned with Elena and Juan Sandoval, Katherine had herself talked into imputing only the best motives to all concerned. After all it was her wedding day—night.

In her opinion the ceremony in the empty little room was beautiful. The priest spoke in Spanish. She and Gaetan spoke in Apache, and for the first time she heard Gaetan speak the word "love," even if only as a ritual part of what he had once called hard promises. They *were* hard promises, and he was giving them to her.

When all the words had been spoken, she watched the priest make a record of the marriage in a small book he took from under a larger one in the desk drawer.

"You keep separate records for ceremonies such as ours, Father?"

"Yes, I do. Castigate me if you will, but the government would imprison me if they knew, and if the church didn't excommunicate me, it would at least defrock me."

After folding the marriage certificate and tucking it inside the pouch at her waist as if it were a holy relic, Katherine sat at the priest's desk and wrote her letter to Tom.

My dearest brother,

I am in a small Mexican town called Cavispa, where Father Miguel Carillo showed me both the poster you distributed in your search for me and a wanted poster of the Mexican government.

Tom, I am safe and well and happy. Apaches saved me from stagecoach robbers intent on my murder, and I have lived with them since that time. I married a wonderful man in the way of his people last year, and Father Miguel married us in the way of our people tonight. If you could meet my husband you would agree he suits me in ways no other man ever could. My life is with him and his people now.

You must know that I only did what I had to when the Rurales took me and an Apache companion prisoner. They intended us unspeakable harm. I believe what we did to escape them would be found justified by any jury in the United States, although I have no such hope for a trial in this country and will do everything possible to avoid such unhappy circumstance.

Please pass on my news and my love to Father, Mark, Peter, Lewis, George, and Aunt Meg. I pray that you are all well and happy.

I have assured Father Miguel that in return for delivery of this letter, you will pay him the reward you offered, whether for himself or for his church, as he wishes. I know you will do that, Tom.

Your loving sister,
Katherine

Finished, she read the letter out loud in English to Gaetan. She had no doubt if English was unknown to the priest, he would find someone to translate for him before sending the letter.

"Is that all right?" she asked Gaetan, sticking with English. "I'm not giving anything away I shouldn't am I?"

"It's good. Give it to the priest. We need to go."

"Do I need to tell him if he betrays us, I'll make sure he never gets a dime of the reward even if I have to walk to Colorado myself?"

Gaetan simply shook his head, and the look on his face was in truth enough to keep any wagging tongue still. She stifled an urge to throw her arms around his neck and kiss him in front of the priest and his servants, folded the letter and handed it to the priest.

"*Gracias, Padre.*"

Back at the horses, Katherine stopped resisting the urge and kissed her husband thoroughly. "Thank you. That's the most beautiful gift anyone has ever given me."

"I thought there were other things you liked very much."

"Ah, there are, but those things are different, aren't they? Were you really baptized Catholic?"

"They poured water over everyone they got hold of as soon as they could. To save our souls they said. And when I could understand English, I heard them talking about how Indians probably didn't have souls, but it was better to baptize us just in case. Of course the Chiricahua don't expect to see anyone except other Apaches in the next world either."

"If there is a next world, it's probably going to surprise us all. Right now I'm happy with this life. I'm happy with the gift of hard promises."

He held her against him for a moment. "They're hard promises for you also."

"No, nothing about being your wife is hard for me."

Nothing except knowing she couldn't plan to grow old beside him. Speaking of it would only make him turn away and replace a little of the joy in her heart with pain. She kissed him again.

"The priest has never betrayed one of the people, but no one has ever given him the chance," Gaetan said, turning from her and untying his horse. "If we ride all night, we can be out of Mexico early tomorrow, but you'll be very sore."

"Better sore than sorry," Katherine said. "I don't want to ever see another Mexican soldier up close."

23

Katherine's nerves jangled the whole time she camped alone while Gaetan rode onto the reservation even though her location could not have been more ideal. A wall of brush concealed the entrance to the small box canyon, an eroded section of one steep wall allowed for escape on foot, or she could bring rifle, pistol, or knife to bear on an enemy.

Most important, she was a free citizen of the United States and in her own country, yet none of it mattered. She knew too much about the government, its resources and its determination, and the territory was crawling with soldiers hunting hostiles.

Mexico's Apache policy had been extermination for hundreds of years, and Mexico had never achieved its goal. Except for a few renegade bands like Bácho's, the United States had succeeded in killing or imprisoning its native tribes in less than a single century.

Gaetan returned on the fourth day. He rode comfortably on a cavalry saddle. A second saddle sat atop the pack of the army mule he led. The mule and supplies hadn't been gifts from Apaches on the reservation any more than the saddles, but Katherine didn't ask how Gaetan had come by them, and he didn't burden her with the information.

She adjusted the stirrups on the second saddle and cinched it in place, happy to have it. "So where are we going?"

"Northeast toward Ojo Caliente."

Going to the old home of the Chihinne sounded dangerous to Katherine. When the government abolished the reservation at Ojo Caliente and forced Victorio to go to San Carlos, it had set the stage for his final, desperate war with the United States.

"Bácho and the others have gone back there? How can they hide there?"

"Not there. In the mountains of the Black Range between here and there. Only a few of the people are with him. Nana and Geronimo are off the reservation and raiding, and the warriors joined them."

"Lupe? Echo?"

"I talked to Echo. She's on the reservation and will stay there. Her eyes are very bad. Itsá and Lupe are with Bácho."

She relaxed at the news. Better that Echo stay safe on the reservation than try to keep up with the last of the fugitives, and the thought of seeing Lupe again lifted Katherine's spirits enough.

Over the next days they traveled swiftly but cautiously, staying high along the ridges when possible, crossing open ground at night. Gaetan often left her with the horses and scouted ahead on foot. Twice they hid for half a day until army patrols left the area.

Although he sometimes studied the ground or the land around them intently, he never hesitated over which direction to take. The thought of knowing a land so vast in such detail confounded her, even though she had grown up around sailors who knew the sea as intimately.

They didn't find the people. Itsá found them. He called out before stepping out of cover, rifle across his chest, quiver and bow on his back. "It's good to see you again," he said. "We thought maybe we wouldn't."

Neither he nor Gaetan showed much emotion, but they didn't hide their pleasure at seeing each other again either.

"The Mexicans shot my wife to stop her from killing more of them," Gaetan said. "So we had to spend the winter in Mexico."

The words caused Itsá to spare Katherine an approving glance. "There are fewer of us here. Everyone will be glad to see you—and the mule and what it carries."

He led the way to the Apache camp, and Katherine looked around in dismay. Just eight wickiups sat in the small mountain vale. Only the remote location and vigilance would protect the camp; the trail in wasn't difficult. Then again maybe that was an advantage. Reliance on the difficult access to the village in Mexico had proved disastrous in the end.

People began gathering, their faces set in the same impassive expressions she had first seen two years before. The differences struck her too, shabby clothing, thinner faces, slumped shoulders. She didn't care. Even if they were few and showing the effects of constant harassment by the governments of two countries, they were her husband's people, and she was home.

Spotting Lupe, Katherine called out. She couldn't get off her horse fast enough. She ran to the smaller woman and hugged her hard, laughing.

"I shouldn't do that, should I," she said, letting go. "I should stand back and pretend I'm only moderately pleased to see you instead of dancing with joy."

Lupe smiled. "I'll dance with you. One of the warriors said he saw you fall and saw Gaetan carry you away. When winter passed, and we didn't see you, we were afraid for you both."

"I was shot in the leg. I have an impressive scar, but my husband is a very good doctor and an even better nurse." She couldn't resist winking and was surprised when Lupe laughed out loud, her eyes aglow with an inner light.

Katherine examined her friend from head to toe. Unlike the others, Lupe didn't look thinner. "You had the curing ceremony," Katherine exclaimed. "You had the ceremony, and it worked!"

Color washed across Lupe's cheeks. "Sssh. I think so, but I'm not sure yet."

The women of the camp used the supplies on the mule and the mule itself to prepare a feast that night, and for a while everyone relaxed, enjoyed food in filling quantities and told stories of the old times. Katherine counted twenty-four people, including children. Men like Bácho and Itsá headed the half dozen families, men so determined to stay free they had accepted an impoverished life of hiding and evasion.

Late that night Katherine sat beside Lupe across the fire from their husbands, listening to serious talk.

"I think a few people could hide in the mountains in Mexico so well, they'd never be found," Itsá said. "We never would have been found there except for the one who led the raids bringing the soldiers to us. We'd have to live in the old way, without the things we like from the whites and Mexicans." He lifted his cup, half full of the first coffee any of them had drunk in many months, as if for a toast. "If no one raided, not even the small raids you do far away, they'd never notice us."

Gaetan shook his head. "In the old days, the people traveled all over to gather food in season. Hiding in one place, how can you gather enough to live on?"

Lupe said nothing, but she didn't look happy to Katherine, who decided there was no reason to keep quiet. "Would you farm? Could that make the difference?"

Itsá looked thoughtful, but Gaetan said. "How much grows high in the mountains? The Mexicans do their farming down below."

"I don't know," Katherine admitted. "My people aren't farmers, and I never tried to grow anything."

"It's something we can try," Itsá said. "If I have to, I'll fight to the end beside you before I live on the reservation taking orders from those who killed my son, but if there's a way to escape them, I choose to do that." He glanced at Lupe but didn't say anything about the possibility of another child. "You won't come back to Mexico with us if we go?"

"We may go back to Mexico, but I can't live the way you want to. I'll fight them until they kill me."

Katherine worked at controlling her face Apache-style instead of weeping like the weak white woman she was. Knowing hard promises changed nothing was one thing. Hearing him say it was another. She felt Lupe's hand in hers and took hold, the two of them taking comfort from each other in the face of the destructive determination of their men.

"My wife fears the loneliness. I hope to convince at least one other family to go with us, but we'll go before fall, even if we go alone. By then maybe the soldiers will be back in their forts."

"Only if they think they have everyone rounded up and on the reservations," Gaetan said.

"They don't know about us. They're after Geronimo and Nana."

"They're after anyone they can find. If they stumble on us, they'll settle for us."

Itsá threw the last of his coffee at the fire, the hiss of the liquid emphasizing his anger. "We'll live in the old way, and they won't find us. I know this."

He rose and stalked off, and Lupe hurried after him.

"I'll have to talk to her," Katherine said. "Living alone with you this last winter wasn't exactly a hardship, and I think she has strong feelings for her husband too."

Gaetan got up and stretched, and Katherine watched him hungrily.

"He's a good husband, but I'm a *very* good husband. That makes a difference."

He planned to leave in the morning, off again on his single-handed war against the forces of an entire country. She wanted to glue him to her and knew she had to let him go without protest, so she put aside her fears and worries and laughed. "You are an extraordinary husband, but as a modest Apache wife, I don't make others feel bad by boasting. At least not very often."

He pulled her close, ran his fingers through her hair, and cupped the back of her head in one hand before closing his mouth over hers. For a little while, Katherine's world had no room for fear or worry.

SPRING GAVE WAY to summer, and life progressed in familiar patterns. Gaetan traveled far from where the people hid, continuing to make war and raid, and he still brought back the kind of goods that were staples in the white world but luxuries to people who couldn't get such things any other way. Working with the other women gathering, preserving and storing food for the winter tired Katherine out enough she slept at night instead of lying awake worrying. Most of the time.

Itsá continued to work at convincing at least one other family to go back to Mexico and live an invisible life there. Katherine hated the constant fear and the strain of the precautions they all took now, and she tried to reassure Lupe.

"Last winter when Gaetan and I were alone was better than this. If I could talk him into going with you, I would. We were careful, but not like this. There's more than enough food still in the caches to keep a good many people through a winter without hardship, more than one winter for two people."

Lupe wasn't reassured. "You stayed in the valley with the ghosts?"

Katherine had forgotten her husband not only ate bacon but didn't share his people's fear of ghosts. "No," she said. "We stayed up on the mountain, out of the valley, and the caches are up there too."

The expression on Lupe's face said "up on the mountain" wasn't far enough, but if she needed extra food to support her baby during a lonely winter in the Sierra Madres, she might change her mind, and at least Katherine had planted the seed.

In late summer the people ventured out of the shelter of the mountains to gather mesquite beans after the scouts made sure there were no soldiers in the area. Katherine worked side by side with Lupe. Knowing the men were keeping watch, they felt safe and relaxed for a change. Until the cry came.

"Soldiers! From the east! Soldiers!"

Like all the other women, Katherine dropped her basket. Unlike the others, she grabbed her rifle before running for the hills to the west. More men in blue charged from those hills, and from the north and from the south. Gunfire added to the confusion.

In minutes it was over. Less than two dozen people on foot, most armed only with knives, were surrounded by twice their number of cavalrymen. The people stood quietly, knowing what came next.

Katherine didn't know, but she had an idea. She dropped the rifle in the bushes and the gun belt at her waist after it.

Rearranging the calico scarf holding her hair out her face to cover her head entirely, she caught up her loose hair and tucked it under the back of her blouse.

"Tell them you're white," Lupe whispered. "They'll treat you better."

"No," Katherine said. "They'll figure it out soon enough. I'm staying with you as long as I can."

She knew from stories she'd heard of past roundups that the few men would be separated from the women and children, and Itsá would be unable to stay with his pregnant wife.

The soldiers were black—buffalo soldiers—the officers white, but several other mounted men caught Katherine's eye.

"There are Apaches with them! In uniform," she whispered to Lupe.

"Yes," Lupe whispered back. "Without them the army would never find us. They're traitors."

The soldiers lined the people up and searched them one by one. Katherine kept her eyes almost closed and her head down as a soldier ran rough hands over her in a way no man should be allowed. The urge to kick him to Texas almost overwhelmed her. Two years ago she could never have forced herself to endure such handling, but she didn't want to give these men any reason to take a second look at her, and they didn't.

Watching them search Itsá and the other men, Katherine found herself praying they'd endure it without trying to fight and thanking heaven that Gaetan wasn't here. No one had been killed or even hurt badly—yet.

Some part of Katherine had never completely accepted the Apache stories about the army. After all, people always saw their own side of things and exaggerated. In the days that followed, Katherine saw for herself.

Their destination was San Carlos, hundreds of miles to the west. Day after day, the soldiers herded the Apaches like livestock over the rugged, hot country. She thanked Ussen for the fact no family had a baby still in a cradleboard and took her turn carrying Ya-kos and other small children when their legs gave out.

Several supply wagons accompanied the cavalry. No Apache, young or old, rode so much as a minute in one. Except when they came to water, water rations were stingy. She doubted any soldier ate the weevil-infested food issued to the Apaches. Men and women alike had to squat to relieve themselves in full view of everyone. The women had an advantage in that skirts provided some modesty.

When the forced march started, Katherine sympathized with her husband's people. Long before it ended a fire burned in her belly, and she had become a partisan.

24

AT THE RESERVATION, the troopers herded the people into a stockade. The only times they would be out of the direct rays of the relentless sun would be morning and afternoon when the fence would provide a little shade. They first entered the corral at midday and sat along the fence. Sitting still under the brutal sun should be easier than walking in it, but for Katherine sitting still only allowed for more fuming and worrying.

Hours later the gate opened and a trooper carried two pails of water a few feet inside and left them. No cup, no dipper, just two pails. Rage rose at the back of Katherine's throat until she almost choked on it. Watching the Apaches calmly take turns drinking small amounts from cupped hands and helping the children enabled her to regain control, but the anger continued to burn deep inside.

The next morning another trooper brought two more pails of water and retrieved the empty ones. Another threw salt pork and hardtack into the dirt. The soldiers left. No one touched the food except the flies.

Katherine had believed during her time with Tliish she learned everything there was to know about filth. Now she found out she'd only had an introduction to the condition.

By the third day, the people with children were giving in, taking enough food to stop the hunger cramps in the little ones. Bácho's wife came to where Katherine sat beside Lupe.

"Tell the soldiers you're white. You don't belong here."

Katherine understood the resentment and anger in the woman's eyes. Her own desire to lash out at someone, anyone, grew stronger every day.

"I do belong here. I'm Gaetan's wife."

"No longer. They'll take you away. He'll be free of you."

Katherine fingered the buckskin pouch at her waist where the precious marriage certificate lay concealed.

"No. Nothing will part us except death. Soldiers can't do it, and neither can you."

The old woman spit in the dirt and went back to her daughter. The fact none of them could work up a decent amount of saliva spoiled the effect of the gesture but didn't mask the ill will.

Lupe said, "She's wrong to be angry at you, but she's right that you should talk to the soldiers. You can't help us, so you should make them treat you better."

"I'm worried about you."

"I'm fine. They'll punish us for a few more days and then they'll put numbers around our necks and take us out somewhere on the reservation and tell us to live there."

Katherine almost laughed at Lupe's matter of fact tone. "And then you'll throw up a shaky wickiup and pretend to settle in until the soldiers look the other way and take off again."

"Yes. And my husband will take us to Mexico, and we'll live there the way he thinks will be safe."

Shadows of fear and loneliness flitted across Lupe's face as she talked of it. Katherine wished she could make those shadows disappear and knew she couldn't.

"You'll like it more than you think you will. Being alone with a good husband is—good—and you'll have a son or daughter soon."

Lupe stared into the distance, disbelief clear on her face as it always was when the subject came up. She was a woman of a tribal people and would never be happy alone. Katherine wondered if, in the end, Itsá also would find what he proposed to do too lonely.

That evening, half an hour after placing the water buckets and leaving, the guards returned to the corral and searched faces.

"There. That one." The shorter of the two pointed straight at Katherine, and she got to her feet, resigned and wondering if Bácho's wife or someone else had managed to get word to them.

When the men reached her, the short one grabbed her by the arm and chin. "She's got to be at least half white. Look at them blue eyes."

Katherine jerked her head away. "Get your hands off me."

The young soldier jumped back as if he'd been burned. "Jeez, no matter what they did to her, she can still speak English."

"Yes, and since you're going to take me out of here no matter how I feel about it, I have a lot to say, so let's go see whoever's in charge of this place."

Without turning from the men, Katherine said in Apache. "If you see my husband before I do, tell him I'll find him as soon as I can get away."

Bastian Greville, the agent for the reservation, regarded Katherine with a jaundiced eye even before she launched into a furious denunciation of his treatment of the Apaches. After she warmed up, his long narrow nose and chin whiskers started to tremble.

"I don't need a murderess criticizing me," he said.

Katherine crashed to a halt mid-tirade. "I'm not a murderess," she said in a lower voice.

Greville pulled the poster from the Mexican authorities from a drawer and slapped it down on the desktop. "Traveling in the company of Apaches. You should have sought different traveling companions long ago, Miss Grant."

Sick fear squeezed her throat. Could he hand her over to the Mexicans or would there have to be court proceedings? "Anything I did was self-defense."

Happy to have gained the upper hand, the agent sneered at her. "I'm sure it was. You can discuss it with men of our army. I'm sure their sympathies will lie with their Mexican counterparts."

"It wasn't the Mexican army, it was...." Katherine broke off. Mounting a defense here would be useless. Better to find a way to reach her family, marshal her arguments and be ready to give a coherent defense to whoever would make an extradition decision.

"Is there a telegraph here? I'd like to contact my family."

"Thanks to your Apache friends, our line is down again. You can talk to Colonel Sandlin at Fort Apache."

Riding to the fort in a creaking wagon, Katherine stayed alert for any opportunity to escape. If only the young soldier doing the driving were her lone escort! Stuck on the wagon seat next to her filthy, stinking self, he all but leaned off the seat and kept his face averted as much as possible. The driver was not on his own, however. Four outriders accompanied the wagon, two cavalry troopers and two Apache policeman.

Long ago she had admired John Clum's description of how he started an Apache police force on the reservation during his time as agent. Now, she heartily wished John Clum had been a twin of Bastian Greville in every way. Escaping the troopers might be possible. Katherine had no illusions about the ability of the Apaches to track her even if she managed to disappear while their attention was diverted.

The sight of the fort reminded her of the anger and indignation she had loosed on Greville and helped her ignore the fear freezing her hands and feet on a warm day. The army had obviously appropriated the best land it could find for itself while banishing the Apaches to the worst.

Flowers bloomed brightly around the houses they passed, attesting to both fertile soil and plentiful irrigation water. Older log buildings looked to be giving way to frame buildings with board siding. Pine covered hills around the site would provide enough lumber for either.

The troopers escorted her to what she recognized as the headquarters building. One spoke to an officer near the door, who raked her with curious eyes.

"Wait here."

He returned moments later. "Take her on back. He wants to see her himself."

Colonel John Richard Sandlin's office was large and comfortably furnished. A limp flag hung on one bare wood wall, a map on another. Sandlin stayed seated at his desk as Katherine and her escorts entered, his head bent over the papers in front of him.

The troopers waited at attention. Katherine moved to one of the chairs facing the desk and sat down without invitation. The colonel raised his head, his nostrils flaring as he appraised her.

"Did she cause any trouble?"

"No, sir."

"Good. Find Sergeant Maguire for me and ask him to wait outside. After that you can return to your regular duties."

Something about the hard set of Sandlin's mouth under the curving sandy mustache told Katherine he had already made up his mind about her. Neither meekness nor a play for sympathy would get her anywhere, which ratcheted her nerves up a notch but made things easier.

After the door closed behind the men, she said, "I'm sorry not to meet you in a cleaner, sweeter-smelling condition, but your men haven't been generous with drinking water. They certainly haven't provided for bathing."

The colonel pulled the accursed wanted poster from under the other papers on his desk, turned it so she could read it and pushed it toward her. "Miss Grant."

She didn't reach for the poster for fear her icy hands might shake and betray her. "Does it make any difference to you that because the Commandant of the Rurales didn't know I speak Spanish, he spoke freely to his men in my presence, and he intended me great harm? If I hadn't escaped, I'd be dead by now, dead in a most unpleasant manner. I believe what I did was self-defense."

"And freeing an Apache captive as you made your escape so he could kill several more men, was that self-defense also?"

"They were torturing him, and I...." Her words tapered off. The man behind the cold gray eyes wasn't going to listen. Anything she had to say would just make him more contemptuous.

"You're right not to waste your breath, Miss Grant. No, I don't believe the Rurales would harm an American woman they rescued from Apaches or torture anyone, although considering what the Mexican people have suffered at the hands of the Apaches, it would be hard to blame them. Fortunately for you, I'm not on a jury."

The poster didn't have so much detail on it. He must have communicated with the Mexican authorities about her. She struggled to keep her breathing even, to keep him from seeing fear.

"More fortunately for you," he continued, "our government would be reluctant to extradite an American woman to Mexico for a murder prosecution under any circumstances. And of course your family has been very busy bringing every ounce of its considerable influence to bear to harden that reluctance to resolve. I've heard from superiors on the matter several times."

Katherine sagged back against the chair, light-headed with relief. No wonder the colonel had investigated the charges and her further. Her family could be persistent. Once the shaky feeling passed, she couldn't help but ask, "Was my father here? Or my brothers? Did you meet them?"

He pulled out a second piece of paper, turned it and pushed it toward her in the same manner as the first. "Your brother was here. He insisted on seeing me to give me this personally."

The second poster was the one Tom had distributed. "Tom was here? He gave you this himself? How was he? Is he really living in Colorado now?" Katherine couldn't hold back the tumble of eager questions.

For a moment she thought he might refuse to tell her. Finally he shoved both posters into a desk drawer and answered civilly enough.

"He seemed well, although he told me your family is devastated by what you've done. I wonder what they'll make of you walking hundreds of miles on foot with Apaches and sitting in filth in a stockade rather than speaking a few words to any one of my men and starting back on the road home as soon as possible. I've heard of women who never had the courage to look up after surviving Indian captivity. You don't seem to have that problem."

Katherine not only had the courage to look up but to study him. The sandy hair and slim build would make him look younger than his years except for those cold eyes and the deep grooves on each side of his mouth that hinted at a disapproving nature.

"Once I explain everything that happened, my family will understand," she said. "Until I saw those posters, I expected they had given me up for dead."

"Yes, I imagine surviving captivity with Apaches for over two years takes great skill."

Understanding what he implied and recognizing the distaste in his expression, Katherine laughed out loud, still a little giddy to know courtrooms, trials and prison weren't looming in the immediate future.

"Surviving the Apaches was the easy part. Surviving the stage robbers and the Rurales was the hard part. I can see you don't want to deal with me, Colonel. If you aren't going to turn me over to the Mexicans, why am I here? I'm of age, and I'm not Apache, so you have to treat me like a human being. I'm not wanted for anything in the United States. Why don't I just walk out of here, and you can forget you met me?"

She started to get to her feet.

"Sit down, Miss Grant."

Katherine sat and waited.

"With anyone who has gone through what you have, there's a question of competency. I think it behooves us to keep hold of you until your family can take you in charge."

The thought of seeing Tom again, spending time with him and having help finding Gaetan appealed to Katherine enormously. "Good. Send Tom a wire, and I'm sure he'll be here in a few days. You probably even qualify for the reward." She didn't try to keep the contempt out of her voice over the last.

"Members of the military do not accept rewards for performing their duty," he said stiffly, "and having met your brother, I don't believe one so young is an appropriate guardian for you. I'll write your father."

Katherine stared at him in disbelief. "Write? My father is likely to be on the other side of the world and not in this country for months, a year even. A letter addressed to him will sit until he gets back. At least his secretary would try to reach him with information in a wire, but that's ridiculous. Wire Tom."

Satisfaction flitted across Sandlin's face. "I wouldn't trust you to anyone of lesser stature than your father, Miss Grant. You'll be staying here with us until he comes for you, and I'd strongly advise against trying to escape from us the way you did the Rurales." His smile said he'd love to see her tried in an American court for attempting that very thing.

So, forbidden to turn her over to the Mexicans and resenting the fact, he was taking it upon himself to punish her. Katherine got to her feet. "I understand completely, Colonel. I'm sure I'll be very happy here."

She started for the door.

"You will wait for an escort to your quarters, Miss Grant, and before I summon Sergeant Maguire, perhaps you'd like to tell me where you saw those posters previously."

"Mr. Greville showed them to me at the reservation."

"He says you showed no surprise."

How could he know...? "So he lied to me. There's no problem with the telegraph there."

Sandlin shrugged. "I'm sure he felt it was necessary. Where did you see the posters?"

How nice that the colonel appreciated necessary lies. "One of the Apaches found them somewhere, recognized my picture and brought them to me."

"Ah, and was there one of the Apache bucks who considered you his—wife?"

"Yes."

"His name?"

"Chishogi. He was killed by the Mexican army last fall." Much as she hadn't liked Chishogi, Katherine threw a mental apology to his spirit as she said it.

"No others?"

"No."

"I see."

No, he didn't, but that was all right. Escaping from a man who couldn't see would be easier.

GAETAN MOVED ACROSS the reservation with as much caution as if in Comanche or Ute country. When he had returned to the camp in the Black Range, he knew immediately what had happened. The only surprise was that after surrounding the people, the soldiers hadn't attacked and killed as many as possible before forcing them to surrender. Even before Victorio's last desperate campaign, the U.S. Army had decreed that any Apache caught off the reservation would be shot on sight. He followed the trail to San Carlos.

Everything on the reservation looked barren and shriveled. The dusty surface of the parched earth puffed around the hooves of the horse and pack mule with each step. Stopping a polite distance from the wickiup where Echo lived with a widowed daughter, he called out, waiting to dismount until the old woman appeared and beckoned.

"So you're back, and you want to find your wife."

He didn't understand how Echo could know everything that occurred on the reservation and in the renegade bands, but he accepted that she did. "Have you heard? Do you know where Bácho and the others are?"

"I know where they are, but no one knows where Katherine is. The soldiers took her away, and no one has seen her since. I think the police know, but they don't say." Echo made a face as if she'd tasted her own black medicine.

Fear caused an unfamiliar clenching in his stomach, and his mouth tightened. Echo patted his cheek, not needing to see to know. "She's a strong woman. She'll be fine, and she'll escape them the same as she escaped the Rurales."

He turned to unload supplies from the mule. Maybe Echo spoke the truth, but why would Katherine need to escape from her own people? The Mexicans were the ones she feared. She smiled when she said the Mexicans would put her in prison or in front of a firing squad, but it was a tense smile because she believed it to be true. He had thought Echo would know where Katherine was, even hoped she would be here.

The unfamiliar fear began to transform into familiar blackness. Not knowing where she was, how she was, left a sick emptiness deep inside. If the whites kept her from him, he would leave a death trail from here all the way to the ocean she talked of so often.

25

KATHERINE'S PRISON CELL showed distinct signs of its origins as a storage shed, but that didn't make it any less formidable. She wasn't going through one of the log walls. The single window had no glass in the frame, but it did have iron bars bolted in place. Meek and obedient behavior might induce the guards to relax eventually, but for now knowledge of how she had escaped the Rurales kept them vigilant.

For furniture she had a cot and a chair, both so flimsy that breaking them over a man's head wouldn't do much more than make him mad. Thinking of madness, Katherine wondered how long she could stay in this stark little cell before she started raving. Or rotting.

The single advantage to her prison was its location. Through the open window came everyday sounds of life at the fort. Voices, marching boots, trotting horses, bugles. On the second day, when she heard female voices, Katherine started shouting.

"Help! I'm locked in here, and I need a bath. I'm filthy and bored. I need a bath. I need a book. I need to talk to a woman!"

The women's voices stopped immediately, and Sergeant Maguire, her jailer in chief, put in an angry appearance, his ruddy Irish complexion even redder than usual. "You need to be quiet. You can't be yelling and scaring people like that."

"Or what? You'll gag me? Beat me? Starve me? Or maybe you'll lock me up somewhere and just let me rot away? You tell Colonel Sandlin I'm going to keep yelling until I get to bathe, not just once either but regularly for as long as I'm locked up here. I want clean clothes, and I want a book or something to keep me from going crazy. If I go crazy, you'll be sorry."

She deliberately treated him to the smile that wasn't a smile. He gave her a hard stare right back before backing out of the room faster than usual. Katherine listened to the key turn in the lock and waited for the sound of the bar across the door dropping into place. It didn't come. In spite of his tough attitude, the red-haired sergeant could be rattled. What a nice thing to know.

The next time Katherine heard voices outside the door, one was a woman's. When the door opened, a small blonde old enough to be Katherine's mother walked in followed by a trooper carrying a wash basin and pitcher. Sergeant Maguire brought up the rear, providing grim escort and protection.

"I'm Colonel Sandlin's wife," the woman said. "I've brought you...." She looked at Katherine, looked around in dismay, and said, "Oh, dear, you need more than.... Oh, my, this won't do at all. You come with me."

Maguire blocked the doorway. "I'm sorry, ma'am, but you can't do that. She can't leave here."

The little woman tipped her head at the glowering Irishman. "That's ridiculous. She has to have exercise and air. I'll talk to the colonel."

The three of them disappeared, leaving the wash basin, pitcher, soap and a towel. The sound of the bar dropping into place outside never came. Katherine washed her face and neck, almost groaning with pleasure as the warm water sluiced across her skin.

Within the hour, Katherine stood in a back room off of the kitchen of Colonel Sandlin's quarters watching as a soldier poured one last bucket of hot water into a tub almost as beautiful as the one she had never stopped yearning for.

"I can't thank you enough," she said to Mrs. Sandlin. "I've dreamed of bathing in a tub like this again for more than two years."

The woman looked startled. "That's what you dreamed of? I would think...." A pink stain flushed across her pale cheeks. "Well. Now I'll leave you to it. Sergeant Maguire is guarding the door, but he'll stand to one side so he won't be able to see you. I'll be with the sergeant, and you can have every confidence in that."

Behind Mrs. Sandlin's back, Maguire rolled his eyes.

"These clothes ought to fit you well enough for now," Mrs. Sandlin continued, smoothing clothing folded over the back of a nearby chair. "Only Lieutenant Foster's wife is anywhere near your height, I'm afraid."

"I'm willing to wear a sheet like a toga if it's clean," Katherine said.

Mrs. Sandlin and the sergeant left the room, and Katherine hurried out of her filthy clothing and into the bath she had longed for. Bubbles floated on the water's surface. The fragrance of lilacs filled the warm air over the tub as she lathered the wash cloth and ran it slowly up and down an arm.

Images of Lupe and the others in the corral rose in her mind. She dropped the cloth, hugged her knees and wept.

"Miss Grant."

Katherine jerked her head up and wiped her eyes with the back of a soapy hand, the sting bringing more tears. "I'm sorry. I'll hurry."

"You don't have to hurry. I just wanted to be sure you're all right."

"Surely you're not supposed to be alone with me."

"Sergeant Maguire will be here in an instant if I so much as raise my voice." Wrinkling her nose with distaste, Mrs. Sandlin picked up the clothes Katherine had piled on the seat of the chair. "I'll have one of the men burn these."

A corner of the buckskin pouch peeked out from among the folds of dirty cloth.

"No! You can't have that."

Shouting in her panic, Katherine lunged to her feet in the tub with a slosh that cascaded water everywhere and yanked the precious pouch out of the astonished woman's grasp.

Maguire was in the room before Katherine finished shouting, rifle pointing at her as she stood naked in the tub clutching the pouch, soapy water dripping down her body. To her further humiliation, a whimpering sound she had never made before escaped her throat. She hunched back down in the water that was left, head bowed, doubled over to cover herself, but keeping a death grip on the pouch.

"Out. It was all a misunderstanding," Mrs. Sandlin said. "Out."

The colonel's wife made to follow Maguire out of the room with the dirty clothes still in her arms. "You wash," she ordered Katherine. "I'll be back as soon as I dispose of these to help you with your hair. Stop worrying about that—whatever that is. Is there anything else we need to preserve?"

"The moccasins please," Katherine whispered without looking up. "I don't want to wear shoes that don't fit."

Mrs. Sandlin dropped the moccasins on the floor and left without another word.

The rest of the bath was a chore, not a pleasure. Katherine submitted to Mrs. Sandlin's help with her hair and made no effort to hide herself from the other woman as she climbed out of the tub and accepted the proffered towels and robe.

Mrs. Sandlin chattered away about people and places Katherine didn't know or care about as she worked on the mass of damp hair until it hung smooth and tangle-free. Katherine recognized the kind intention to change the atmosphere in the little room, but her spirits stayed on the floor.

All she could think about was how happy Colonel Sandlin would be to know that for a few minutes at least, she had been reduced to the state he believed she should have been in to start with, ashamed to raise her head. The sooner she was out of here and back in her private prison, the better, even if it meant facing Sergeant Maguire.

Left alone to dress, she tied the buckskin pouch around her waist over the chemise, threw the corset and corset cover aside and put on the tall Mrs. Foster's dress over a single petticoat. The bodice was several sizes too large, the hem too short. Her moccasins covered the extra ankle. She almost laughed at the thought. As if a few inches of exposed ankle could matter after today.

"I'm ready to go now," she called out.

Mrs. Sandlin appeared in the doorway. "I indulge in a cup of tea at this time every day, Miss Grant. I would appreciate your keeping me company."

More chatter. Katherine appreciated the sentiment but didn't want to endure more chatter. "Your husband wouldn't want you talking to me, Mrs. Sandlin."

"As a matter of fact he specifically warned me against it, but when I explain, I believe he'll agree. Why don't you call me Emma Grace."

Following Emma Grace Sandlin to her kitchen, Katherine couldn't help but notice the absence of Sergeant Maguire.

"Where is he?" she asked, taking the indicated seat at a small table.

"Outside. And if it's any comfort to you, I told the sergeant if I ever hear so much as a hint that he has mentioned what happened today to another living soul, I will personally see that he is transferred to the most remote and hazardous outpost the army has at the time."

Such a grim threat from a small, maternal woman in a pink silk dress covered by a voluminous apron sparked a first tiny flicker of humor in Katherine. Right here in Arizona had to be as remote and hazardous a post as the army could offer. Maybe the whole incident would strike her as humorous—in ten or twenty years. "Thank you."

She accepted an oatmeal cookie and watched Emma Grace pour tea.

"My husband is a soldier. In a conflict between civilians and the Rurales, his sympathies are all with the Rurales. He also reacts very badly to political pressure. When you saw him he was already incensed about both of those things. I understand why you would want to keep the things that happened to you private, but he says you were insouciant and disrespectful. Why didn't you tell him that you were tortured and forced to do the things you did?"

Now it was Emma Grace who couldn't raise her head.

"When I first walked in his office, your husband made it clear his mind was made up, and he didn't want to hear anything I had to say. I was upset and angry over the way I was treated on the reservation and worried about extradition to Mexico. I wasn't about to beg for understanding, and I'm still not. And I wasn't tortured or forced to do anything."

"I saw the scars, Katherine. A blind woman couldn't miss seeing such terrible scars."

"Oh, those." Katherine hadn't even thought of the scars amid the overwhelming embarrassment. "Those scars are from bullet wounds. The one under my breast is from a Rurale bullet that suppurated, and my husband—well, he wasn't my husband yet, but still—my husband had to drain it. Of course he did the cutting with a knife and enlarged the wound, but he saved my life. The regular Mexican army gave me the scar on the leg. Your husband would applaud, I'm sure."

At the last words, Emma Grace's expression mimicked Aunt Meg at her disapproving best. "My husband is a good man."

"I'm sure he is," Katherine said in a tone that left no doubt she thought nothing of the sort.

"Will you tell me what's in that leather purse that you value so highly?"

If she refused, the good colonel would probably have his troopers not just looking at her body but putting hands on her to rip the pouch away and take the contents.

Unwilling to even contemplate that, Katherine got to her feet, raised the hem of her dress and petticoat, reached up and removed the precious certificate. Unfolding it with care, she placed it on the table.

"I love my husband. He gave me this as a gift. If you tell the colonel, he will cause terrible trouble for the priest and my husband."

Emma Grace stared down at the marriage certificate, eyes wide, mouth half open. "This isn't the name you gave my husband. You gave my husband the name of a dead man, not this name."

Ah, so the good colonel had investigated the name Chishogi. "The army is already hunting the Apaches the way my father does big game. I don't want them hunting my husband in particular. Will you tell the colonel?"

After pouring more tea and pressing another cookie on Katherine, Emma Grace finally said, "I don't keep secrets from my husband, but if he doesn't ask me the name, I see no reason to bring it to his attention."

Katherine refolded the paper, put it away and headed for the front door without asking permission. Sergeant Maguire followed her back to the log building in silence. As she crossed the threshold, he hesitated before closing the door behind her. "I'm sorry, Miss Grant."

"We're all sorry," she said and listened as the key turned in the lock and the bar dropped in place outside the door.

As Gaetan expected, soldiers were thick in the area where Bácho and his people had been settled. He visited Bácho under cover of darkness but not even dim firelight masked how much the old chief had aged since they'd last talked.

"I don't know if we'll leave here again," Bácho said wearily. "Sometimes I think there's no place left to go, and I'm not sure the hiding is any better than staying here."

If Bácho was broken and ready to give up, the end was no longer somewhere in the distant future but close. Knowing the enemy would win was one thing; knowing the victory would be soon was another. Gaetan pushed the thought away. The time didn't matter. When it came he would die fighting them as he had always planned.

Katherine's voice came to him on the heels of that thought as if she whispered in his ear. *Dying is easier than living sometimes.* When she had said those words, he felt as if she'd slapped his face, even though she wasn't speaking of him. The words still rankled. He wanted to argue with her. He wanted—her.

"Have you heard where the soldiers took my wife, Grandfather?"

Bácho frowned at him. "They probably gave her back to her people, the whites who live far to the east. You're divorced now."

"She's my wife. We'll never be divorced."

"She's back with the whites and will forget all about you. How long will you waste your time waiting for a woman who will never return?"

Gaetan didn't have an answer. She had given him the hard promises willingly. More than that, with joy. Would being back among the whites change her? He didn't want to believe it, but the calmness Katherine had given him was slipping away, the old rage searing through his belly. How long would he wait? How long could he?

26

KATHERINE SPENT THE next day alone with her thoughts and the book Emma Grace had given her. An unfamiliar soldier delivered meals and wash water. The day after that Sergeant Maguire came to escort her to Colonel Sandlin's office barely in time to stop her from more yelling out the window. After a single glance to check for smirks, Katherine walked with her head up and ignored the sergeant.

Colonel Sandlin sat behind his desk, his face and posture stiff. Emma Grace sat in one of the chairs facing the desk, red-eyed and clutching a handkerchief. In Katherine's opinion anyone married to a martinet like the colonel would need a large supply of hankies. Reluctant to bring more misery down on Emma Grace's head, Katherine waited politely until Sandlin pointed at the remaining unoccupied chair.

Silence stretched over the three of them until Katherine couldn't stand it. "Are you all right?" she whispered to Emma Grace.

"Me?" Emma Grace dabbed at her nose with the handkerchief. "Of course I'm all right."

"My wife becomes emotional when she discusses things about which she feels strongly, Miss Grant, and she feels strongly about you." Sandlin leaned back in his chair and crossed his arms over his chest. "We've reached the point where she's decided she'd rather live with our oldest son and his puritanical wife than a man of such a closed and miserably pinched mind as I. Therefore, I'm going to pry a small crack open in my pinched mind and listen to whatever fairy tale you have to tell."

"She told me you're a good man," Katherine said, hoping to soften the pinched mind a little.

"Did she? I don't imagine she expressed that sentiment in the last twenty-four hours."

Had she just glimpsed something other than ice in the gray eyes? "My husband bounces me on my bottom when he's reached his limit," Katherine blurted without thinking.

"Does he? The dead husband? How does he do that?"

Katherine snapped her mouth shut and tried to press deeper in the chair.

Emma Grace waved her handkerchief and said, "Don't let him do that to you. He already knows, and he agreed to hear your story long before we got to my opinionated daughter-in-law. What we've gone round and round over is whether I can sit in. He thinks you're going to play to his sympathy by telling terrible things I shouldn't hear. So please hurry and tell us before he changes his mind."

"Oh." Katherine wondered if he knew Gaetan's name and decided to proceed on the assumption he didn't. Rather than think of the name of someone else beyond the army's reach, she'd just go ahead and use Chishogi. After all, she'd already apologized to his ghost.

She started talking.

Two pots of tea, one pot of coffee and a half dozen slices of current cake later, Katherine finished the story. She only edited a little. These people didn't need to know everything, and she still didn't like Colonel Sandlin.

"What happened after we got to San Carlos is unconscionable," she said. "Is it your doing?"

"No," Sandlin said. "The agent is in charge of what happens on the reservation, but I won't claim I'd do anything different. We have to impress upon these people that they have no choice. They have to stay on the reservations and follow the rules."

"Why?" Katherine said. "What gives you the right?"

"The fact we're going to kill them if they don't. Be reasonable, Miss Grant. You had the protection of one of their people from the beginning. Without that you can't imagine the savagery you would have endured. We have to stop it."

"The savagery is on all sides so far as I can tell. People always give as good as they get. There was savagery in the Civil War, and the combatants were countrymen before and after."

"Nothing that happened in the late war...."

"Andersonville," Katherine said. "Fort Pillow."

Sandlin glared at her, but he didn't try to argue further. "I bow to the wisdom of you ladies," he said. "I'll have a wire sent to your brother today."

"Thank you." But Katherine looked at Emma Grace as she said it.

Itsá and Lupe showed the effects of hard times in a different way than Bácho. Itsá's face was tight with a fury Gaetan recognized. Lupe no longer looked sturdy and capable but fragile, as if she might blow away in a strong wind.

Gaetan unloaded the last of the supplies near the wickiup the couple had thrown up to further the illusion they planned to live on the reservation. He worked in silence until Itsá burst out with furious words.

"We scouted the area well that morning. There were no soldiers for miles in any direction. I'm sure."

"It can happen in the mountains. We've done the same to them many times."

Some of the tension left Itsá but not the anger. "We'll be safe in Mexico. If we hide well, we can live without being hunted all the time."

The Mexicans had been hunting Apaches hundreds of years before the Americans appeared, but Gaetan said nothing.

Before long the scent of coffee filled the air. Gaetan stirred a single spoonful of sugar in his coffee and asked the question that had brought him here. "Do you know what happened to my wife?"

Lupe's head came up, and a spark of her old spirit flared. "The soldiers took her. She hid from them and stayed with me all the way here and for the first days in the stockade, but then I think someone told the soldiers she was white because they came for her. They came just for her and took her away."

"No one knows where they took her?"

"First they took her to the agent. The police say she shouted at him, but then they took her somewhere else, and no one knows where."

Shouting at the agent sounded like Katherine. The agent must know where the soldiers took her. Maybe he even told them where to take her, and if he knew, he could be made to tell. Making him tell would cause the people on the reservation trouble, but still Gaetan tucked that piece of information away for future consideration.

"The last thing she said before they took her was for you. She said to tell you as soon as she got away from them, she would come to find you."

The fire that had burned hotter each day until it threatened to consume him, abated a little, but only a little. He took another swallow of coffee. Hearing what she had said was good, but she was still with his people then. She had been with the whites for many days now.

"One strange thing did happen the day they released us," Itsá said. "The police asked us if we knew of the man who led the raids from Mexico. They asked about him by his name, and they called him the husband of the white woman. They wanted to know if he really was dead, if the Mexicans killed him last fall."

The words stabbed right through Gaetan. Containing the swift surge of relief took effort.

"What did the people tell them?"

"That it's true. The Mexicans killed him last fall."

"What about the white wife?"

"No one knew of such a thing so we said nothing."

"Why would she tell them such a thing?" Lupe asked, showing she understood the source of the misinformation. "Why would she tell them a lie?"

"She's white. She thinks lying well is a good thing," Gaetan admitted. "This time she did it to protect me. She thinks if they know my name, they'll hunt for me. They don't want one of their women married to an Apache."

"Why would they care any more?" Itsá said, puzzlement on his face. "They took her away, and they won't let her come back, so she isn't married to you any more."

Yes, she is. Gaetan swirled the last of his coffee around the cup before swallowing it. Hearing Katherine's lie had calmed him almost as much as her presence.

"Killing me would be much easier than stopping Katherine," he said.

27

COLONEL SANDLIN'S capitulation was not total. Katherine spent the next days in the company of Emma Grace, but still under Sergeant Maguire's watchful eye. The door to the storage shed prison remained locked at night.

Tom arrived on the fifth day, covered with dust and beard stubble, nothing about his manner or dress hinting he'd been born east of the Mississippi. Katherine flew across the parade grounds at the sight of him, her arms around his neck before he made it all the way off the horse.

He lifted her in the air and swung her in a circle. To her surprise, when he put her down and held her away to look at her, she saw tears glinting in blue-gray eyes so like her own. Tears fell freely across her cheeks, but she was the girl.

"The next time you get mad at us all, do something less dramatic, will you, Kate?"

Katherine laughed at the sentiment and the nickname she had forbidden her brothers to use when she turned twelve.

"I don't think I could ever be mad at you again."

She endured quizzing about her health, state of mind and brown skin with good humor. The sight of him and sound of his voice delighted her.

"Oh, it's good to see you," she said when he slowed down. "I really didn't expect what you did. I thought you'd give me up for dead, not move to Colorado and paper the West with posters with my photograph."

"The whole family searched for hundreds of miles in every direction for months, and none of us ever gave up, but what happened to you was a catalyst. A lot things have changed. George is married."

"George! Who would think he'd be first. Where did he find a girl to put up with him?"

"In England. She's the third daughter of a third son of some blue blood or other, and George is going to take over as head of the London office when old Carruthers gives it up. He's apprenticing now. And Peter's turned landlubber too. He married one of the Bell girls, Amelia, and he's devoting himself to raising the best hunting dogs in the country."

Ah, Peter and his hunting dogs. *Stay! Heel!* More tears blurred Katherine's vision for a moment. "But the rest of you are still traveling the world?"

"Not me. When I saw the Rocky Mountains, I finally understood how Father feels about the sea. I have a ranch in Colorado, and it's home in a way nowhere else has ever been. You'll love it too, I know you will. It's so remote the nearest town is a hard day's ride away, but there's such beauty and *majesty.*"

Katherine examined him. Features she had always rued as too strong in her own face made Tom ruggedly handsome. All her brothers were tall, but Tom seemed taller than she remembered, broader in the shoulder and more confident than ever before. Her youngest brother had grown up.

"Is there more keeping you than the land? The fourth daughter of a fifth son maybe?"

The self-conscious grin that spread across his face answered before he did. "The first daughter of a rancher only half a day's ride away. My horse can make the trip on his own with me asleep in the saddle."

After introducing her brother and Sergeant Maguire, Katherine led Tom back to her prison to wash up at the washstand Emma Grace had insisted be added to her furniture. For the first time since he'd been assigned to watch her, the sergeant walked in a different direction. Knowing he would be reporting to the colonel in minutes didn't concern Katherine. She sat on her cot, watching as Tom splashed water in the basin, peppering him with questions about family and friends as he washed.

Finished drying off, Tom rolled his sleeves back down and buttoned the cuffs. He settled on the flimsy chair warily and changed to more serious subjects.

"Why are you here? This looks like a jail cell. What's going on, Kate?"

"*Katherine*," she said, done with nostalgia. "What did the wire say?"

"Just that you were here, you were fine, and I should come get you."

Katherine told him what was going on and watched his jaw clench and eyes narrow. "You wipe that look right off your face," she said sternly. "Waving family influence in Colonel Sandlin's face caused half the problem in the first place."

Before she could confess she caused the other half herself, Tom whooped with laughter. "I can't believe I lived to see the day! My sister telling me to ease off and tread gently."

She had to laugh with him, even if sheepishly. When he was ready to listen, she started the story from the beginning, and when she finished, waited for questions. He had only one. "You're going back to him, aren't you?"

"Yes. Will you help me find him?"

"Ah, Kate. Katherine. You're going to get yourself killed. How can I let you do that?"

"I haven't been any closer to being killed in the last two and a half years than in that big storm off Africa when I was ten and you were eight. For that matter the time I was standing behind Father when his rifle misfired just as the lion charged was pretty exciting."

Tom hung his head, and she kept quiet until he looked up. "I couldn't stop you if I wanted to, could I? Maybe it's time he met a brother-in-law. Can I meet him and live to tell about it?"

"Of course you can, but you won't like him, and he won't like you." She hugged him again where he sat. "Thank you. Thank you for searching for me so hard, and thank you for coming to rescue me right away, and thank you for helping."

"How are we going to find him?"

"We need to ask on the reservation, and I need your help for that. I lost my temper with the agent, and you'll have to smooth things over. Maybe I could slip onto the reservation and find the people I need without permission, but it would be easier with permission. I think the best thing would be to tell him I want to say goodbye to some of the Apaches I knew who helped me. I'm sure if you turn on the Grant charm you can sell him on that."

"So, a few fibs, a lot of charm, and you'll have your way?"

Katherine considered her brother a moment. "Maybe I'm wrong. Maybe you and Gaetan will become fast friends after all."

AFTER INTRODUCING TOM to the Sandlins, Katherine spent the afternoon adding to letters she had already written on Mrs. Sandlin's stationery.

The one to her father was longest and had been the most difficult to write. Although shorter, Aunt Meg's had proved the trickiest. Each letter to a brother brought a different joy. She gave all of them to Tom, including the one she had written for him.

"I didn't give anyone the whole story. You'll do that for me, won't you?"

"I will. I go back for a few weeks when they're in home port. That's one reason I got the telegram about you so fast. Everyone in town knows I'll make it worth their while to get family news to me as fast as possible."

After a dinner with the Sandlins marked with reserve on both sides, Katherine hugged Emma Grace goodbye. "I can't thank you enough," she told the other woman.

"I wish you'd plan on breakfast with us before you leave in the morning."

Katherine shook her head. "Tom has provisions with him. We'll be on our way before reveille."

"Well, you take care of yourself and have a safe trip home."

Colonel Sandlin gave Tom a stiff handshake and turned a perceptive eye on Katherine. "Let's not do this again, Miss Grant."

She gave him the smile that wasn't a smile, "I certainly hope not, Colonel Sandlin."

The sky had lightened but the first rays of the sunrise were half an hour away as Katherine finished dressing while Tom went to saddle the horses. Walking out into the shadowy world, she found two surprises waiting, a sidesaddle on the horse Tom had brought along for her and Sergeant Maguire holding the reins.

"I thought you'd be off to more important duties, Sergeant."

He bobbed his head in agreement. "That I am, but I wanted to wish you well, missus. Good luck to you."

Unable to answer immediately, Katherine accepted a leg up, hooked her right leg around the pommel, and finally met the sergeant's eyes, their bright blue already distinct in the strengthening light.

"Good luck to you too, Sergeant," she said thickly, and put her heel to the horse.

Tom caught up and reined in by her side. "What was that? Were you fond of the sergeant?"

"Not until now. He's the first person who ever called me 'missus,' and he did it on purpose."

"That just proves he knows where we're going. There's not much doubt Sandlin knows too. The question is will he try to stop us?"

"Maybe. If he does we'll just have to try another way." Katherine grinned at her brother. "If lying doesn't work, we'll sneak. And if sneaking doesn't work, we'll start shooting."

"Ah, come on, Kate. At least let me work in some family influence between the sneaking and the shooting."

She was almost glad enough for his company to let him get away with it, but not quite. "*Katherine*," she said.

Without Tom, Katherine wouldn't have had a prayer of inducing a particle of cooperation from Bastian Greville. The agent glared at her as he talked to Tom.

"What your sister needs is a husband with a strong hand, although I suppose it's too late for that. You need to get her back East and keep her there."

The only thing that enabled Katherine to sit still with her head bowed, her mouth shut and her hands folded in her lap was astonishment at the quality of Tom's performance.

His voice was somber and sorrowful as he replied. "Yes, sir. She's the only girl in the family and the baby at that, so I confess we spoiled her. You can bet on the fact that we won't be doing any more of that."

Bet the fortune you're making selling supplies meant for the Apaches, why don't you, Katherine thought with venom. *I'd love to cost you every dime.* Still, the fact that Tom was doing just fine with a few fibs of his own tickled her—the baby of the family reassigning his own position to her was a particularly clever touch.

"If any of them helped her, it was an accident, you know."

"I'm sure you're right. That's what everyone says about Apaches," Tom said solemnly, "but I can't stand the weeping. You know how it is. Giving a few savages some tobacco and candy won't hurt anything, and it will buy me a peaceful trip home."

"How are you going to take her in hand if she gets her way that easy now?" the agent said, his long nose twitching with suspicion.

"Oh, I won't," Tom said, boyish embarrassment all over his face. "That's a task for my father and older brothers. I just haven't the heart. She's so—broken." His voice fell to a whisper on the last word.

"That's an act. You should have heard her screeching at me no more'n a couple of weeks ago."

"That was before Colonel Sandlin was through with her." Tom's voice stayed low and mournful as if speaking of an untimely death. "He kept her in solitary confinement in a *prison* cell."

Katherine glanced up and caught the smug satisfaction that flashed across Greville's face, and the calculation as Tom added, "The whole Grant family would be *most* grateful for your help, sir, as I'm sure her godfather, Senator Brown, would be."

Her godfather, the grizzled sea captain who was her father's best friend, would be upset to find Senator Brown had replaced him. Katherine bent her head lower than ever and bit the inside of her cheek, struggling to hold onto her chastened expression.

In the end Tom wheedled permission to visit the Apaches of Bácho's band out of the reluctant agent.

"I know you wouldn't be giving them liquor," Greville said as he handed over signed permission, "but you remember they can't have weapons, ammunition, or money either."

"An excellent policy," Tom said. "I feel safer already."

Katherine choked down her laughter until they had ridden far enough to be out of earshot, and then she laughed until her stomach hurt. Years ago, Tom's inability to dissemble had given away many of their childish pranks and schemes. Thank goodness he had developed some of the family talents in the last years.

As they rode, she sobered. During the time at Fort Apache, she'd forgotten how miserable the land assigned to the Apaches was. Even this late in the season, the temperature had to be a hundred, the land barren and vegetation desiccated. The occasional gusts of wind didn't cool but bombarded with bits of sand and gravel.

To further soothe Greville's suspicions, Tom had asked for directions only to where Echo lived with her widowed daughter. They found the medicine woman in the shade of her wickiup grinding dried herbs.

After hugs and greetings, Katherine introduced Tom. Even though she had told him Echo only spoke Apache, he gave a courtly bow. "I'm pleased to meet you, ma'am."

Echo looked up at Tom with cloudy eyes. "He sounds like a nice man. Does he look like you, this brother?"

"He is a nice man. He's a wonderful man, and yes, he looks like me, but he's handsome."

"Good. Your husband has been here looking for you. You don't want him to think you have a white husband now."

A giddy relief surged through Katherine at the news. "He knows he's the only husband I'll ever have. When was he here? Will he be back? When will he be back?"

"He comes when he comes. He visits Itsá too, so you should go there."

"We will. Tell us which direction, and we'll go there right now, except...." She switched to English. "Tom, could you leave us alone for a little while? I need to talk to Echo."

Tom looked around the barren landscape. "Where could I go? I can't understand a word you're saying. Talk away."

Avoiding his eyes, she said, "Go for a walk, why don't you? She's a medicine woman, and I need to talk to her about something medicinal."

"For heaven's sake, if you're sick why didn't you say so when we were at the fort where there's an army surgeon. You're not going to let this old lady burn chicken feathers over you or something, are you?"

Katherine crossed her arms and waited.

"All right," he grumbled. "It's such a lovely day for a walk. I'll just go find a rattlesnake to admire."

As soon as he was a good distance away, Katherine sat beside Echo. "Something's happening to me I need to ask you about. Can a woman wish she could have a baby so much her body starts to act as if—as if it's happening?"

Echo patted her cheek. "Do you wish it that much?"

"Yes," Katherine whispered. "Every time he.... I think what a waste. I think a man like that should have children, but I couldn't bear for him to have a second wife either, and he can't do that. We made vows to each other, and he can't."

"You bleed sometimes?"

"Yes, a little, once or twice a year. The last time was in early summer. He was gone. I was glad he was gone when it happened."

"Hmm." Echo asked a string of questions so personal and so perceptive Katherine squirmed. "Do you feel anything inside? A flutter like butterfly wings?"

Heart pounding so hard she could feel it in her throat, Katherine said, "Sometimes in the last days, but it could be just from food, couldn't it?"

"Yes, food can disagree, but from all you tell me, I think you need to be good to yourself. You'll know for sure soon, but I don't think your body is lying to you."

"My aunt took me to doctors, and they all said it couldn't happen. Four of them said it."

"Pfft. White doctors." Echo waved a hand in the air, dismissing them all. "White men are all liars. Why would white doctors be different?"

Let her be right. Please dear Lord, let her be right, and I'll never tell another fib so long as I live. "You won't tell him, will you? Please don't tell him."

"You'll be sure soon. There comes a time when you know the butterfly wings aren't from food. You tell him then. Now you better get your brother back. He's not Apache, and the sun will kill him if he stays out there much longer."

28

Gaetan returned to Itsá and Lupe under the cover of darkness, still edgy and frustrated from his last encounter with white men no more than twenty miles from the eastern edge of the reservation. Usually if miners or settlers spotted him before he did them, he turned their clumsy attempts to hunt him down against them in most satisfactory and bloody ways. Today he had hidden and run rather than kill so close to the reservation and bring trouble on the people.

Staying close to the reservation undetected called for exceptional caution, and the necessity only added to the anger rising hotter in his belly every day. Before the building rage exploded, he needed to be so far away even the traitorous scouts couldn't track him and the army couldn't blame others for anything he did.

Maybe Bácho and Itsá were right. Being back with her own people had changed her. Maybe even if they were wrong, the soldiers had forced her to go back to New York, to the ocean, and her family would keep her there. His hand closed so hard over his rifle, the rear sight tore into his palm—an ordinary sight on an old, single-shot rifle, unlike those the whites had used against him today that fired many times in rapid succession without reloading.

He tied his horse to the only bush in the area large enough, walked closer to the wickiup and stood listening for any out of place sound. No fire glowed in the night, but reassuring scents of tobacco, coffee and beef came to him on the hot air, so he moved closer, called out.

Itsá's welcome confirmed no one else was about. Gaetan settled across from where the couple sat in the dark.

"The night's too hot for a fire," Itsá said, "but the coffee's still warm. The beef is from the agency, and it's bad, but we have more."

Gaetan accepted the coffee, turned down the food. The hunger that ate at him had nothing to do with food.

"She was here," Itsá said after the courtesies had been fulfilled.

Some of Gaetan's coffee spilled over his hand, an accident, nothing to do with the news. He put the cup on the ground so it couldn't happen again and kept his voice steady. "When?"

"Yesterday. She brought a white man with her. She says he's her brother." Itsá paused a moment before adding, "It's probably true. It's hard to tell with whites, but his hair and eyes are the same. He's tall."

Lupe said, "Of course he's her brother. He's the youngest of her brothers, and he's called Tom. The soldiers locked her up at Fort Apache. They wouldn't let her go until the brother came."

"My wife thinks he's handsome for a white man," Itsá said, teasing her.

"I do not," Lupe protested. "He's easier to look at than most of them is all. His eyes are like Katherine's."

Determined not to give away any of the feelings roaring inside his head, Gaetan picked up the cup and emptied the last of the coffee on the ground before asking, "Where is she now?"

"Maybe with Echo. When she left here she said that's where they were going, but I don't know if they stayed there. The agent gave them permission to visit some of the people, but I don't know how long she can stay."

Back at his horse, Gaetan clenched his jaw muscles so hard his teeth ached as he conjured up mental images of a tall, handsome brother, a brother who could find out where the soldiers took Katherine and who could make them let her go.

After a while, he untied the horse and walked toward the San Carlos River. Shallow and wide, the river wasn't a good place for bathing, but the brother would be clean. He would stink of strange odors like all whites, but he would be clean, and his clothes wouldn't have worn or ripped places. Instead of moccasins with soles almost worn through, he would wear glossy boots that shone in the sun.

Gaetan couldn't replace worn clothing tonight, but he could make the brother and everyone else understand Katherine was his. And he would be cleaner than any white man when he did it.

When he approached Echo's wickiup more than an hour later, a fire still burned in the night. Four shadows sat around it far enough away to avoid the heat. Scents of food hung in the air. The low rumble of a male voice mingled with higher female ones—Echo and her daughter, Katherine and the brother. Katherine's voice carried to him, light with laughter. In all the times he had pictured her in his mind over the many long days, never once had he pictured her laughing.

He walked into the circle of light from the fire and watched her until she saw him. Joy lit her face. She jumped to her feet and ran almost straight through the fire to get to him and wrapped herself around him in a way no Apache wife would or should. Against his will and everything he planned, he held her hard for a moment, buried his face against the place her neck and shoulder came together.

Her words were low in his ear, her voice thick with tears. "I was afraid. I missed you, and I was afraid. I love you so."

He said nothing, pushed her away and went to meet the brother.

The brother was on his feet by the fire. He wasn't that tall. Their eyes were level. His face was so hairy no woman could think him handsome.

He heard Katherine whisper to Echo. "What should I do?"

"Nothing," Echo said, not bothering to lower her voice. "This is for men. We sit and tend the fire."

"But they're like a pair of dogs just before they start fighting. All stiff."

"They'll work it out. Drink some coffee."

"They can't even talk to each other! I mean Gaetan can understand Tom, but he won't talk to him. He won't speak English."

"So they fight. When it's over, I'll put medicine on them."

The brother stuck his hand out in that strange way whites had. Gaetan ignored it.

Drawing his hand back, the brother said, "She told me you suited her in a way no other could. I suppose I see what she means. I'm her brother. Tom Grant."

Gaetan spoke each English word carefully after sounding it in his mind to be sure it was right. "She is *my* wife. The soldiers had no right to give her to you."

He heard Katherine gasp but didn't so much as glance at her.

The man should look nervous, but he didn't. "No, they had no right. They had no right to hold her in the first place, but they did. I'm glad we found you. She would have dragged me over every inch of Arizona and Mexico looking."

Even by the slight light of fire and moon, his eyes really did look like Katherine's. Gaetan could even see signs of strength there, but not the fierceness. The desire to kill him dulled a little. "I am found. You will go now."

"In the morning. If I took off tonight, she'd be dragging you all over looking for me tomorrow because I'd be lost."

Gaetan sat at the fire and accepted the cup and then the plate Echo pressed on him. He looked at Katherine finally. "Are you all right?"

"Yes."

The sparks in her eyes as she looked at him boded well for the rest of the night. He wanted his wife. He wanted her in ways that would leave no doubt that she was *his*, in her mind or the brother's—or his own.

The brother didn't sit again. He said, "I think I'll turn in now. Early start and all that. If you'll thank Mrs., well, err, thank Echo for me for the dinner, Kate. I'll, um, stay where we left the saddles. Do you need anything from our supplies?"

"*Katherine.*"

Gaetan liked the prickly way she said that, but she went on all too pleasantly. "No, I don't need anything. We can talk and sort things in the morning before you leave. Goodnight, Tom."

Finished eating, Gaetan said a few polite words to Echo and her daughter, rose and started off into the night. Without looking, he knew Katherine was at his heels, ready to berate him for ignoring her and for rudeness to her brother.

To make sure her mood matched his, he flipped one hand off to the side. *Heel!* She made a satisfactory hissing sound, not only catching up with him, but passing him.

He grabbed her arm, forced her to halt and started pulling off his clothes where they stood, ready for hot words. Her silence gave him grim satisfaction.

They were close enough to Echo's wickiup and where the brother had unsaddled his horses that everyone would hear anything louder than ordinary conversation. And they could all listen to him reclaim his wife and brand her by the sounds and actions he would force from her.

She knew him well, would recognize his intentions. He waited for her to try to walk away, anticipated resistance. Instead by the feeble light of the new moon he watched her shed her own clothes, sit to pull off her moccasins. Completely bare, she got to her knees, arranging her skirt and both their shirts over the hard ground. The skin of her back gleamed in the silvery moonlight as the mass of her hair fell forward around her face.

The thick heat in his groin surged to aching fire. Before he could crouch to seize her, she sat on the makeshift bed and raised her arms to him. "Gaetan." The way she dragged out the husky sound told of a need as great as his own.

Shoving her down, he took her mouth in a bruising kiss, expecting to provoke at least a self-protective shrinking he could use to feed his anger. Neither temper or roughness affected her as it should. She kissed him like a starving woman determined to devour him. The heat of her hands seared across his shoulders and down his back. The musky scent of her desire burned into his senses.

As he left her mouth and took the skin of her neck in his teeth, for the first time he understood that her fierceness gave her value, but what drew him and held him was acceptance. As a boy the teachers had forced him to obey and learn to save their own souls, not the one they doubted he had. As a man his own people looked at him with suspicion because of what the teachers had done.

Katherine alone accepted. She accepted his body in every way he gave it. She accepted his spirit as it was, not as a woman must wish it to be. When they married, she accepted there could be no future and gave hard promises. Tonight his anger could not make her turn away.

In spite of all the fierceness, in spite of knowing him so well she must know his intention to brand and to hurt, she welcomed him. He pulled his teeth from her skin and touched her with his tongue, tasting the salty sheen, kissing more gently as the anger drained away like poison from a wound.

He caressed her with lips and tongue, moving from her breasts to her stomach. Primitive triumph brought a growl from him when sensitive skin quivered and rippled under his kisses.

Dimly through the fog of his own passion, he heard the sounds of Katherine's pleasure and knew she muffled her cries against her arm. The shame of what he had planned in half-crazed anger pierced him like a bullet. To dishonor his wife by letting others hear such a private thing between them would be unforgivable. Even though Katherine would forgive him, he wouldn't forgive himself. He slid his arms under her and their clothing, gathered her into his arms and walked into the night.

After one small kiss to the side of his jaw, she stayed quiet, her arms tight around his neck, her head on his shoulder, her breath feathering across his skin. Far from the others, he eased her to her feet. This time he arranged a bed from their clothing. When he finished, she knelt down too, scattering small, sweet kisses over his face, down his neck and across his chest. Her hands explored his body as if he had become new to her.

He stopped her and pulled her hard against his chest, aware of the first touch of peaked nipples, then the way her breasts flattened against him, soft yet firm. He kissed her deeply, wanting only her pleasure now, recognizing it in the first purring hum resonating in her throat.

If a man could taste wind and fire, they would taste like Katherine. When he stood in high places looking down on things made small by distance, he tried to feel what the eagle felt soaring free on the wind. He was an earthbound man. Only his spirit could ever soar, and only Katherine raised him so high.

He left her mouth, trailed kisses down her neck, sipped a bead of sweat from the hollow of her throat. Her hands wove into his hair, her fingers stroked his neck and back.

Her skin glided smooth and damp under his lips and palms. The inside of her most secret places was wet and ready for him.

"Gaetan." She moaned his name in passion.

"Gaetan." She whispered his name as a plea.

He entered her slowly, determined to keep a tight hold on the lust pounding in his veins. She wrapped her legs higher, took him deeper and deeper. Her hands dug into the muscles of his rear, urging, telling him what she wanted and what he needed were the same. He obeyed and thrust harder, driving into her not with anger but with a desperate raw need. He felt her climax, her body arching, tightening and contracting around him as she cried out against his neck. He shuddered with the intensity of the explosion that wracked his body and spirit and wrung a deep cry from him.

"Katherine." *I was afraid. I missed you. I love you.*

29

Tom ate breakfast with them before saddling his horse and preparing to leave. Katherine hugged him hard around the neck. "I wish you and the rancher's first daughter could live next door."

"And where would next door be?" he asked soberly.

"Oh, you're right. It's impossible. I'll see you again, but I hope not for a long time." She had already promised to find her way to his ranch when it was over. What *over* meant was one more thing she refused to contemplate.

"You won't lose what I gave you?"

"No, I already memorized the directions, just in case, but I won't lose them or the money."

Gaetan would not like the small wad of greenbacks that now rested in her buckskin pouch along with the marriage certificate and directions to Tom's ranch, and Katherine hadn't made up her mind whether to tell him about it or not.

One last hug, and as she backed away a step to let Tom get on the horse, Gaetan walked up beside her. Surprise kept her quiet when he held out his hand in the same manner Tom had done the night before. Tom took the offered hand warily.

Katherine's surprise changed to astonishment when Gaetan said, "Thank you."

Tom accepted the turnaround more easily, grinning. "Don't let her run you ragged."

He swung up on the horse and started for the agency, turning once to wave.

Ready to give her husband a large piece of her mind, Katherine said, "So you wouldn't speak English to me even when our lives were in danger, but you can speak English to my brother? How exactly do you explain that?"

"With him it was necessary."

"But with me it wasn't? Instead of just saying 'be quiet' you put a knife across my mouth!"

"You wouldn't have listened. Is this what he meant by running me ragged?"

"No, we're only walking right now." She glared at him for a moment, and then the sheer delight of being able to fuss at him overwhelmed her. Moving close she leaned her forehead against his shoulder and breathed deep. She smelled wood smoke, traces of the dust carried on the ceaseless wind, and the essence of Gaetan and smiled against him. "You can't know how I missed you."

"Yes. I can." His arms closed around her for a brief moment. "We need to go. If the agent realizes your brother left without you, the police will be here soon."

"I bet Tom fools him. He's really gotten quite good at that since I saw him last."

In spite of her words, she hurried to say goodbye to Echo and her daughter. "Thank you. I hope we can get back to see you."

"You worry about yourself and your husband and the butterfly," Echo said, sending her on her way with a smile.

Katherine went to help Gaetan saddle the horses and found him eyeing the flashy bay horse with two hind socks and the sidesaddle that Tom had left with dislike.

"You can tell this is a white man's horse. It's so fat, it would be better for eating than riding."

"We are *not* eating my horse. He'll be lean and ready to race in no time."

Abandoning the subject of the horse's condition, Gaetan rocked the sidesaddle with the toe of his moccasin. "You can ride this?"

"Yes, it's really a more secure seat than you'd think. The sooner we get a regular saddle, the better, but it will do for now."

"Hunh."

She ignored the twitch in his lips as he watched her mount and arrange herself and her skirts. "Go ahead and laugh. It's better than bareback. Where are we going?"

"Off the reservation before they catch us."

They set up camp high in the mountains east of the reservation. Able to see for miles in the directions of most likely approach, they felt almost safe, but the few supplies Tom had carried and given them wouldn't last two people long. Tom had also given Katherine his pocket knife, but the only weapons they had were Gaetan's knife, rifle and pistol, and they had little ammunition for either of the guns.

After much debate, Gaetan left Katherine the pistol and went hunting. He returned three days later, a deer draped over the withers of his saddle horse. A second horse trailed behind carrying a saddle for Katherine, a rifle, saddlebags and flour sacks bulging with supplies. No wonder he had used the one rifle as an excuse to keep her from going with him. He had been hunting more than meat.

The days alone had given her an understanding of the fear that haunted Lupe. The fluttering sensations persisted, and she was beginning to believe. That night, secure beside Gaetan in their blankets, she asked about the future. "What are we going to do?"

He turned toward her, his fingers caressing her cheek. Asking in the dark had been a way to keep him from seeing her fear. She hoped nothing his fingers could detect of her expression nor her voice gave her away, but perhaps they did.

"Are you afraid to go back to Mexico?" he asked.

"No. Being caught by soldiers down there is more dangerous for me, but the chances are less, aren't they?"

"Yes. The Mexicans are too poor to hunt us all the time. The Americans are rich and impatient to kill us all."

"Or make you live on reservations."

His hand left her face, but not before she felt him stiffen. He would never consider living on a reservation as living.

"I'm not afraid to live in Mexico," she said. "I know you're a lot more careful than Chi– than the one who almost got us killed."

"Bácho is reluctant to leave again, but there are others who will persuade him, I think. If not, some will go without him. Piishi talks of it. Too loudly maybe. If he's not careful spies will tell the agent about him."

"Spies? There are spies on the reservation?"

"It's easy to bribe people when they have nothing to do and not enough to eat."

"So some will try to get back to Mexico in the spring, and we'll go with them?"

"We'll go with them, but it will be soon. Almost all the warriors have guns again now. The agent and soldiers will think like you that we'll wait till spring, so we'll go now. We can use what's in the caches in the old place to get through the winter, bring it to a new camp."

"And who's going to be the one who walks past the ghosts to get to the caches?"

"Bácho will make ghost medicine, and everyone will work fast."

Katherine laughed, the fear of being alone through pregnancy and childbirth receding. In fact happy expectations for the future left her thinking about things other than sleep, and her own fingers did some caressing, not just of his face.

Over the next month Katherine only saw Gaetan for a day or two. Resoling moccasins, weaving baskets and preparing for the trip in every way kept her hands busy. She even managed to weave water jugs and waterproof them with piñon pitch on her own, but she couldn't manage to banish troublesome and unwanted thoughts.

Late fall brought cooler days before Gaetan returned with the news they had been waiting for. Bácho had made up his mind. He and his small group of followers would leave the reservation in two days.

At first light on the designated day, Katherine helped pack what little they would take with them on the spare horse. For the first time she carried the saddle Gaetan had brought back for her out of cover and lifted it onto her fat bay horse. The slanting rays of the rising sun picked out a dark stain along the edge of the cantle. Scraping with a fingernail removed most of the substance, but also brought out the deep rust color.

She opened a water jug, poured a little water over the stain and rubbed. More water, more rubbing. By the time the water no longer came away red, the small stain was a large wet spot. Pregnancy had sharpened her senses. The coppery scent of blood rose around her as if gouts of it covered the saddle, and she gagged.

"Are you ready?" Gaetan called.

"Almost."

What Gaetan did when he was away from her topped the list of things she didn't want to know. She had accepted his enemies as hers. The sinking of her stomach foretold of change even before the small flutter that followed it. She finished saddling, tied the water jug and saddlebags in place and got on the horse, making sure her skirt covered leather now darkened by water.

She reined her horse in behind the one Gaetan led, and they headed out. Soon they'd be settled in Mexico. She'd tell him about the baby and argue him around if he tried to behave like a Chiricahua husband. Life would be good. It would.

THEY JOINED THE people on the flight south before the day ended. Of the twenty-seven people, only nine were warriors, and the small group traveled in the traditional Apache way. Women and children went ahead, and the men stayed behind between the expected source of danger and their families.

Scouts ranged in all directions. Not everyone had a horse. The warriors were mounted and half the women. People traded off. Women rode with the smallest children at their backs.

Large with child, Lupe insisted the birth was at least two months away and walked beside Katherine more than she rode. Watching how often Lupe pressed a hand into the small of her back and arched away from it, Katherine suspected walking must be more comfortable than riding. Her own back had begun to ache now and then in unaccustomed ways.

In spite of whatever discomfort she felt, Lupe had the look of serene confidence that had always marked her in the past, and Katherine understood. Maybe no medicine woman like Echo accompanied them, but the women in the group had helped with many births, borne many children of their own. Their knowledge and experience brought comfort going to a world where no one could hustle to bring a doctor when things went wrong.

"I'm glad Itsá decided to stay with the people until after the baby comes," Katherine said. "Maybe he'll change his mind about going off on your own in the spring too."

"Maybe. He'll do what's best for us all. I wish you could come with us, but Gaetan...."

"Won't change," Katherine said, wishing she could take back the sharp tone of the words the second they left her mouth.

Lupe said nothing, and Katherine silently thanked her friend for forgoing either sympathy or the opportunity to say I told you so.

More than the rough terrain and need for water affected the route of their flight south. Twice they made large loops off the direct route to avoid men spotted by the scouts. This wasn't a war party or a raiding party, but an escape. Losing track of her count of the days, Katherine thought at least ten had passed when a renewed energy in the pace of the people signaled their approach to the border and safety from at least U.S. troops.

"Will we celebrate tonight or wait until we cross over in the morning?" Katherine asked Lupe late in the afternoon.

"We won't celebrate until we're hidden away in the mountains."

Lupe showed no sign of any premature jubilation, and her instincts proved right as night fell and word circulated among the women. The Mexican army lay in wait along the border. U.S. cavalry was closing in fast from the north.

Something worse than confusion or fear spread among the people. The women cooked over small fires, and the flames showed faces with expressions all too like that of Señor Estrada as he obeyed the stagecoach robbers and went to his death. The warriors came for food and soon everyone, men and women, gathered in council around the largest fire.

Katherine stayed on the outskirts and listened as Bácho spoke of surrender with resignation and Itsá spoke of escape with passion. Gaetan said nothing. When the talk died down, he rose and walked away. She found him, an unmoving shadow alone in the night, and sat beside him, unsure of her welcome, yet determined to say what had to be said. In a little while.

The moon appeared, a faraway cold light, but enough that she could see the outline of strong, beloved features. From behind them came the sound of a woman's voice, high and keening. A man spoke harshly, and the sound stopped.

She sat as motionless as Gaetan, close but not touching. Something small moved nearby in the creosote brush, unaware or uncaring about human presence. Finally Gaetan shook slightly as if coming out of a trance. He put an arm around her, and she scooted against him, rested her head on his shoulder.

"Can we still get away?"

"Yes, the Mexicans are to the southeast and southwest and the Americans are coming from the north. We can go east or west, but tomorrow Bácho will send our scouts to find the army scouts. They'll carry a white flag and let the soldiers know he'll surrender."

"They've lost heart. I see it in their faces. They shouldn't have tried this time."

"No. They're ready to become good Indians."

"And you're not."

He didn't answer her. He didn't have to.

"Itsá and Lupe will come with us," he said. "A few can get around the Mexican army easily. When we get to Mexico, he'll do what he always planned."

"She's afraid."

"I know. It will be easier for her if you're with her."

"We can't live with them. He wants to hide, no raiding."

"We could have another winter like the last one. I can wait until spring."

She closed her eyes, tempted, so tempted. "I'm going to have a baby too. In spite of everything the doctors always said—in the spring."

His arm tightened around her slightly but other than that he didn't react. She hadn't surprised him.

"I wondered when you'd tell me," he said.

"You knew? Did Echo tell you?"

"No one told me. You're my wife. I know your body, and there are changes."

Katherine lifted her head from his shoulder and stared at the dark eyes gleaming in the moonlight. Kissing the corner of his mouth, she settled back against his shoulder. "I wasn't sure those changes meant what I hoped at first. I guess that's one more thing Aunt Meg was wrong about. She always said men are oblivious about things like that. Of course her husband was a lot more like Henry than you."

Another glance showed teeth gleaming along with eyes.

"Is that why you didn't tell me? You weren't sure?"

"Lupe told me once how it is with the Chiricahua, that as soon as a woman knows, her husband leaves her bed and stays away until the child is weaned, and that's why children are so far apart. I was afraid that might be one of the things you choose to believe in."

"A man would be foolish to choose that thing unless he has many wives."

Resting her head back against him, she fought against the ache in her throat and the cowardly desire to wait to say what else she had to say until tomorrow, or forever. If she waited for the strength to hide the pain, she'd never speak.

"I always thought when it came to this I'd go with you, support you in all the ways an Apache wife does, but seeing Tom again, even the Sandlins and the sergeant I told you about—I can't fight my own people, and I feel the same thing Lupe feels. I'm afraid. Last winter was the best time of my life, but spring will come again, and I can't be alone so much. I can't do it, and I don't want our child to do it."

Pausing, she waited for him to argue with her, tell her all the ways she was wrong, but he said nothing.

"When I told you I would never leave so long as you live, I meant it, and I meant the hard promises, but now I'm proving you right. I believed I never lied to you and never would, but I did because I can't keep those promises. I can't go with you. I love you. I'll never stop loving you, but I can't go with you."

He hadn't moved, but his voice was tight. "Where will you go?"

"To Tom. He gave me a map, and he gave me money. I should have told you about the money. I'm sorry. I hoped we'd never get to this place."

Oh, how she had hoped. That something would work out, that something would change and this moment would never come. "Will you talk to Itsá for me? He won't listen to me, but maybe if you talk to him. They could come with me. It would be safer than Mexico and a better life. Tom says it's so remote that strangers never come there and he has trouble finding men to work for him. The hiding wouldn't be any worse there than in Mexico."

"Your brother would allow this?"

"Of course he would. The only problem might be if the girl he's courting won't go along with Apaches in her backyard, but if she's like that, there are other places."

"The faraway places you told me about where people like us can live."

"Yes! Places where children can live to grow up. Places where they can grow up without being afraid all the time, being afraid with good reason."

"I'll talk to Itsá."

Tears rolled down her cheeks and turned the shoulder of his shirt into a soggy mess, and she didn't care. She waited for him to leave her, get up and go talk to Itsá and Lupe, but he didn't move.

Dwelling on the coming parting was useless, and there was still a little time. She knew he would take her north, keep her safe until she was with Tom. She raised her head and tried to put lightness in her voice.

"Sneaking away will be like the beginning again, won't it, like getting away from the Rurales all over."

He answered so softly she could barely make out the words. "No. It will be different. I didn't love you then."

Her heart stopped in her chest before it started again with a painful thump. He continued in a more normal voice as if he hadn't said anything extraordinary. "You said once that dying is easier than living. When you said it, I felt as if you called me a coward."

"But I wasn't talking about you! I never meant you. I never thought that."

"I know, but the words still buried their way inside like arrows, and they come back to me often. I said fighting them to the death would take revenge for what they take from us, but I know it never will. We are too few. Nothing we do is of consequence to them. To them we are already *indeh*."

"That not true!" Katherine said angrily. "You're alive. The people here are alive, and they're going to go to the reservation and stay alive."

"I know. And I think now that's the only victory left to us. To live when they want us to die is to win a little."

Did he mean what she thought? Could he? Terrified of the answer, still she asked. "Do you mean that? Are you saying you'll come with me?"

The silence stretched so long her small flicker of hope died back down. She had misunderstood him, or he would take back the words.

He swiveled to face her, so close she could make out his features in the moonlight. "Before you came, only the killing mattered. My brother told me I was wrong, that I could make war and enjoy good things like other men, but I never listened. By leaving you with me, in death he made me listen. If the people are right and there are ghosts, his ghost is laughing at me. If dying is easier than living, I will take the hardest path. I will choose to grow old beside a fierce woman."

She kissed him. Fiercely. Before she could do more, one of the scouts returned with frightening news. His excited voice carried in the night.

"The American soldiers kept coming in the dark. They're close, and they're taking positions around us."

Gaetan rose and pulled her to her feet. "I'll talk to Itsá after we get away. No more talking."

Katherine had heard all the words she needed.

There were no gullies here, but a slight swale ran to the northwest, not a direction the army would be expecting strays to try to flee. No one dictated the order. They fell into line as if they'd practiced, Gaetan first, Katherine behind him, Lupe behind her, and Itsá acting as rearguard.

Gaetan moved out silently. So did Katherine. No sound came from behind her. She walked bent double and then she crawled.

The slight sound of a horse shaking its head, its bit rings jingling, came from their right. Gaetan dropped down all the way. So did Katherine.

They inched through the cavalry scouts on their bellies, Katherine's nose almost touching Gaetan's moccasins. No fear crept along with her, only joy. After all, they'd be free by morning. They'd done this before.

Afterword

October 1915
Long Island, New York

KATHERINE LEANED BACK on the stone bench, enjoying warm fall sunshine and the sight and sound of generations of Grants buzzing around the family home. Children laughed and screamed, parents called and cautioned.

After three tries, she had given up on an accurate count of everyone attending the reunion. Her five brothers and their wives were easy, as were their sons and daughters. She even felt confident of her tally of grandchildren, but then there were cousins from Aunt Meg's branch of the family, and a few people floating through the crowd didn't seem to be related at all. Seventy was a nice round number and close enough.

The person Katherine considered the most important one at the reunion appeared around the curve of the driveway, walking slowly as he examined each of the more than dozen automobiles parked in a long line.

Gaetan's fascination with all things mechanical had served them well over the years. Once she had worried that staying at the ranch with Tom would lead to resentments over charity given and received even though her money had purchased more land. Instead, she watched with wonder as Tom, Gaetan and Itsá forged a partnership that turned a rich man's toy into a successful enterprise. Tom dealt with the outside world, Gaetan with all machinery and construction, and Itsá with the livestock.

Gaetan finished his examination of the shining new Pierce-Arrow convertible sitting ready to lead the coming procession to the reunion picnic. He walked toward her, straight and tall, moving as easily as ever. Like her sons, brothers and nephews he wore gray flannel trousers, an Oxford shirt and a dark blazer. Unlike them, he didn't look casual and civilized but intense and only half-tame.

His hair contributed to the dangerous aura. Thick and glossy black except for a few intriguing streaks of silver, it still hung past his shoulders. But the real difference was the essence of him, still wild and so very Apache.

He sat beside her, and she switched from leaning against the back of the bench to leaning against him.

"You look like an old grandmother sitting there in the sun wrapped in a blanket," he said.

"I am a grandmother." She pointed to where the children played on the lawn. "The brown ones are mine."

"You mean the good looking ones."

She didn't have to respond to that. They *were* good looking. "Maria worried that a stone bench like this would be cold and brought me the shawl a while ago. The least I can do is keep it around my shoulders for a while."

Lupe and Itsá's daughter was Gaetan's favorite daughter-in-law. Knowing the shawl was Maria's idea, he wouldn't say anything else critical about it.

"And there's nothing for me to do," Katherine said. "We packed enough food for an army and every single thing anyone could think of ever needing at the beach. It's all in the automobiles ready to go the minute my brothers give the word. I don't want to play croquet while we wait."

"Hunh. The woman in that big soft bed with me last night didn't feel like a grandmother who sits and watches."

"Really? What did she feel like?"

"She felt like the woman who once helped me steal horses. She felt like a woman who would not wait for slow brothers or ride in a convertible with the sun and wind locked out because they act like old men."

Katherine stopped leaning against him and twisted on the seat to look at him, considering. Two of her bossy nieces had taken it upon themselves to run the reunion and everyone in it. They had decreed that the "original Grant siblings" would ride to the beach together in the splendor of the Pierce-Arrow.

Her brother George, whose many years in England hadn't changed him a particle, had fussed so much over the thought of wind blowing through what was left of his hair that everyone agreed to leave the convertible top up on the automobile to appease him.

Gaetan had proved remarkably tolerant of her family over the years. He joked occasionally that a Chiricahua man was obliged to join his wife's family, and her family was his burden. Still, Katherine wouldn't leave Gaetan alone with George for a minute. Well, not without gagging George first.

She studied his face, recognizing the intent there. "Can we get the top down before we go?"

"I already unfastened it."

"Then what are we waiting for? They may decide it's time to leave any minute."

The top was folded back and secured, Gaetan behind the wheel and Katherine beside him before anyone noticed what they were up to. The sound of the engine starting all but drowned out the first astonished shouts. By the time her know-it-all family started running toward them, Gaetan had the car in gear and accelerating down the drive.

Katherine curved one hand around the hard muscles of his thigh, leaned back against the glove leather upholstery, and laughed.

"They'll be right behind us."

"No. They won't."

He was right, she realized. Not only would it take a while for the family to organize and squeeze into the other vehicles, but her staid brothers would follow at a far more sedate pace. The road stretched before them, straight and smooth, and the roadside scenery disappeared behind in a blur. The big automobile purred as it ate up the miles.

"Easier than horses," Gaetan said. "And faster."

The wind had torn her hair loose from its pins. Katherine had to pull strands away from her mouth before answering. "Except no one ever caught us over the horses, and we're going to get caught this time."

"That worries you?"

"Of course not. No one will even have the courage to yell at us. They're afraid of you."

"Victor and Jerome aren't afraid."

No, their sons weren't afraid of their father, but they were so much like him they would be too busy laughing to even pretend to disapprove.

The beautiful straight stretch ended, and Gaetan slowed, following her directions through several turns until they came to a flat, graveled field. He drove to the far side and parked.

"Shall we wait here?" Katherine said.

"No. I want to see the ocean, and I want to see it without the others."

"You saw it yesterday on the way to the island."

"That was only a little seeing."

Katherine left the shawl on the seat as she got out. Gaetan threw his blazer across it. They walked to the first of the sand dunes that separated the parking area from the beach where the family intended to hold the reunion picnic.

"I wish Lupe and Itsá had come with us," Katherine said between quick breaths as they climbed. "I know she'll never leave the mountains, and he'll never go anywhere without her, but I wish it anyway."

Gaetan said nothing but reached his hand out to her. The warmth of his callused palm closing over hers comforted more than any words.

They crested the last hill and stopped, taking in the sight before them. The tamer water they'd crossed yesterday coming to the island had indeed been only a harbinger of this.

The ocean stretched as far as the eye could see until it blended into the sky at the horizon. Sun glinted off gray water. Waves broke and frothed white on the beach, the sound a low roar that provided background for the shrill cries of seagulls.

The breeze tugged at her hair and whipped her skirt around her, cool, but too fresh and alive to hide from under shawls or jackets.

"You told me of the sound, but you never told me of the smell."

"Didn't I?" She sucked in a deep breath of the salt air. "I don't know if I could describe it to someone who's never been near it."

"No. It's like the mountains."

Katherine almost questioned his meaning and then understood. "It is. Majesty Tom calls it."

"We won't swim in it."

"It's too late in the year and too cold."

"Hunh."

A man who broke ice and bathed in a creek would have no problem swimming in the ocean in October, and they both knew it.

"We can take off our shoes and stockings and walk along the beach. You'll see how cold it is."

She no longer remembered exactly when either of them had given up moccasins for hard-soled footwear, but Gaetan still wore moccasins around the house, and she still kept them repaired.

Leaving their shoes on the crest of the hill, they made their way to the edge of the water, walking barefoot on the cold, wet sand, laughing as incoming waves caught them, drenching the cuffs of his trousers and hem of her skirt.

He cupped his hands and caught a little of the water, tasted it and made a face.

"Did you think I made it up when I said it's salty?"

"No, but I wanted to see for myself. I didn't think it would be so very salty." He looked out to the horizon. "The ship will really take us so far from shore we'll see only water?"

The plan had long been to cruise several days down the coast and back. "Unless you've changed your mind. We don't have to go if you don't want to."

"It didn't seem real until now. I believed you, but it didn't seem real. I won't change my mind—unless I get seasick. If that happens, you'll change your mind too."

Katherine frowned at the thought.

"I won't die because we left the mountains."

"Of course you won't. I know that," she said, denying the fear that had traveled east with her.

"I worry about you too sometimes."

As a matter of fact Tom's descriptions of Gaetan's behavior when she had been in labor with each of their sons could make Gaetan disappear while the rest of the family rolled with laughter. But this was different. Her worry was *real*.

Maybe the government had finally released the Chiricahua it held for twenty-seven bitter years as prisoners of war, but her brothers couldn't seem to understand that didn't mean Apaches could travel freely.

The Eastern Grants wanted a family reunion in New York. Katherine wanted her husband, sons and grandchildren safe. She had made excuses and found problems with every suggested date.

Her brothers had finally come up with the idea of sending a private railroad car for the Apache branch of the family so she couldn't claim the cross-country trip would be dangerous. After that Victor and Jerome and their wives and children had joined in the reunion campaign.

She had held out until Gaetan admitted he'd like to see the entire country and the ocean, but still she worried. At least this time of year heat and humidity no longer threatened.

"In spite of everything, Nana lived into his nineties and Geronimo almost to eighty," Gaetan said. "Naiche still lives. A trip like this with my wife taking care of me won't kill me."

"Good. Because I want you to be a grizzly at a hundred and ten."

"A man married to a fierce woman has to be a grizzly."

"A woman married to a grizzly has to be fierce."

He pulled her to him. His kiss was neither fierce nor grizzly-like but a loving reminder of promises made and kept and always to be kept.

Excited voices sounded behind them. The whole family streamed across the dunes toward them. Maria carried the shawl. Victor had Gaetan's blazer.

"Do you think we could steal another automobile and get away by ourselves again tomorrow?" Eying the approaching crowd, Katherine added, "Maybe in a way so they don't miss us for a few hours. That straight stretch of road would be worth doing again, and there are other good roads on the island. The cruise isn't until Wednesday, and I don't like playing croquet."

Gaetan's eyes met hers, a look she had first seen many years ago glittering in their depths. The corners of her mouth pulled straight back. Neither said more as they turned and walked back along the beach.

Author's Note

It is my hope, of course, that readers enjoy the story of Katherine and Gaetan. I have done research for all my historical romance novels, but this is the one where the story behind the story pulled me in and almost didn't let go. Many years ago Dee Brown's book, *Bury My Heart at Wounded Knee* changed the way I look at the world, but one of the pictures affected me in a very different way than the text. I'm female after all, and the picture of Victorio has never lost its fascination. It's such a very strong and very masculine face. From my reaction to that picture, Katherine and Gaetan's story was born.

In doing the research for *Dancing on Coals*, I found a lot of contradictory information, and I freely confess to having used the source that fit my story best. For instance, some sources say that the Chihinne (Victorio's people, later led by Nana), Chokonen (Cochise's people, later led by his son Naiche), Nednhi (Juh's people), and Bedonkohe (Geronimo was Bedonkohe) were all Chiricahua. Other sources say only Cochise's people were really Chiricahua. I used the former version for my story.

Other things left me with writer's dilemmas. The best source of Apache names is probably the list of names of the Chiricahua the government rounded up after Geronimo's last surrender and transported to Fort Marion, Florida, for the beginning of twenty-seven years of imprisonment. I couldn't bring myself to use the names of those real people who fought so superbly and were made to suffer for it so terribly.

My plan was to use Apache names for animals or things for my characters, but that plan also presented problems. Special fonts are required to write the Apache language properly, and the names most easily found are from the Western Apache dialect, not Chiricahua. In the end I made an authorial decision and chose names without regard to dialect and wrote them in ways I hope English-speaking readers will find easy to deal with. However, I think some readers may enjoy knowing what's behind those names. So, still written in my highly editorialized way:

Nilchi – wind
Chishogi – buzzard
Agocho – pigeon
Kloshchu – rats
Tliish – snake
Debechu – sheep
Goshé – dog
Bácho – wolf
Itsá – hawk
Ya-kos – cloud
Datilye – hummingbird
Jágé – antelope

I think the name Gaetan is my own invention. If not, I read it somewhere so long ago I no longer remember.

That's the end of the confessions I feel compelled to make. Other things readers may have more trouble believing are true. The Rurales were a rough bunch. Not only were they said to fill their ranks with criminals straight from prison, rumor had it that a Rurale with a black hat instead of gray had been in prison for murder. Exaggeration? Probably, but they were not a modern well disciplined police force.

The abuse at Indian boarding schools, the bounties on Apache scalps, the numbers around the neck at reservations, the edict that any Apache caught off the reservations would be shot on sight—true. Did Katherine have good reason to worry about her family traveling from Colorado to New York in 1915? Yes, she did. Courts upheld the intent of the Fourteenth Amendment to the United States Constitution to exclude Indians. Legislation passed in 1924 finally granted them citizenship, which meant the right to travel freely. Until that time an Indian traveling off reservation needed a pass from the agent.

Free or wild Apaches did continue to live hidden in Mexico's Sierra Madres in the way Itsá planned until at least the 1920s. Several children were captured and taken from them, and other evidence has been discovered. It must have been not just a lonely life but one of severe deprivation. I wanted better for Katherine and Gaetan and for Lupe and Itsá and so sent them north instead.

Ellen O'Connell